Jeopardy

*1066: Three Queens,
One Throne
and a Poet*

Kathleen
Jones

First published in 2025 by The Book Mill

Book and cover design Copyright © JD Smith Design

ISBN 978-1-0686991-2-2
E-ISBN 978-1-0686991-3-9

The Book Mill
www.thebookmill.co.uk

It's 1066. The old king lies dying and England is without an heir. Four war-lords are eyeing up the prize. Four women stand to gain or lose from the result. What must they do to survive?

Queen Edith, childless, about to be stripped of her position in the court, supports her brother Harold Godwinson's bid for the vacant throne in an attempt to keep some of her power.

Eadgifu Swan-neck, Harold's Anglo-Danish wife of twenty years, sees her place taken by a new wife, married in the Christian church –

Ældyth, formerly Queen of the Welsh, who is the most beautiful woman in the kingdom, now forced to marry Harold. It's the price both women have to pay for the support of Ældyth's brothers, the powerful earls of the north, to put Harold on the throne.

At the centre of it all is Hannë, princess of Denmark, a gifted musician, captured as a slave and given to the English court as a gift. She is disguised as a boy for her own safety, playing her lyre every night in the hall, never sure from one moment to the next, what will become of her.

Contents

Godwin the king-maker married his daughter
to a man he'd raised to the throne with a small
army. No matter Godwin had once murdered
the king's brother to put another man on the throne.
No matter the king loved Godwin's son
better than the Queen.

This is how it starts —
the founding of dynasties, murder and weregild
the trading of women and the survival of the tribe.

Kings of the English, 978 to 1066

In Order

Æthelred II (the Unready): 978-1013, House of Wessex, m.(1) Ælfgifu of York, 9 children inc. Edmund II (Ironside).

Sweyn Forkbeard: 1013-1014 (Danish)

Æthelred II (the Unready): 1014-1016, m.(2) Emma of Normandy, children Edward II, Alfred and Godgifu.

Edmund II (Ironside): 1016, House of Wessex, son of Ælfgifu of York and Æthelred II. Grandfather of Edgar the Ætheling.

Cnut the Great: 1016-1035, son of Sweyn Forkbeard, (Danish) King of England, Norway and Denmark.
    m.(1) Ælfgifu of Northampton, mother of Harold I (Harefoot)
    m.(2) Emma of Normandy, widow of Æthelred II, mother of Harthacnut, and Gunhilda of Denmark.

Harold I (Harefoot): 1035-1040, (Anglo-Danish) son of Cnut and Ælfgifu of Northampton.

Harthacnut: 1040-1042, (Norman-Danish) son of Cnut and Emma of Normandy.

Edward II (the Confessor): 1042-1066, House of Wessex, son of Æthelred II and Emma of Normandy, m. Edith of Wessex.

Harold II: 1066, Harold Godwinson, Earl of Wessex, brother of Queen Edith. The last Saxon king of the English.
   m.(1) Eadgifu Swan-neck, 6 children, Godwin, Edmund, Magnus, Gunhild, Gytha, Ulf
   m.(2) Ældyth of Mercia, 1 child, Harold Haroldson

Part One

The Virgin Queen

'Hear my words, destroyer
of the dark black sea-horses,
sea warrior under canvas,
for I can shape them to bring
glory to your name. A king
must have one praise-singer
under his roof and out of all
song-smiths, that should be me.'

Snorri Sturluson, *Olafs Saga*, (trans KJ)

11th day after Yule, 1066

It was the coldest winter anyone could remember. Crows had fallen frozen from their perches overnight and the rivers and the marshlands were thick with ice. In the palace of Westminster, torches flared against the blackened walls of the corridors. In the death room, firelight and candlelight offered flickering glimpses of the tapestries that hung on the walls and reflected from the polished wood of the carved bedposts. The thick hangings around the bed pulsed in the draughts.

Under a mound of embroidered coverlets and furs King Edward was dying. His six-foot frame, now an emaciated shell, stretched from headboard to footboard. A Benedictine brother was bending over the king to bathe his forehead with lavender water. The room was loud with Edward's laboured breathing.

'How long?' a woman asked. She was dressed simply in dark wool with a white veil over her hair, but the golden circlet on her head revealed her royal status.

The monk straightened up. 'I thought we should lose him several hours ago, my Lady, his fever was so great. But he has rallied. There's more strength in him than we guessed.'

'He's in the hands of God.' Edith crossed herself. Her pale, youthful face, framed by the veil, turned to one of the men standing at the foot of the bed, who put his arm around her protectively. Harold Godwinson, Earl of Wessex. They were very alike; both tall and blond in the Saxon way – brother and sister, earl and queen, children of the late Godwin, a power-hungry Saxon thegn raised up by Cnut the Great. Before his death Earl Godwin had been the most influential man in England – king-maker, opportunist, land-grabber, lord of half England; the man whose ambition had placed both Harold and Edith where they were now. But, with the imminent death of Edward, what would that ambition be worth?

Cold, hungry, tired of standing in that room anticipating the inevitable, both Godwins made their way to the great hall, where dinner was being served. It was Twelfth Night, the last of the feasts of Christmas, a time of celebration, but with the imminent death of the king, the atmosphere was sombre. At high table, in the space next to Harold where the king usually sat, his place was empty. There were other vacant seats too. Archbishop Stigand had remained in the bedroom with Edward, as well as some of the other high officials. Edith noticed that there seemed to be more hearth-carles in evidence; not sitting eating at the lower tables, but standing on guard with their helmets on and weapons at the ready. Everything felt uneasy.

'Are you expecting trouble so soon?' she asked her brother, who was sitting beside her. She had taken beef and bread but eaten little of it. Every morsel stuck in her throat.

'It's possible,' Harold said, looking up from his platter. He spoke very quietly. 'I don't expect it from outside the kingdom while the king's alive, particularly at this time of year – armies don't move in winter. But who knows what loyalties our family can command from within.'

Edith's gaze moved around the hall. At one of the lower tables the Normans were sitting, a small group now, only a residue of the retinue Edward had brought with him when he came out of exile in Normandy twenty-four years ago to claim his throne. But they were still a force to be reckoned with – a reminder that Edward's mother Emma had been sister to the Old Duke of Normandy. Who would they back when the king was dead? The current Duke William was known to be an ambitious man with his eyes on the English throne.

Edith's eyes moved down the table to where Edwin, Earl of Mercia, sat with his brother Morcar, Earl of Northumbria – two dark, powerful northern war-lords, grandsons of Earl Leofric of Mercia – their father Godwin's arch rival for power while he lived. Edwin and Morcar were still young men, the latter little more than a boy, but they were dangerous. She looked at Edwin's thin, greedy face, the opulence of his robes, the rings on his fingers as he put the knife into his venison. Edwin's dark, hooded eyes were inscrutable. He would only support the Godwins if it was in his own interests.

'And what of our brother Tostig, Harold? Do you know where he is?'

'The last news I had was that he and the Lady Judith were still in Flanders, taking refuge with Count Baldwin. I've heard nothing to the contrary since.'

'Surely you can trust Tostig to support you?'

Harold's expression was one of contempt. 'His absence here speaks for itself. He's known the king was gravely ill for the last two weeks, but has he come? No.'

'It's not easy to cross the channel in winter.'

'You're too quick to make excuses for him Edith. If Morcar can get here from Northumbria, Tostig could have travelled the short distance from Flanders.' Harold looked troubled. 'Since the beginning of our father's disputes with the king, I've never been sure of Tostig's loyalty. First, he married a close kinswoman of William of Normandy against Edward's wishes. Then, when Tostig lost Northumbria to Morcar, he turned his back on us, his family. The last letter I had from him accused me of withholding my support. He informed me that he intended to get his lands back by any possible means. But how could I support him when the Northumbrians refused to tolerate his rule? They chose Morcar, not I. To try to enforce Tostig's claim would have meant civil war.'

Edith reflected that it was just another twist in the long and tangled history of their family. Fifteen years ago, the Godwins had fallen from grace. It had begun when their eldest brother Swein had murdered his cousin in an argument, sacked Leominster and abducted the Abbess. Edith could still hear the king's explosion of temper that had had everyone cowering. In a rage, Edward was capable of anything. Their father, Earl Godwin, was already unpopular for his open hostility to the Norman influences at court, particularly the Archbishop of Canterbury, Robert de Jumièges. That position was made more precarious by a jealous Earl

Leofric whispering in the king's ear. Godwin had become too powerful in the eyes of the other nobles and, possibly, even the king himself.

Something strange and unexplained had happened on the eve of Tostig's marriage. Edith had never dared to ask her husband what it was. In the space of a day, her father and brothers were exiled; Tostig, Swein and Gyrth with their father to Flanders; Harold and Leofwine had fled to Ireland, while she had been sent, under guard, to the Benedictine nuns at Wherwell, where Edward's half-sister was Abbess, before, eventually, being sent to Wilton where she had been educated as a girl. The archbishop had advised the king to divorce her. Edith had wished, many times since then, that Edward had taken his advice.

She took a mouthful of Rhenish wine to quieten her stomach and suppress the sense of dread she had felt all day. 'Edward can't live much longer, Harold.'

'Rest easy, sister. We're surrounded by my own men.' He glanced towards the hearth-carles standing just inside the door. 'And be careful what you say. There are too many listeners here.'

~ ~ ~

My name is Hannë, though that is not the name they know me by. They call me Hari, if they call me anything. Slaves, even slaves who can sing and compose sagas, are still slaves. Three years ago, I was seized from my father's hall by that renowned Viking, King Harald the Landwaster, then given by him to Earl Tostig Godwinson when he was a guest at the Norwegian court. When he came back to England, Tostig sent me as a gift to King Edward, with secret instructions to keep the earl informed of what was being talked of at court. Tostig feared – rightly – that he was to be deprived of his earldom by his brother Harold.

Whenever I catch sight of myself in a mirror, or a reflection in a goblet at table, I say my real name over and over, silently in my head, to remind myself that I was once Hannë Magnusdottir, the cherished daughter of an important family in Denmark. But now I am dressed in the garb of a servant, and I look the very image of a pretty young boy, which is what Harald saw when he raided my father's hall. It is certainly what the men of Tostig's court saw and, during the brief time I was in Northumbria, it was a struggle to keep myself chaste. I had not realised that an unprotected young boy is in as much danger as a girl.

It was to avoid rape that I hacked off my hair, muddied my face and dressed in my brother's clothes when the Landwaster's horde was at the gates. We had heard of his reputation, the raids all along the coast of Denmark – how the old and the very young were put to the sword, the women loaded onto his ships as concubines for his warriors. Young boys were usually taken as slaves and that seemed a less miserable fate. From my hiding place behind the tapestries, I saw him standing at the door of the hall, blocking out the light, seven feet tall, with his famous blond hair tumbling over his shoulders; the face that looked as though his cheekbones were chiselled from wood; I saw the muscles of his sword arm, the golden dragon rings that encircled it; breathed his body odour – that strange smell the Vikings have, of sheep grease and sweat and the iron after-bite of their victims' blood. I witnessed my father and brothers cut down with axe and sword, the massacre of their thegns, the red flood running across the threshold. One of Harald's men was raping my sister across the table. I put my fingers in my ears to shut out the sound of axe on bone, the screams of the women.

Too young to be killed as a warrior, I was taken from my hiding place as a slave, herded with other youths onto the ships dragged up on the shore. As we left, the wolves were already slinking out of the forest to feed on the fallen.

There were more than fifty vessels on the strand, each with as many as forty oars. If it had not been for the occasion, that fleet would have been a beautiful sight; their prows carved into the shape of swans or serpents, elaborately painted and touched with gold. When the sails were unfurled and filled with wind, the wave-horses of the Norwegian king inspired shudders of fear and awe in the beholder. Huddled in the centre of the ship, next to the barrels of looted treasure, roped to them with my hapless kith, I faced the stern and had no choice but to watch my homeland disappear behind the waves as we rode far out onto the ocean. The flames lightened the sky, sparks flying up into the dusk, until we rounded the headland and it passed out of sight.

By good chance, my own lyre was among the goods taken from our hall and, when it was discovered, I was ordered to play for Harald and his thegns on the long journey back to Norway. And when we arrived at court I was appointed scop to the king. To be scop is a great honour. And also a curse. One of my first tasks was to compose a praise-song for Harald celebrating his conquests. I saw his lips twist as he ordered me to do it, as if he knew the horror that he inflicted on me and enjoyed it. If you had asked me before, if I could sing the praises of the king who murdered my father, I would have declared myself willing to cut out my tongue, rather than let the words pass my lips. But it's strange how the need to survive compels us to do things that we find repugnant. It wrenches the soul from its dwelling place, leaving only emptiness behind.

Keeping my true identity hidden has proved easier than I feared. I found, by starving myself, that I could avoid the onset of the monthly courses that would betray me. Not that it was hard. Whenever someone plunged their knife into a joint of meat on a platter, I could see my father's breast cleft in two, and the blood running along the floor of the hall. My breasts have remained those of the child of twelve I was when Harald seized me. And I can piss against the wall with the best of the men.

When I was first brought to the English court by Tostig's messengers, the queen asked to see me in her private chamber. She scrutinized me up and down, as if she could see what was under my clothes, and then she began to question me. At first it was about my home, the Landwaster's raid, the fate of my kinsmen. Where had I learned to read and write? At least I could answer those questions honestly. Then it was about the Norwegian court. She seemed curious about Harald and his family. What did the Norwegian king look like? she asked.

My instincts were to be wary in what I said. I told her that he was taller than any man I had ever seen, with blond beard and hair that reached well below his shoulders. He was still a handsome man but had a scar on his cheek and one eyebrow higher than the other, which gave his face a hard, almost cruel look. I said nothing else.

'And what of his queen? Is it true that she's the daughter of the King of Kievan Rus?'

'She is, my Lady. They say that Harald sacked Byzantium to get enough gold to marry her.' They had told me in the Norwegian hall that Ellisev's father had demanded a golden ring as her bride price. Now she has rings on both arms and a weighty torc around her neck said to be worth a small kingdom.

'And is she beautiful? I'm told that he's taken another wife.'

'Queen Ellisev only gave him daughters, so he married another woman who has two sons. But it's Ellisev the king prefers. She's quite old now, but whenever he returns from one of his battles he takes her to bed straight away without removing his boots.' It was true, I had witnessed it myself. How he picked her up in his long arms like a child and swung her above his head, before carrying her off to his chamber, the blood scarcely dry on his skin.

There was a strange expression on the queen's face. But she began to ask more questions – some of them I barely understood; my knowledge of the Saxon tongue having been learned from songs and stories. But the queen herself spoke Danish, her mother, it seems, is a Dane and, when she saw my puzzlement, began to ask me things in my native language, about my family and their status in Denmark, which I was hard-pressed to avoid. I gave the impression that my father was simply a thegn, wealthy, but of little importance. I wondered why she asked me these things. What did she already know, or suspect? But her last question was unexpected. Was I familiar with the story of Olaf Tryggvason? she asked.

Who doesn't know the story of the first Christian king of the Norse and one of their greatest warriors? I told her that I did. That's good, the queen said, for it is the king's favourite tale and he never tires of it in hall. I thought it a strange story for a Saxon king to be fond of, but I didn't tell her that.

Then the queen said, 'I expect that my brother Tostig will have asked you to write to him to tell him of your arrival and the king's reception of his gift.'

I said nothing, wondering how she had known what I'd been told by the earl.

She went on, 'You will write, but you will bring it to me first so that I may read it before it is sent. Is that understood?'

I nodded.

Edith is a dangerous woman.

I sleep in the lower hall, with everyone else and their hunting dogs. We put our bedrolls down on the floor as near the fire as we are allowed and wrap our cloaks around ourselves. You get used to the noises; the dogs scratching for fleas, the scuffles, the night cries. There's no privacy. I try not to think of my former position, the wooden bed with the embroidered hangings, the sheepskins to keep out the winter cold, my waiting maids. Dwelling on what you have lost does nothing to warm the body or the spirit. I miss clean linen most. The English are not of the cleanest habits, at least among the lower orders.

On the night the old king died there was fierce competition for places close to the fire and I was too late to secure one, having played late in hall to try to lighten the mood, though it proved impossible. People were talking quietly in corners, watching each other. There was an atmosphere, like the feeling before a battle, when you know something is coming, but not when, or what will happen.

Arthur was in the lower hall, curled up in one of the corners where I took my bedroll. He is one of the younger brothers of Edwin and Morcar of Mercia, but by a concubine, rather than a wife, so he's not accorded their status. He usually sleeps in their lodgings, but tonight, he tells me quietly, they have all remained at the palace. 'The king can't last long,' he says. 'My brother Edwin is in the king's chamber with the archbishop, Earl Harold and the queen.'

I lay down a little distance from him. Arthur is a couple of years older than I am, with the shadow of his first beard on his chin. We've become good friends, but sometimes he looks at me oddly in a way that makes me want to blush, except that I mustn't. And being near him gives me the strangest feelings – feelings that make me realise that I am still a girl, almost a woman, even if dressed in boy's clothes.

As I thought about what was unfolding, I began to feel very precarious. What happens to a slave when the master dies? Under the protection of King Edward, I had been safe for a while. But what would happen after he was dead? Tostig had fled to Flanders when he was made an outlaw after a quarrel with the king and his brother Harold. Would I have to seek refuge with him? I scarcely realised that I'd spoken aloud.

`You could come to us,' Arthur said. 'My brother Edwin likes the stories you tell, and his only scop is so old he can barely hold his lyre.'

'But will I be allowed?' I asked, unsure of the rules.

'I'll ask Edwin. He'll know.'

Arthur is kind, but it's shameful to be passed around like an animal, or a chattel; to belong, not to yourself, or your family, but to an overlord.

~ ~ ~

After dinner, in her private chamber with Harold, Edith dismissed her waiting maids who scuttled out like frightened children.

'Tell me!' Edith said, bringing her brother some wine and a basket of sweet breads. 'I saw messengers arrive a few hours ago. What did they say?'

'Harald of Norway is wintering in Orkney, presumably weighing up whether to claim the throne. If he comes south, he'll have a formidable army, particularly if Malcolm, King of the Scots, decides to join him. Malcolm's not our friend. He gave his loyalty to Tostig, not me.'

'But Morcar is Earl of Northumbria now. Surely he's in a position to repel them from the border?'

'Would you trust either Morcar or Edwin?'

Edith had to agree with him. The Mercian earls were no friends of the Godwin family. Who knew which way their allegiances would swing? She felt chilled and moved nearer to the fire, but it was something inside her, rather than the temperature of the chamber.

'Things have never been right since the king sent you all into exile,' she said. The memory of her sudden, inexplicable banishment fifteen years ago, when her father had fallen from grace, and the possibility that it might happen all over again within a few days, made her fearful. Edith's twenty years as queen consort had taught her that old grievances have a way of re-surfacing. The bones of the wronged did not lie quiet in their graves.

There had been only a year of exile, before her father and brothers had raised an army and demanded reinstatement at the point of a sword. Robert de Jumièges was replaced, and Edith had been recalled from the Abbey at Wilton where she'd spent eleven miserable months. The Godwins were forgiven, but only for political expediency. Edward had discovered that he couldn't control the petty squabbling of his nobles without them. Nor could he endure a court without Tostig to adorn it.

Shortly after their return Tostig was made Earl of Northumbria and Swein had died on a pilgrimage to Jerusalem to ask for forgiveness for the murder of his cousin and the abduction of the Abbess. Then their father had died of a seizure and Harold, the next in line, had inherited all his land, his titles and his wealth. Edith and her brother had become the most powerful people in the kingdom. She was the Queen and Harold became *Dux Anglorum*, duke of all England, second only to the king. Tostig, who had been the king's favourite, was no longer a constant presence at court, often absent in his role as Earl of Northumbria, something that suited Tostig, if not the king. But only a year ago, the Northumbrians had decided that he was too brutal and petitioned the king to dispossess him. The thegns and ealdormen had chosen Morcar as their earl, and Tostig had fled the country blaming Harold for his lack of support. The Godwin family was no longer the unified force it had once been and that disturbed Edith. Fate could turn on the spinning of a coin.

'It can only be a matter of hours before my husband dies,' Edith said. 'Then, as soon as the weather softens, all the claimants to the throne will descend upon us like ravening wolves.' England, rich and peaceful, but without an obvious heir, was a glittering prize. Edith feared that Harald of Norway, Sweyn of Denmark, William of Normandy, perhaps all three, might try to claim that prize by force. And then there was Edgar the Ætheling, Edward's fourteen-year-old cousin, currently the king's guest at Winchester. Would some of the English nobles attempt to put him on the throne?

Edith knew what happened when there was no true line of succession. After the death of Cnut the Great there had been confusion and violence. News of it had even reached the convent at Wilton Abbey where, still only a girl, she had been sewing her sampler and learning her psalter. She knew all the stories of the rivalries between Edward's half-brothers. His mother Emma's marriages to King Æthelred and then King Cnut had created a tangled web of relationships. There were plots and ambushes, killings and banishments, until Edward returned from Normandy, evaded would-be assassins, and secured the throne.

'I'm afraid, brother. Really afraid.' Edith could hear her voice trembling and despised her own weakness. 'What is going to become of me if your plan goes awry?'

'Don't fret, sister. I intend to seize the throne as soon as Edward takes his last breath,' Harold said. 'You'll be safe enough. The Godwins protect their own.'

'But do you think the Witan will allow you to be king?' Edith asked. This was something they'd discussed often in the last few months as Edward's health declined. It was that supreme council who would choose the king, regardless of seniority. Which of the claimants would they support? Or would it be Harold, king in all but title?

'In God's name, why not?' Harold held out his glass, impatient for more wine. 'Since the king lost interest, we've been regents, ruling the kingdom between us. Besides, I'm the richest man in the realm after the king and can mount more warriors than anyone else. Who's going to oppose me?'

'Edwin of Mercia for one.'

'But the other nobles will support me in the end. No one likes Edwin and it avoids turmoil and uncertainty.' He put down his glass. 'Dear God! If only you'd had children, Edith, we needn't be in this position.'

'That's unjust Harold!' She put her hand to her mouth. 'And unwonted coming from you. You know what he was. But everyone has accused me of being barren, and he was happy to let that be known. It's always the woman's fault if there are no heirs. If you knew how many nights I've ached for a husband who would give me children. I've worn my knees raw praying for it. But Edward couldn't even bear to touch me!'

Her voice was shaking again with the effort of holding back emotion, but she went on, 'He was forty-two when he married me. Did no one ever question why he'd never had a single concubine before that time? A single bastard child? Why he made Tostig, our beautiful brother, his constant companion? The hunting trips they made together? His failure to give Tostig an earldom that would take him away from court, until his hand was forced? He loved Tostig. They were inseparable!' Edith had a memory of the two men, a grey head and a blond head, bent together absorbed in their game. Had they also been lovers, as the common tale went?

'At least Archbishop Stigand's your friend.' Harold said. 'He's been quick to spread rumours of your husband's piety. The ordinary people believe him to be chaste to the point of sainthood.'

Edith snorted with bitter laughter and said, 'Many others think differently. I've always thought that *that* was what our father held over him, when our family was reinstated – for you know as well as I that the church regards such love be-tween men as a sin that incurs eternal damnation, whatever the common law says. Old Archbishop Robert de Jumièges hinted to me once that Godwin had sworn that he could give testimony against the king and Tostig if we were not given back our lands and privileges. Our father was very good at political manipulation.'

Harold was staring into the fire and made no response.

Edith was sure she was right. In the years that followed, the king had been afflicted by sadness and seized every opportunity he could to invite Tostig to court, or to accompany him on hunting trips or on a progress to Winchester or York. Edward had visibly pined for his company. After Tostig had gone into exile last year, Edward had never recovered. From that day on he had suffered what she thought of as an illness of the mind and spirit. It was as if, without Tostig, he had given up on life. He had lost interest in state-craft and spent his time and money building abbeys instead, as if to expiate a great sin.

It was past midnight when one of the stewards came to summon them back to the king's chamber. Edith was dozing in her chair, tired to the point of exhaustion.

The room echoed with the prayers chanted by the monks. It was now Epiphany, perhaps a fitting date for a king to die, particularly, Edith thought bitterly, if he was rumoured to be a saint. Archbishop Stigand had a chalice of wine and a vial of holy water on the table beside the bed. As soon as Edith and Harold were in the room, he anointed the king and read the last rites over him. Edward seemed to come to his senses as the archbishop touched his tongue with the wine and murmured something. He appeared to be asking a question. Stigand stood to one side and said, 'Your wife is here, your majesty.' Edward looked up at Edith standing next to the archbishop and shook his head, saying, in a quavering whisper, 'No wife.' His lips parted as if gasping for air and then he gathered himself with visible effort and said,

'We have lived as father and daughter, by God's truth.' Then he was consumed by a fit of coughing and closed his eyes.

'That, at least, is a fact,' Edith said under her breath to Harold, standing beside her. She had to grind her teeth together to control her anger. Even on his death bed, Edward had denied her, just as he had failed her in his marriage bed.

'But he's saved us by his words,' Harold murmured. 'At least we won't have to wait nine months to see if you produce an heir.'

Why, Edith thought, did the men always think of themselves and their own interests? For that was how her marriage had come about, arranged by a father who had seen her only as a means to power. Soon after her parents had brought her home from the convent where she had been educated, she had heard her father talking about Cnut's succession with Earl Leofric in hall, as she and her mother served the wine. She heard her father say 'I've seen Edward Æthelredson and I can swear he's throne-right-worthy. He's served his time in European wars and learned state-craft at the Duke of Normandy's court.'

And Leofric had replied, 'He's a Saxon, at least. The last of Æthelred's brood,' and then with great sarcasm, 'I just pray he's not as ill-advised as his father was.'

'Not with us to counsel him.' Godwin had laughed and leaned back in his chair, staring down at his wine. 'He's a man in middle life, has spent his manhood in foreign courts, he knows nothing of how things go here. The power will be ours.'

Leofric had less confidence, but in the end her father had prevailed. And so Edward had been made king. Edith, as Godwin's eldest daughter, had been the price of his support. She had been married in Winchester and crowned Queen of England, the daughter of a mere earl with no royal blood at all. They had changed her name, which had come from her mother, because it was felt to be too Danish, and so she had become the Lady Edith.

The memory gave her no pleasure. After the feast, they had brought the king to her chamber, where she lay, in her best linen, with her hair brushed on the pillow. The archbishop – the Norman Robert Jumièges in those days – the king's steward, her father and Earl Leofric and their retinues and a scop playing the lyre, all standing at the foot of the bed, while Edward knelt at the prie-dieu and the archbishop blessed the bed and prayed for issue. And then they had drunk the bride cup and turned back the covers for Edward to join her. He had insisted that the candles be blown out, so there was only firelight to show her face, once they had left the chamber and closed the door. Had she been frightened? A little. But there was no need. He kissed her once, fumbled her breasts without enthusiasm and then turned over and fell asleep. In the morning he had given a purse of money to each of the maids of the bedchamber and sent them away. There was no-one to testify to her virginity. Even her chief maid-in-waiting, Mathilde, was one of Edward's Norman ladies.

Now, the king seemed weaker, his breathing quieter. The archbishop moved away and Harold took his place beside the bed, holding the king's hand. Edward said distinctly, 'My feet are cold.'

Edith felt for his long, thin, feet at the end of the bed. They were as cold as death itself. She rubbed them, warming them between her palms, trying to suppress her revulsion at the scaly skin of his heels, the curved horns of toenail. A wife, performing a last rite for a man old enough to be her father.

Harold was bending over the king, his ear close to Edward's mouth. Edith could see the king's lips moving.

'What's he saying?' she asked. Edward had become very still.

'He commended his kingdom to me and asked me to take care of his queen, did he not archbishop?'

Stigand looked startled and, for a few seconds, confused. But then, ever the astute politician, looking at Edward's face beginning to relax with approaching death, he said, 'Indeed, my lord. He gave all into your care.' Stigand made the sign of the cross over the bed.

Edith, watching her husband's face, counting the breaths, realised that she'd been holding her own breath for a long time. Edward was dead.

~ ~ ~

When Harold returned, exhausted, to his quarters, Eadgifu, the woman they called the Swan-neck, was waiting for him. She flung her arms around him, smiling, lifted up her face, and said playfully, 'Well, my king?'

Harold removed her arms and pushed her away from him. 'Don't call me that, Swan, you'll invite ill-fortune. I'm not king yet.' He sounded harsher than he meant to be and felt her recoil. 'Forgive me, I didn't mean to be unkind. I'm just very tired.'

'How's Edith?'

'Stricken.' Harold dropped his fur robe on the carved chest at the foot of the bed. 'But, I think, more for the loss of her position than her husband. Edward's taken little notice of her since he brought her back from Wilton. She's grieving for what could have been.'

There was a small silence, and then Eadgifu Swan-neck asked, 'And what will it mean for us?'

'I intend to be king, if the Witan will agree it.'

'And will I be crowned with you?' Eadgifu's voice faltered as she put into words the anxiety that had been troubling her all day. She was Harold's wife, but she knew there was no certainty that she would be crowned as queen.

There was a pause before he answered. 'That's my wish,'

Harold said, running a weary hand over his face. But there was constraint in his voice.

Eadgifu knew why. They had been hand-fasted after the Danish fashion and not married in the Christian church. She said quietly, 'I fear the archbishops will never agree to it.'

'If I'm king, I may do as I please.' Harold's voice was curt. 'And now, Swan, I must go to bed.' He began to tear off his clothes, clumsy with tiredness.

Eadgifu recognised his mood. He could be difficult, unapproachable, when he had things on his mind. She lay awake for a long time after the candles had been blown out. Twenty years of her life had been invested in the man who now lay unconscious beside her. Twenty years and five children. She had kissed him and sent him off to battle, embraced him when he returned, celebrated his fortunes when they were rising, tended his wounds when they were not, and endured his absence in exile when he was banished. Why should she not be queen? It was true she was only of royal blood through her mother's line, and her father wasn't an earl, but she was a great-granddaughter of Æthelred and a considerable landowner in East Anglia in her own right. The richest woman in England. Surely that counted for something?

She thought about their first meeting, shortly after King Edward had created Harold Earl of East Anglia. He had come to her father's hall and she had served him wine. He was twenty-four, as tall and muscular as any Saxon war-lord, but it was his eyes, a piercing blue, that had mesmerised her. His physical presence made her hands tremble as she filled his goblet at table. Harold told her father that he had been granted this eastern earldom by the king, to prepare for a possible incursion by Magnus of Denmark, and he wanted to have her father's support for the battle and approval for the levy that would supply the necessary troops. Her father had offered his daughter's hand in marriage, to be given with a dowry of money, men, and a fully equipped ship to repel the Danes. Despite advice to the contrary, her father regarded a connection with the Godwins as potentially useful. And Harold had not been unwilling. There had been an instant mutual attraction. Eadgifu's mirror told her what the scops already sang, that with her fair hair and long, slim neck, she was the most beautiful girl in all the lands of East Anglia. Her name meant 'precious gift' and her dowry was considerable. She was a worthy wife and she had brought Harold power in the east, where he most needed it. But, more than that, it was a love match.

In the morning, Harold was up and gone long before the winter sun made an appearance. Arrangements were being made for the Countess Gytha, his mother, to travel to London from her home in Wessex. She was old now, but Eadgifu knew that her mother-in-law would not be able to resist coming to watch her son crowned. She was a proud woman – one daughter a queen, and now her son was to be king. That was an achievement for a Danish noblewoman and she never lost an opportunity to make everyone aware of it. Neither Edith nor Harold could tolerate her for long, but Eadgifu liked her plain-speaking ways.

King Edward, already washed and dressed by the Benedictine brothers, was laid out in state on the bed in his chamber. Eadgifu went there first to pay her last homage. He looked very peaceful, his skin almost transparent in death. The monks had combed his long white hair and beard and laid his hands over a large gold cross studded with gems, placed on his chest. With the gold coronet on his head and his embroidered robe, he looked the very image of a saint in one of the illuminated books of prayer Queen Edith kept in her room. *So much for power and wealth*, Eadgifu Swan-neck thought to herself as she looked at him, *so quickly ended*. But perhaps it was the biting cold in the now fireless room that made her shiver.

Afterwards she walked along the quiet corridors to her sister-in-law's chambers. Two of Harold's hearth-carles were outside the door. The Godwins protect their own, she thought wryly. Inside, the queen was sitting in a chair beside the fire, surrounded by her waiting maids. The dowager queen, Eadgifu corrected herself, just as Edith raised her eyes. Something had gone from her. She looked diminished and almost uncertain as she got to her feet to face her sister-in-law. The wife of one king looking at another, Eadgifu thought. The Swan-neck bowed her head, out of habit, and then they embraced.

'So,' the dowager queen said. 'You hope to step into my shoes.' There was an edge to her voice. 'But don't expect me to stand aside. I've ruled this kingdom alongside my husband and brother for the past fifteen years. Harold will still need my counsel. You can't do that for him.' It was a warning.

Don't take on the Godwins, someone had once said in her father's hall, when he was wondering which way to take his loyalties just after King Harthacnut had died. Don't take on the Godwins – they're like a nest of vipers. I married a Godwin, Eadgifu thought, and yet I can never be family, I will always be on the outside.

'The king's funeral's tomorrow,' Edith said, 'And then the Witan are meeting to decide on his successor. We must both hope.'

'It should be clear. There's no one else with Harold's experience, or his power.' The Swan-neck's voice was full of pride.

'Edwin and Morcar are the stumbling blocks. Harold will have to buy their support.'

'But what can he offer them? Since Tostig was deposed, they already have almost half of England between them.'

The dowager gave her an odd look. 'I think you should prepare yourself.'

'For what?'

'You are, after all, only Harold's concubine in the eyes of the church.' There was no mistaking the bitter jibe. Eadgifu felt the colour rise up her neck and flush across her cheeks. She had to clutch her fists to prevent herself from slapping her sister-in-law across the face. 'How dare you say that to me! I'm his wife,' she said, as soon as she could trust herself to speak. 'And I have five children to testify to the fact.' Then she turned to sweep out of the room.

'The king's wife today,' her sister-in-law called after her. 'But who knows what you'll be tomorrow.'

~ ~ ~

The old king died in the night. It began as a whisper with the hearth-carles at the door and spread from sleeper to sleeper, rousing us all, and I found it impossible to go back to sleep. I got up, shivering, wrapping my cloak tightly round me and, glancing down, I saw Arthur staring up at me in that strange, almost puzzled, way he has. I went out to the latrine, and when I came back into the hall, the stewards were putting bread and meat on the tables and others were warming flagons of spiced ale with a poker at the fire. Bed-rolls were being stashed under the benches and there was an air of excitement. Arthur had gone, but he returned as I was nibbling a slice of bread. 'I've talked to my brothers, and Edwin has agreed that you can come to us. Harold already has two scops so he's sure you'll be allowed.' Arthur was beaming. 'From now on you're under the protection of the house of Mercia.'

I ate with them that evening in their palace near the river. Edwin was reported to have brought twenty ships with him from Mercia, all moored nearby ready for battle, or flight. No one knew what his intentions were, but he had brought an army with him just in case.

Just as they were finishing the meal, there was a bustle in the outer hall, the sound of feet, the clatter of metal. Edwin's steward pulled back the curtains and announced Earl Harold of Wessex. He came into the hall with his hearth-carles – not one to go anywhere without protection. He was dressed like a king in dark robes with gold embroidery and a fur cloak over all – a magnificent figure.

I was playing my lyre quietly beside the fire where Arthur was sitting and no one asked us to leave or seemed to notice us at all. Harold was invited to sit down and one of Edwin's household brought wine and bread. It's a sign of safety – you can't murder someone who has just eaten bread at your table, at least until they're outside your gates. They began to talk about the Witan and Harold asked, straight out, what their intentions were.

'It's a dangerous situation,' he said. 'The risks are very great, unless England has a strong king with widespread support in the country. Have you thought about the options?'

It was Morcar who spoke first. 'There's Sweyn of Denmark, who can lay claim to the crown through his kinship with Cnut. And Harald of Norway, too.'

'But he's just a Viking,' Edwin broke in. 'A chancer with his eyes on the prize of an empty throne. The Landwaster has no legitimate claim.' Edwin swirled his wine around in his cup and then said, 'The real threat is from the king's cousin, William of Normandy.' He looked straight across at Harold and asked, 'Is it true that Edward promised the throne to him?'

Harold looked uncomfortable. 'I can't be sure. It's supposed to have happened when Edward banished my family in '51. I was in Ireland with the King of Leinster and knew nothing of what he was doing at the time.'

'But it's said that you went to Normandy and swore an oath to William that you would support his claim when Edward eventually died?'

'You know, as well as I, that I was on my way to Flanders to negotiate the release of my youngest brother Wulfnoth, who's still being held by William as a hostage. Edward actually warned me not to go, and he was right. It was a foolish errand. I was shipwrecked on the coast, captured by Guy de Ponthieu, who intended to hold me to ransom, and then rescued by William, which put me under an obligation. He treated me very well and I fought two campaigns with him, winning one for him against the Bretons. He knighted me for that, but he wouldn't release Wulfnoth. It's true that I'm in his debt, but . . .' he paused and looked Edwin in the eye. 'Do you think I would compromise the throne of England so lightly by making such an oath? Do you think I would sabotage my own chances? I'll not be any man's thrall.'

Morcar said, 'In any case, an oath sworn under duress is void, however many holy relics you put your hand on. And it wasn't in Edward's gift to promise the throne to anyone. It's in our hands, in the hands of the Witan.'

'And then there's Edgar the Ætheling,' Edwin said smoothly. 'As the grandson of Edmund Ironside, Edward's half-brother, he has the best claim to the throne. Edward sent for him from Hungaria so that he might put him forward.'

'A youth of fourteen?' Harold said scathingly. 'Would you trust an untried youth to lead an army against any of our enemies?'

'And then there's yourself, of course,' Edwin said, ignoring his question. 'Earl Godwin's son. Not a drop of royal blood, but the most powerful man in England after the king; *Dux Anglorum*, regent, brother of the queen, battle-hardened, trained in state-craft. Is that your claim?'

'It is. But I'm not so arrogant that I would put it forward to the Witan without your support.'

'And what are you prepared to offer us in exchange?' Edwin's eyes were hooded, his face inscrutable.

'What are you asking?'

'That you marry our sister, Ældyth – Queen of Wales until you slew her husband, Gruffydd, while you were subduing the Welsh last year.'

Harold looked grim. 'And what will she say to marrying her husband's murderer?'

'She will do what we tell her.'

'And if I agree?'

'Then we will give you our support at the Witan, on condition that you marry her according to the rights of the Church and that she's declared the queen consort and the children of your marriage your rightful heirs.'

Harold was very quiet. Very still. At length he said, 'I understand.'

'And there's another condition,' Morcar said, suddenly. 'That you get rid of the Normans at court. There are too many of the bastards.'

Harold's eyes narrowed. 'And what about the Danes? Are you going to purge them too?'

'Are you worried, Harold Half-Dane?' Morcar's voice was mocking.

Edwin laughed and made a gesture to quieten his brother. 'Sleep easy. It's too late for that. You'd have to remove half the nobility of England. No wonder Harald of Norway thinks he'd be at home here.'

Edwin turned back to Harold. 'And what of our sister? Will you marry her?'

Harold said nothing for a few moments, and then – as if coming to a decision – said, 'Will you give me time overnight to think about your proposal? Marriage is not a thing to be entered lightly.'

Edwin nodded. 'You may give us your answer tomorrow, before the Witan meets.'

~ ~ ~

When Harold came back from his meeting with the Mercians, he was very subdued. Eadgifu was almost asleep but woke as he turned the covers back to climb in beside her. She turned toward him automatically but was surprised to be taken in his arms and held very tightly. And then he began to kiss her in a way that brooked no refusal, forcing open her mouth with his tongue and crushing her breasts with his hands. It was so unlike him – he was normally a gentle lover for such a big, passionate man. But this time he turned her over, spread her legs and entered her so fiercely she had to stifle a cry. Afterwards, she realised that he was weeping on her shoulder and knew that something had happened and that she dared not ask.

In the morning he was gone and then there was the king's funeral and when that was over, Harold went straight into the Witan. She saw his cavalcade from the window, returning to the palace, the royal standard of Wessex with its golden dragon flying in front of him, and knew that he'd been chosen. About an hour later a messenger came to say that the king wanted to see her.

When she went into the chamber she bent very low in front of him. He looked tired and there was a grim set to his jaw.

'Sit down', he said. 'There's something I must tell you.'

Eadgifu sat in the chair next to him.

'In a few hours, I'll be crowned king in St Peter's Church.' He paused and then said, with difficulty, 'But I'm afraid you will not be beside me.'

Eadgifu felt her heart turn to stone.

'The Witan was unanimous. Edwin and Morcar agreed to support me, but on one condition.'

'Which was?'

'That I marry their sister, Ældyth of Mercia. There was no other way. I needed the support of all the earls.'

Eadgifu tried to swallow and thought she would choke. 'And what is to become of me? And our children? Are we not legitimately married?'

Harold said nothing.

Eadgifu felt rage building inside her. 'What is to become of our sons, Godwin, Edmund, Magnus and the little ones? And me, the twenty years we've loved each other? Have I to stand by and watch you bed some young girl, more beautiful than me? In front of a court that will enjoy my humiliation?'

He let her continue, his eyes downcast. An honourable man, Eadgifu thought, caught in a trap, but her anger compelled her to go on. 'And will Ældyth enjoy fucking the man who killed her husband?'

'That's enough Swan.' He sounded sterner than she had ever heard him. 'Sometimes there are things we have to do that aren't pleasant. Do you think I don't love you? That I wouldn't rather see out my years in your bed?'

Eadgifu was crying now, unwillingly showing her weakness.

'Of course our marriage was legitimate. We were married in the Danish way, as was your father, my father and all our kin.' His voice was shaking and there was something that sounded like anger underlying his words. 'That all changed when Edward brought his French priest to England and made him archbishop. The devious Robert of Jumièges ruled that marriage was no longer a civil contract, but a Christian sacrament. Because of that, if you aren't married in church you can legally marry again.'

'We married in *More Danico*,' Eadgifu said. 'And now you are marrying in *More Politico*!' She laughed unsteadily.

'These are hard times for both of us,' Harold said. 'But we must bear it.'

For the sake of a kingdom, Eadgifu thought, bowing

her head. *He has cast me off for a crown.* She should have known all along, for the ambition of the Godwins ran deep in every vein and it had been talked of privately.

'I promise,' Harold said, 'that you will not suffer. You'll be treated with the same respect due to my wife, and our sons will have every right to succeed me. I'll see to that.' He paused. 'There's a precedent. You must remember that King Cnut was first married, after the Danish fashion, to the daughter of an ealdorman of Northampton, before he married Queen Emma in the Christian way. And the son of his first marriage became king after his death, before Emma's children. You have no need to worry.'

Eadgifu said nothing. There was nothing that could be said. She got up and curtsied very low, and when he held out his hand, she kissed it, feeling his fingers tremble under her lips. Not husband and wife any more, but king and subject.

~ ~ ~

Edith declined the litter, leaving it to her mother Countess Gytha. She herself would walk in the procession behind her husband's coffin. It was no distance from the palace to St Peter's and she had had no fresh air for days. Veiled, wrapped in a fur cloak, surrounded by her ladies and Harold's hearth-carles, she felt safer than she had inside the palace, which had suddenly seemed full of dark alcoves and doors that opened and shut without anyone going in or out. People stopped talking whenever she appeared. It was intolerable.

Harold had told her not to come to the funeral – it was unnecessary – and she was outraged. She wanted to be there, to hear Archbishop Stigand pronounce the last words, to see Edward's mortal remains placed in the tomb, to face the knowledge that all her hopes and dreams had come to nothing. *I'm forty*, she thought, *and my life is over.*

Was she too old to have a child? She still had her monthly courses, although few women gave birth as old as this. And what of love? It was one of her deepest regrets that she had never known passion. When she looked at her sister-in-law, Eadgifu Swan-neck, she was almost sick with envy. The way Harold looked at her; the way her belly swelled so regularly. He had made no secret of the delight she still gave him.

Could such a thing as that ever be hers? It was rumoured that her termagent mother-in-law, the Dowager Queen Emma, had had an affair with a bishop between her marriage to Edward's father and her marriage to King Cnut. There was also a rumour that there had been a child, a girl, spirited away to Normandy to be reared. Nothing would surprise Edith. A woman who could conspire to kill one of her own sons in order to put another son on the throne, was capable of anything. She remembered Edward telling her, when they were first married, how Emma had abandoned him and his brother in Normandy and seen nothing of them for thirty years. And then, when he acceded to the throne, he had had to take three of his most powerful Earls and their armies to Winchester to dispossess Emma of the crown jewels, the treasury and the deeds of all the land she had refused to hand over to him after his coronation.

Edith stood with her head bowed before the coffin, as the Archbishop of Canterbury read the funeral mass, and remembered Emma's fierce face, the woman who had made her own life as a young queen so utterly miserable. Emma had refused to relinquish her role as regent, or as chief adviser to the king, ruling his life and that of his new wife with little regard for their feelings. In the end Edward had banished her from court. Edith felt a twinge of sympathy for Emma, because that was now her own situation. Whoever Harold married in the Christian church would be queen and she, who had previously held so much power, would be redundant. Eadgifu Swan-neck, who had little interest in politics, would have been no competition at all. But Ældyth, sister to the Mercian Earls, Queen of the Welsh, if everything Edith had been told was true, was another matter entirely.

Harold's coronation followed the funeral so quickly there was barely time to sweep away the mason's dust from the sealing of the tomb. It seemed strange to see her brother in the gold cope, kneeling at the altar to make his oath before the archbishop. Not Stigand of Canterbury this time, but Ealdred, the Archbishop of York. There had been much discussion around the choice, but Stigand, though appointed to the See of Canterbury by Edward, was not recognised by Rome and Harold was determined that there should be no challenge to the legitimacy of his coronation. Ealdred was an old friend, a diplomat priest and a well-tried general who had supported Harold on his Welsh campaigns. Now he had been chosen to place the crown on Harold's head.

Archbishop Ealdred prompted him with the words and Harold's voice was steady as he repeated the three promises in his low, sonorous voice. 'In the name of the Holy Trinity, I promise three things to the Christian people who are subject to me: first, that God's church and all Christian people in my dominions preserve true peace; the second is that I forbid robbery and all unrighteous things to all orders; the third, that I promise and command justice and mercy in all judgements, so that the kind and merciful God because of that may grant us all his eternal mercy, who lives and reigns. Amen.'

Without warning Edith's eyes filled with tears. She knew from his voice that Harold meant every word of the vows. Then she watched her brother being led to the coronation chair while the choristers sang an anthem. Harold bowed down on his knees before the archbishop to receive the holy oil and have the crown placed on his fair head. Gold on gold.

He was almost lost among the massed ranks of bishops and priests, a sea of golden copes and mitres. Harold had his eyes closed as the archbishop made the declaration, and everyone shouted 'God save the King!' Edith knew what it meant to him, what the kingdom meant to him. England was everything. He had fought to secure it as one united realm, determined that it should not revert to separate, warring kingdoms. He had talked of founding a line of Saxon kings to take England forward in peace and prosperity. Harold was seated on the throne and the earls and bishops lined up, one by one, to kiss the king's ring on his finger and swear their oaths. She watched her brothers, Gyrth and Leofwine kneel before him and the thought of Tostig, and his absence, made her heart ache.

Where had it all gone wrong? Edith thought that his fortunes had started to unravel the moment the king, pressed by their father Earl Godwin, had made Tostig Earl of Northumbria. Godwin's ambition had not taken into account that he was clearly unfit for such a great responsibility. Tostig was rash, quick to anger, fonder of hunting than state-craft, a lover of feasting and playing board games with the king. But after the reinstatement of their family Tostig had failed in an attempt to subdue an uprising and been humiliated when an exasperated Harold had had to bring his own carles and do the job himself. Then Tostig had replaced the laws of Cnut, part of the fabric of the earldom, with West Saxon law which was wholly alien to the northerners. The breaking point came when Tostig, because he had failed to understand the relative poverty of the northern earldom he ruled, taxed the Northumbrians too hard in order – he said – to raise an army to defend against Viking incursions. Edith had told Tostig herself that these northerners were subjects of an old, venerable kingdom. They were Norsemen, not Saxons. Their lives were harder; they saw things differently. He needed to be patient and listen to what his ealdormen were telling him. But he didn't, and so the Northumbrians had raised an army and had him expelled. Nursing his humiliation he had fled to his father-in-law Count Baldwin in Flanders, rather than return to court, blaming Harold for everything.

If only he had come today, Edith thought, Harold would have made all fair between them and given him an Earldom somewhere where he couldn't do any harm. Since Harold's own domains were being passed to Gyrth and Leofwine, there would have been places Tostig could have filled, if only he would swallow his pride.

When the last of the Earls and Bishops had paid homage to the new king, Edith supported her mother to the throne and, after Gytha had made her homage, she knelt to kiss her brother's hand. Their roles had been reversed.

The evening meal served both as funeral meat and coronation feast. Such haste was, she had overheard one of her waiting maids say, a bad omen. Edith found her usual place at High Table occupied by the youthful Earls of Mercia and Northumbria, Edwin and Morcar. On the other side of the king, Edgar the Ætheling, grandson to King Edmund Ironside, had been brought from Winchester to swear his oath of fealty to Harold. He was a quiet boy, Edith thought, unremarkable. He looked lost among so many powerful nobles; a youth ripe for manipulation. Further down were Harold's younger brothers, Gyrth Earl of East Anglia and Leofwine Earl of Kent, and, below them Harold's two eldest sons, Godwin and Edmund, nineteen and sixteen, young thegns already trained in the military arts of their father. She wondered if Harold had told them that they were no longer going to be Æthelings – princes of the blood – but to take their places among the dispossessed.

Edith was taken, by the steward, to a place lower down, beside her sister-in-law, Eadgifu Swan-neck, who looked as though she had been crying all day.

'I hope to God,' the Swan-neck said, taking a long draught from her cup of wine, 'that he doesn't expect me to witness his wedding!'

'He's a kinder man than that.'

'And he'd better not think of sending me to an abbey! I'll cut his balls off first.'

'Hush.' Edith put her hand on her sister-in-law's arm. 'There are too many ears around us. And I suspect he won't do that. He'll want you near him. Can't you see that, every now and then, he looks across at you? You are his true wife, whoever else he marries.'

'He's promised the Mercians that he'll marry their sister, Queen of the Welsh.'

Edith nodded. 'He had no choice and, I suspect, neither did she.'

'I wonder how many brides are forced to marry the man who sent their husband's head in a basket to the king? I hope she gets joy from bedding him!'

~ ~ ~

Harold didn't come to her chamber that night, which was just as well, since Eadgifu would have sent him packing, king or no king. She hadn't known that she would feel such pain. Childbirth had been agony, but a different kind of suffering, with the hope of happiness at the end of it. But this was endless and not to be endured, knowing that she would see another woman in her husband's arms, his bed, her place at table, and her children pushed out of the succession. The worst of it was, that she had begun to suspect that she was carrying another child. The thought made her want to vomit.

She had been eighteen when they married and her nick-name had been 'Eadgifu the Fair'; now she was thirty-eight and the years and the children she'd birthed had all taken their toll on her body. She had put on weight, there were threads of grey in her hair, and her mirror told her that the skin of her long neck had begun to sag below the chin. The Welsh queen, Ældyth, was very young and rumoured to be beautiful, as dark as she herself was blonde. What man of Harold's age and position wouldn't desire such a wife? It was pointless to try and rationalise it. Eadgifu cried herself to sleep.

Part Two

The Welsh Mare

Happiness came back   the hall was thronged
and a banquet set forth

Even a queen   outstanding in beauty . . .
should weave peace . . . heal old wounds
and grievous feuds

Beowulf Trans Seamus Heaney

Chester. A cold, blustery winter's day with flurries of snow, too cold for walking in the garden. Ældyth was entertaining her daughter in the solar, above the great hall. Nest was just beginning to learn her letters and enjoyed looking at the illustrated books of saints that Edwin had in his collection. Ældyth thought that her brother was not a religious man, nor a lover of books, but one who liked to advertise his wealth with precious objects. Sitting on the window seat in the alcove, she had the perfect view of Edwin's estates beyond the gates, the rolling fields and farms, all belonging to him. From the Welsh borders to the northern sea, Mercia was his earldom, his kingdom. It was all very well-tended, prosperous, not like the barbarous lands of the Welsh, though she had grown to like the magnificence of the mountains and the rocky coastline.

'Be careful,' she said to Nest, who was tugging at one of the illuminated vellum pages. 'These books are very precious.'

'I like this one,' Nest said. 'It has a snake round the edges.' The serpent was their family emblem. Nest liked angels too, with their swan-like wings and golden hair. Her own hair was dark, like her mother and her Welsh father.

Nest didn't remember him and Ældyth was sorry for that. Gruffydd had been quite old when she was married to him by her ambitious father. She'd never met the Welsh king, never seen him, until her father and her brother Edwin took her to his palace at Rhuddlan as part of the peace-keeping bargain in some war or other. A girl of thirteen, and all she knew of her bridegroom was that he had the reputation of a brutal, pitiless ruler, despatching his enemies with the same unconcern as a farmer killing the Sunday goose. But, after the horror of the first night in his bed, Gruffydd had become fond of her and had treated her well, and he had given her Nest and never once complained that she had not provided him with a son. He said that he had enough from his previous marriages to start several wars, without adding another to the brood..

Since Gruffydd's death in battle, hunted down like an animal by Harold Godwinson, she had lived here in her brother's house, with no occupation other than reading the books in his library and the education of her daughter. It was only an interlude that she knew wouldn't last forever. Edwin, she supposed, would find her another husband to promote his interests. She was still a prize worth having. Ældyth looked down at her daughter, innocently turning the pages of the book, five years old, but already dark-eyed and pretty, and wondered what fate awaited her, how long her childhood would be allowed to last. *We are born to be pawns in a man's game*, Ælbyth thought. To be beautiful was a curse.

Nest put down the book and climbed up on the seat in the window, pressing her face to one of the small panes of glass near the top. 'Someone's coming,' she said.

Ælbyth put her own face to the glass and could see a cloud of dust rising from the road approaching the gates. Not just one person, but a whole cavalcade of horses. Was her brother Edwin coming back so soon? What did it mean?

But it was Morcar who stamped into the great hall, trying to warm his frozen feet at the fire, throwing off his gloves, shouting for someone to bring him spiced ale.

'Welcome brother,' Ælbyth said. 'This is a surprise! What's happened?'

'Edwin sent me to fetch you,' Morcar sounded querulous. 'I've had a nightmare journey in this god-awful weather. But I can't rest. You need to get ready to leave tomorrow.'

'Why? What's the reason for this haste?'

'The king's dead. You're to come with me to London to marry Harold Godwinson.' He paused. 'You're to be the Queen of England.'

~ ~ ~

The atmosphere in the Mercian hall is very cheerful tonight – a great deal of beer and French wine has been drunk and a scuffle has already broken out between two of the hearth-carles over a board game. Everyone is waiting for the arrival of Morcar, who has been sent to fetch his sister, the Queen of the Welsh, who is reported to be the most beautiful woman in the kingdom.

'Hey, scop!' Edwin calls out, pointing to me sitting at the

lower end of the lower table. 'You call yourself a scop – so give us a riddle.'

The Saxons love a word puzzle even more than the Norsemen, and the more lewd they are the better. I've learnt a great deal in the past two years that gently bred girls know nothing of. So, I stand up in the centre of the hall as he commands me and, when they fall silent, I begin, 'What is soft in the evening, rises during the night . . .'

'Oh, we know that one!' a hearth-carle calls out. 'Give us something we haven't heard before.'

That's tricky, since they know so many. But after two more false starts, I think of one I heard King Harald recite in his hall.

'A young and beautiful woman, keeps me locked
in the chest beside her bed; she takes me out sometimes,
raises me up with gentle hands and offers me up
to her lord, to quench his desire. When he takes me
he sticks his head hard inside me, pushing
it upwards into the narrowest part.
This is my fate, dressed as I am, to be filled
with something rough if the lord
who possesses me is virile enough.'

I sit down and wait for them to guess the meaning. There's a lot of discussion and crude laughter. Eventually it's the Earl's chaplain who solves the puzzle.

'Is it a helmet?'

I nod and Edwin takes a silver cup from his table and tosses it towards me. 'That's for your wit,' he says. So now I have a silver cup, but who knows if I can keep it. When he's sober tomorrow he may take it back.

I go sometimes to the palace with Arthur. His brother Edwin is one of the king's Council and Arthur attends him as a thegn. The court is in turmoil. Harold Godwinson refuses to sleep in the old king's bedchamber – which is understandable given that the Dowager Edith still occupies the queen's apartment next door. So he is to stay in his own quarters, which means that his wife, now reduced to the status of a concubine, has had to move into other rooms to make way for the arrival of the new queen. The Swan-neck was so hysterical it could be heard all over the palace. Harold took himself off to St Peter's with the archbishop on church business to avoid it.

But I have now to compose a lay for Earl Edwin, celebrating the marriage of his sister to the king. He's making me earn his silver cup. And, this morning, the Dowager called me to her chamber to ask if I would compose a praise-song for her husband. I bowed and agreed, having no other choice. I wonder what she would have said if I'd told her the rhymes that are being chanted in hall when she and her kinsmen aren't there.

> Edward the fair, pure and mild
> never gave his wife a child.
> Confessed so often of his sin
> God has shrunk his lower limb.
> And we all know his love for churls
> Norman bishops and English Earls.

No one dares to say it aloud, but the crude gestures they use when they sing it leave no doubt.

~ ~ ~

It was late in the afternoon when Morcar's cavalcade reached London. Ældyth felt frozen to the core in spite of her fur robes and the warmth of the horse's body between her legs. Her ladies rode behind her. Morcar had insisted that only two could accompany her, since the king would want to appoint ladies from his own court to wait on her. She had brought her cousin Merwenne, her closest friend, as well as Angharad, widow of Hywel, a Welsh Prince, because she had the highest status of any of her ladies, and because it was a political gesture designed to placate the Welsh.

As they crested the last hill, the city sprawled below them enclosed in immense walls and surrounded by marshland – haunted, in the evening light, by the cries of wild geese and swans returning to their roosts. By the time they reached the narrow streets, there was barely enough light to see and the hearth-carles had to light their torches to make a way through. Ældyth was surprised to see so many fine stone buildings among the jumble of wooden houses. In the centre, the tower of the new church rose against the sky, catching the last rays of light, like a finger pointing to God.

At Edwin's palace he was there to greet her and she was taken straight to the chamber that had been assigned to her. Inside the room, the fire had been lit and the bed prepared, and three ladies came forward to greet her.

'These are to be your waiting women,' Edwin said. 'It's been agreed with the king.' He beckoned them forward.

The first to approach was a woman Ældyth thought was probably in her thirties, richly dressed but rather plain, broad in the hips, with dark hair plaited round her head.

'This is Hilde, wife of Earl Leofwine Godwinson.'

Hilde bowed to her. There was no hostility in her eyes, as Ældyth had feared, but only frank curiosity. Then Edwin presented a younger woman, nearer to her own age, blonde-haired and with a lively smile. 'This is Theo, wife of Earl Gyrth Godwinson.'

So, she was to be surrounded by Godwins, Ældyth thought, who would report her conversations, visitors, everything she did, to the king.

Then Edwin's voice changed, taking on a more reverent tone, and he bowed as he presented a dark girl of about sixteen or seventeen. 'And this is the Lady Margaret, sister to Edgar the Ætheling, grand-daughter to King Edmund Ironside. She is to be your chief Lady of the Bedchamber.'

They all bowed to each other and Ældyth introduced Merwenne and Angharad, who had been standing quietly just inside the door. She turned to Edwin. 'I hope that the king intends to let me keep my own waiting women?'

'He has no objection.'

This was going to be an interesting situation, Ældyth thought – women from two royal households, waiting on a third, their every movement watched by the Godwin family.

When she'd refreshed herself, Ældyth was taken to Edwin's hall where she was seated at high table between her brothers and offered food she had little appetite for. A saddle of mutton sat on the board in front of them and Edwin was greedily taking his fill. *I am like that sheep*, Ældyth thought, *being meekly taken to the slaughter*. She shivered as the word came into her mind. Her first husband had been cut down in battle by the long-swords of Harold Godwinson's men. And now she was to marry him. To be twice a queen in such circumstances was not a good omen. She was a blood-maiden; her marriage tainted by the blood of Gruffydd. Where would it end? Tomorrow the Christian priests would bless her union with Harold, but there was a darker force, something they called Wyrd, older than Christianity, that steered men's destinies. If you offended the three sisters who controlled it, no power on earth could change the fate they decreed for you. Ældyth felt that she was surrounded by danger.

England, Morcar had told her on the journey, was facing a turbulent time. They were staying overnight in a monastery, in cold, comfortless rooms. Very soon, Morcar said, the kingdom would be fighting for its survival. Harold Godwinson was the only man who could hold it together. 'So, you will do your duty,' he had said tersely. 'The future of our family, and of the country, is at stake.'

In the morning, her ladies dressed her in a gown of blue wool, held at the waist by a belt of gold studded with garnets. She wore the gold circlet on her head, that proclaimed her Queen of Wales. It was woven from strands of gold intertwined in the shape of serpents, with eyes of garnet and claws of lapis lazuli. Then her maids put a blue cloak lined with beaver on her shoulders and she was ready. Her brother went first, with his escort of hearth-carles carrying the Mercian standard, and she followed, accompanied by her ladies.

Only a small group of people stood in the king's chamber when she was ushered in by his steward. There was the archbishop standing to one side in a red cope sewn with gold thread. Two well-dressed men beside him bowed to her and nodded to her ladies. She guessed, from the strong family resemblance, that they were the earls, Leofwine and Gyrth, the king's brothers. Seated in a chair beside the fire, a woman rose to greet her as she entered. She looked youthful, but there were lines on her forehead and, from the way she held herself and the golden circlet on her head, Ældyth presumed that this was the queen dowager. A woman to be reckoned with, she thought, as she met the shrewd eyes that were examining her from head to toe.

Then Harold Godwinson himself came forward to greet her. She had known who he was from the moment she entered the room. He had a presence that dominated everyone else; a great bear of a man, taller than anyone else, with golden hair threaded with silver, and moustaches after the

Saxon fashion. He had an air of self-containment, of power being held in check. But when he looked down at her, his piercing blue eyes were kind, which she had not expected. She bowed and kissed the ring on his hand, almost faint from relief. On the journey she had been afraid that he would be unattractive. She knew that he was around forty years of age, a time of life when men developed bellies and began to lose their hair. Ældyth had a horror of facial warts and unsightly scars. But Harold's face was unmarked and his belly only slightly thickened.

'Did you have a hard journey?' he asked.

'Better than it could have been.' It seemed odd to be making polite conversation. 'The ground was frozen, so we made good time.'

He grunted agreement and seemed to be trying to think of something else to say. Not a man of words.

The Dowager Queen was more articulate. 'I hope you find your quarters comfortable. Robert the Staller will take you there shortly. And then I hope we will have time to talk. I'm glad that you speak the Saxon language.'

Ældyth held Edith's gaze. 'What else would I speak, my Lady?' Edith's inference that she was uneducated was an insult. Ældyth wondered if it was calculated. At home she spoke the Mercian dialect with her family, and in the Welsh court she had spoken Welsh. But, like all civilised people in England, she also spoke the Saxon tongue. Ældyth decided that the Dowager Queen was someone to be wary of.

'The wedding is this afternoon,' Harold said, 'and you will be crowned Queen of England at the same time.' The archbishop bowed his assent, and Harold added, nodding to Edwin, 'Your brother will bring you to church'. He turned to one of the men standing just inside the door and gestured to him to come forward. The man bowed, almost to the floor, and presented the king with a box.

Harold opened it and held it out to Ældyth. 'My bride gift to you.'

It was a collar of gold, worked, after the Saxon fashion with an inlay of garnet and one sapphire, deep blue and large as a pebble, set in front. It was exquisite.

'Thank you, my lord.'

She bowed her head and Merwenne came forward to place the collar round her neck. Ældyth could feel the weight of it pressing on her shoulder bones like a yoke. She glanced up at the man she was about to marry and saw that his eyes were anxious. They were intelligent eyes that held something in them that looked curiously like pity.

~ ~ ~

The new queen is quite unlike any of the other women here, and the most beautiful woman I've ever seen, either here or at the court of the Norse king. She is tall and dark and very slim, not like the plump blonde Saxon women. But it's a cold kind of beauty, polished, like a knife blade. All bone, one of the men behind me said, sniggering to his companions as he added, 'I wonder how the king'll like lying on a sack of stones'. Queen Ældyth holds herself very still and her dark eyes are watchful. Her wedding – a blood wedding, they said – is the talk of the halls. How she had been escorted into St Peter's by her brother's hearth-carles, married by the Archbishop of York and then crowned with the same crown that Queen Emma had worn for her marriage to Cnut. A nice touch to please the Danes, some said. Then she had left the church with the king, escorted this time by his hearth-carles. It's all very different to the way it used to be done at home – a simple handfasting in hall in front of the fire, the drinking of the bride cup, the swearing of the oath, the exchange of gifts.

The wedding feast was as jolly as it could be in the circumstances; a funeral, a rushed coronation, a forced marriage, and – hanging over it all – the threat of an invasion, which everyone says is sure to come. But we tried to be cheerful. One of Harold's old scops sang some wedding pieces I hadn't heard before, and then Edwin asked me for the praise song I was supposed to have composed, since that night in his hall. For some reason I'd had trouble finding something suitable and skillful enough to please a king and a queen and two powerful princes. But in the end I thought of the lay my father's scop had composed for the marriage of my eldest sister to Ealdorman Wulfstan in better days. I had to leave out all the references to Frigg, wife of Odin, the goddess of marriage, this being a Christian court but, changing names and places, I thought it would do.

> Tonight, two houses will be woven
> Mercia and Wessex into one
> a king as fair as any hero in a tale
> strong in battle, gentle in his hall
> a queen whose beauty is renowned
> perfection worthy to be crowned ...

And so it went on in a similar style with more clichéd lines. It was a work-piece, without inspiration, but they seemed to like it well enough. What else could I have said? What was there to celebrate? It wasn't a love match. And I was expected to sing the praises of a woman I'd never seen. There was some disappointment on the lower tables, that I hadn't managed something with a few more double-meanings and salty phrases, but King Harold, I've noticed, doesn't care much for such things. He's a serious man.

Tonight, sitting between Edwin of Mercia and his new queen, he looked uncomfortable, wary, like an animal at bay.

~ ~ ~

After the feast, Ældyth was taken to her chamber by the steward, and handed over to her ladies. They took down her hair and brushed it loose, dressing her in a white linen shift covered with a sleeveless robe edged with marmot fur. She was almost dressed when they heard the approaching procession and her maids hurried to put away her clothes and the small items of her toilet. The jingle of mail from the hearth-carles who escorted the king drew nearer, a scop was playing a tune on the lyre, and then the archbishop banged on her door with his staff. The Lady Margaret, prompted by Angharad, opened the door to let them in. Harold was simply robed in dark fur over his night-shift. He took Ældyth's hand and led her to the prie-dieu where they knelt for the blessing. Then holy water was sprinkled on the bed by the archbishop and the covers turned down for them to get in. She felt almost naked in her shift before the king's retinue as the maids removed her robe. The steward brought the bride cup, which they had to drink from together, and her hands were shaking so much some wine spilt on the bed sheets. She heard one of her ladies gasp at the spreading stain. As red as blood. But then they were all gone and she was alone with the king.

He didn't immediately turn to embrace her and, after a few moments awkward silence said, 'I'm aware that this is difficult, maybe even unpleasant for you. It hasn't exactly been my desire either. I must tell you that I haven't slept with any woman since I was hand-fasted to my first wife. I've been faithful to my vows for twenty years, so this doesn't come naturally to me.'

'We must do what we're compelled to do,' Ældyth said. Duty, her mother had once told her, came before love.

It was easy enough to arouse him, after the candle was blown out. Ældyth had not been the wife of an ageing man without learning how to stimulate a husband. It surprised her that Harold should find it difficult, but in the end it was accomplished, and they lay, silent, side by side, husband and wife.

In the morning he was awake early and took her again, wordlessly, but this time with more enthusiasm. After he had returned to his own chamber to dress, Ældyth turned her face to the pillow and prayed to God that he would give her a son, so that it would all be over and he could go back to his concubine.

~ ~ ~

Eadgifu had stayed in her chamber over the last few days. The cold still had everything in its grip and she had kept herself close to the fire. Her new apartments unsettled her. The main room was smaller than she was used to. She couldn't bring all her tapestries with her and some favourite items of furniture had had to be left behind. It felt rather bare until they could be replaced. Eadgifu hadn't been to hall since Harold's marriage, eating in her own chamber, relying on her maids to bring her all the gossip. It seemed that Harold's new wife wasn't entirely to his liking, and that he'd only spent two or three nights in her bed since their marriage. That gave her some pleasure. Eadgifu had wished the Welsh queen terrible things when she'd woken in the middle of the night alone, but then she'd been ashamed of her thoughts because it seemed that Ældyth had been ordered to marry him by her brothers. *And*, Eadgifu thought, *I wouldn't wish that on any girl.*

Yesterday her eldest son had been to see her and Godwin had seemed quite bewildered that one day he could be his father's legitimate heir and the next a bastard in the eyes of the church. Apparently, Harold had promised him an earldom when he came of age, in an attempt to heal the breach. In the meantime he was practising for the battle that was almost sure to come. Godwin told her that Harold had had a watch placed in Sandwich for any sign of Duke William's fleet on the water and that, when it arrived, he was to go into battle for the first time as one of Harold's thegns. Edmund was furious because his father had told him he was too young and must stay behind. Neither of them were happy about the way things were.

The nursemaids had told her that Harold visited the nursery almost every day to see the younger children and she was glad that he wasn't neglecting his duty to them. Eadgifu had seen no sign of him, though she'd hoped, perhaps, that he would come.

This morning the steward knocked on her door and when Eadgifu's maid opened it, her mother-in-law, Countess Gytha, was standing outside, resting her arm on the shoulder of one of the pages. Eadgifu stood up and asked her to come in, while the maid brought the most comfortable chair and cushions for her to sit. She was offered mead and sweet breads, which Gytha was happy to accept, always, Eadgifu thought, being one to enjoy her food. Being a little queasy, Eadgifu asked the maid to bring an infusion of mint and fennel, which she'd found through long experience always settled her stomach.

'Breeding again?' Gytha asked, her Saxon words still with that Danish inflexion, even after so many years.

Eadgifu nodded. 'It's a little inconvenient.'

Gytha laughed. 'Harold will welcome another child. I doubt the Welsh Mare will give him very many. All skin and bone and hips the width of your hand.'

Eadgifu smiled for the first time in weeks. The Welsh Mare. That was good. She was also heartened, dishonourably, she admitted, by Gytha's insinuation that the new queen wasn't likely to be fertile. At least she herself had given Harold three handsome sons and two healthy daughters.

Then Gytha looked at her daughter-in-law quite sternly.

'You must get over it, you know. It's the fate of women in our station of life. I was lucky that I wasn't given to some ageing prince I couldn't bear the sight of. Godwin was an attractive man when he came to ask my father for my hand, though he was only a very insignificant earl in those days. He came to Denmark with King Cnut and saw me at court. I was sister-in-law to Cnut and he could see the advantage of the connection – there was always some calculation with Godwin. And then I had to leave my home, my family and friends and come to a strange country that was often hostile.'

She stopped to take a sip of her mead, staring into the fire a moment. It's a story Eadgifu had heard often enough. Gytha had lately begun to repeat herself, but Eadgifu let her go on because remembering past glories seemed to comfort her now that she lived in retirement. Eventually Gytha said, 'On the whole I was happy enough, though Godwin had a talent for getting into trouble. We were exiled once. But he was as cunning as a fox and somehow always managed to wriggle out of whatever trap was set for him. And now our eldest daughter is the Dowager Queen and our second son King of all England.' There was so much pride in her voice.

Then she laughed again. 'It's not for us to know what our destiny will be. It's in the hands of the gods.' Gytha had been brought up in the old religion of Denmark before she had converted to Christianity. Eadgifu had always felt that it was only skin deep and that she still, in her heart, believed in the Wyrd sisters and the existence of Doom. 'Who knows what will happen?' Gytha spread her own hands wide as if dispensing fate, and then suddenly dropped them in her lap and asked, 'Do you intend to stay at court?'

'I'd been thinking of going back to my own manor at Waltham, but then I found I was breeding again. I've decided that I want this child to be born in the palace, to know his – or her – father.'

'Good! You shouldn't run away; you should stay and

fight. Remember that out of sight is out of mind. You must stay to remind Harold of what he has lost. And, if it becomes too much for you, you are very welcome to come and stay with me, in Wessex or perhaps at Hildburgh. I live very quietly these days, but it is a beautiful place – the first manor Godwin took me to when he brought me out of Denmark. Your children would like it too – the air is much healthier than here in London.'

And then she was gone. Eadgifu knew that the dowager queen found her mother impossible, but she genuinely liked Gytha, partly because she was outspoken, and afraid of no one. Perhaps, Eadgifu thought, I might go and stay with her for a little while when the court goes to York before Easter.

Her next visitor was less welcome. Edith, Queen Dowager, made a pretense of coming to enquire about her health. Edith was worried that her sister-in-law was still unhappy, or so she said. Eadgifu made noncommittal replies, but it was clear that it was an excuse and the dowager was here on another errand. The king, she said, not even calling Harold by his name, had noticed that Eadgifu had been absent from hall since his marriage and had requested, according to the dowager, that she appear, because her absence was an affront to the queen. That didn't sound like Harold at all, and Eadgifu wondered whether the request came either from the dowager herself or the new queen.

As she was leaving, Edith turned her head and said, with no trace of malice, but with an odd smile on her face, 'You know that the queen is already with child?' Eadgifu's heart lurched inside her, but she managed to keep control of her temper. Gytha had been wrong. The Welsh queen was as fertile as a brood mare. As soon as the door had closed behind her Eadgifu threw her cup into the fireplace and tossed herself onto the bed. After a fit of weeping she felt calmer. She gave herself a stern talking to. She must think of Gytha's words and rouse herself from this morass of depression and weakness. Perhaps if she were to appear in hall it would please Harold and give the Welsh Mare something to think about. After all, Eadgifu thought with a smile, it's not her name he has tattooed on his body, but mine; the emblem of the swan on the inside of his thigh, in the intimate place where the ancients used to put their hands to swear fealty to their lords.

~ ~ ~

I am learning a new version of the lay of Beowulf. I know it well in my own language, but it is tricky in the Saxon tongue, with its strange stresses and different phrasing, and there is much more religion in it. The old king used to like the part where an ageing Beowulf defends his kingdom from the Dragon, which then kills Beowulf defending its treasure. He particularly loved the part where the king's funeral pyre is lit on the headland for everyone to see and he is celebrated as a hero. The Mercians prefer the account of Beowulf defeating the trolls, Grendel and his monstrous mother. They like the part where Beowulf tears off the troll's arm. But that's how they are.

I've seen the dark queen several times now. Arthur often brings me to the king's hall with his brother when Edwin comes to sit in the Council. His sister also sits at the Council table, with the Dowager Queen and the archbishop and the Godwinson brothers.

Arthur is learning to fight in the palace yard with the other boys. One of them is Edmund Haroldson, the king's second son, only a year older than me, but already bidding fair to be as good a Saxon war-lord as his father. He is broader and more muscular than his older brother, and very skilful with a sword. Arthur spars with him, but Edmund sends his sword spinning away across the yard more often than not. At first the boys tried to get me to join them, but when they felt the muscles of my arm they decided that I was a weakling only fit to carry a lyre. I've got used to the ribaldry and bullying; I never thought being a boy would be so difficult.

While they are all occupied I often sit in the hall near the fireplace and practise. Lately a young girl, one of the queen's ladies who accompany her to the Council, has been coming to sit close enough to listen. She, too, is dark, with her hair plaited round her head, a little taller than me and fuller of figure.

'Will you play for me?' she said today, stumbling over her words and with a very heavy accent. 'Will you play something . . . I do not know how to call it . . . some music from the east?'

'I'm not sure I know any,' I said. 'Where do you come from?'

'From Hungaria. Myself and brother and little sister. But my mother was a princess from Kievan Rus in the east.'

I felt a shock. 'That's where the Landwaster's wife, Queen Ellisev, comes from.'

The girl nodded. 'She is my mother's sister.'

I knew nothing of Kievan Rus, or its music, but there were a few tunes I'd learned in the Landwaster's hall that had pleased the king of Russia's daughter. Perhaps they would please her neice?

I began to play, once I had tuned my strings. The eastern tunes that Ellisev liked need a different tuning on the lyre and they have a very sad sound to them – as though they speak of lost places and families. Which may well be the case, because I noticed that the girl was weeping.

I stopped. 'I'm sorry. I've made you sad.'

'No, no. It's just, that I am so very far away from home

and I do not think we can go back. They will not let us go back.'

'What's your name?'

'They call me the Lady Margaret.'

'You're Prince Edgar's sister?' I'd seen the prince at High Table.

She nodded. 'I'm sorry my English is not perfect. The convent try to teach me, before the king died, but is very difficult language to learn.'

'I had the same problem at first. When I came to this country, I only spoke the Norse tongues.'

And then she wanted to know about my family and how I'd come here and I told her as much as I could bear about the raid by Harald the Landwaster.

'Ah! Him!' She almost spat the words out. 'In Hungaria we call him hadrada – ruthless one. He gives no quarter. I cannot understand why my aunt wants to marry him.'

'Perhaps she had no choice. Like the Welsh queen.'

The Lady Margaret told me about being chosen to wait on Ældyth. 'We look after clothes, brush hair, but mostly we sit and sew while she reads books. How I hate embroidery! I want to learn things, but it is only the queen who is allowed to read.'

'And have they told you what's going to happen to you? The king must have plans for your future?'

'There was talk of marrying me to Godwin, the son of the king, but that has all come to nothing because of the arrival of the new wife. And I am very glad. I do not wish to marry anyone!'

'So, are you going to be a nun?'

She tossed her head. 'If I must. Anything but to marry.'

I was going to ask her reasons, but just then the queen came out of the Council chamber and called her ladies to her. The Lady Margaret raised her hand in a leave-taking as she turned to go and I smiled at her. It would have been good to be able to talk as two girls together, the usual chatter about clothes, court gossip and boys, that I used to have with my sisters. Instead, I have to guard my tongue every time I open my mouth.

All the rest of the day I felt sad and very much alone.

~ ~ ~

The Swan-neck dressed in her finest robe, trimmed with fur at the sleeves, and had her maids put up her hair in a circlet of narrow plaits. She wore the gold rings that Harold had given her when he returned from Ireland, and a necklace of gold cartouches set with garnets that had been her father's wedding gift, wound around her narrow throat. Her maids called her 'my Lady', as they fixed her hair, but she wondered by what title she should be known now. No longer Countess of Wessex; she was nameless. 'I am Eadgifu Swan-neck,' she said to herself in the mirror, watching her maid skewer the last plait with a bone pin. 'No more, no less.'

As she entered the hall she was aware of a pause in the babble as heads turned towards her, but the conversations quickly began again. Eadgifu didn't look towards the high table, where Harold would be sitting with the queen and his brothers, and she held her head erect as the steward lead her to a place below her sisters-in-law and the dowager. It was good that Edwin and Morcar's wives weren't there, or she would have been at the bottom of the table. 'I'm Eadgifu Swan-neck,' she told herself, clenching her jaw tight in defiance. Since the king had not officially divorced her, she was still his common law wife, still the mother of his sons. Eadgifu caught her son Godwin's eye, where he sat at the end of the high table, and saw him smile.

She had been placed beside Hilde, Leofwine's wife. Hilde had always been the most good humoured of the

Godwin women; plump, pleasure loving, preferring her own home and children to life at court. Eadgifu turned to her and asked, 'How do you like waiting on the new queen?'

Hilde laughed, spilling some of her wine. 'Tiresome! The ladies she brought from Wales do all the work and we just sit there, hanging around. Queen Edith liked conversation and making tapestry, which was at least something to do, but Ældyth – she reads books and mopes.'

'Isn't she happy?'

'Difficult to tell. You can't guess anything from her face. Deep as the North Sea, that one. She doesn't talk either.' Hilde pulled a face and then, under cover of the table, she reached over and squeezed Eadgifu's hand. 'She'll never be queen in my mind, ever, until she has as many sons as yours at the table beside her.'

Eadgifu risked a quick glance at the high table. Harold was in conversation with the archbishop and Ældyth was sitting, cup in hand, staring into the distance. But she was beautiful; it gave Eadgifu a pain in her stomach to see how beautiful.

'There's plenty of time, Hilde. Harold's only forty-four.'

'She's too cold and too skinny! The Godwinson brothers like a warmer armful than that.'

'The Dowager says she's already pregnant.'

'She has missed her courses, but only once. You can never tell.'

Eadgifu put her hand, automatically, over her own swelling stomach, feeling light-headed and sick. Two unborn siblings, but what might their futures hold? And what if Ældyth's child was a son?

~ ~ ~

It was late winter, a time when the world was supposed to be inching towards spring. There were snowdrops in the garden beyond the palace walls, their frail white blossoms trembling in the bitter wind coming from the east. In the Council chamber a fire had been lit, but the tapestries on the walls shifted restlessly in the draught that came creeping into the room despite all efforts to keep it out. It should be lighter by now, Edith thought, looking at the narrow window. But there was a gloom inside the room that matched the grey sky outside.

'There's news from Normandy,' Harold was saying. He stroked his face and his expression was troubled. 'Duke William's building ships'.

'Do we know how many?' Edwin asked. He kept tapping his seal ring nervously against the edge of the wooden table and Edith found it irritating.

'The messenger says that every port along the coast is busy. That number of vessels can have only one purpose.'

'But at least we know now,' Archbishop Stigand said. 'He won't invade until they are ready. So we have time.'

'And what of Tostig?' Edwin again. The Godwinson brothers looked uncomfortable and Harold didn't answer as Edwin went on, 'I notice he's not here. Does anyone know his intentions?' The emphasis was on the pronoun.

'He's more likely to attack us in Northumbria,' Morcar said. 'He'll want his earldom back, but we'll be ready for him if he does.'

Edith was angry enough to interrupt. 'I hope my brother Tostig is loyal enough to sue peacefully for his reinstatement. He's not a traitor!'

No one said anything, but she knew that everyone was thinking the same thing. What if Tostig wanted – not his earldom – but the crown? There was a short silence and uncomfortable glances between Gyrth and Leofwine. Harold was looking down at the table. Edith could hear the clerk recording the proceedings, dipping his quill in the ink pot, the scratch of the nib on parchment.

Morcar changed the subject. 'Is the court going to York? Has the king decided?'

'I think so.' It was obvious that Harold was still weighing things up. He was never hasty. 'I'd have preferred to wait until the weather has improved. But, if we're not to have an imminent invasion, then perhaps we can go to York next month. I don't want to leave it until the summer.'

'I think it's essential, for the nobles to meet their new king as soon as possible and swear fealty,' Edith said. 'They need to know that the former Earl of Wessex cares about the north.' She observed the new queen sitting, expression-less, at the end of the table, with her head down. She hadn't spoken once, though her signature would be written on the bottom of the document. Gyrth and Leofwine were also quiet. Neither of them had spoken.

Harold sighed, as if accepting the truth of what Edith had just said reluctantly. 'But we must be ready for the duke when he comes,' he said after a pause. 'I've met him, I've seen him fight and he's a formidable opponent. Ruthless. I've been calculating and, I think, with the help of the earls of Mercia and Northumbria, we can muster a force of about ten thousand men.' He looked straight at Edwin and Morcar. 'Can I count on you?'

'For sure,' Morcar said. 'But I must leave a force behind in Northumbria to defend our territory in the north. You mustn't expect us to leave our flank unprotected.'

'England,' Harold said, slowly and deliberately, 'has never faced such a threat since it became one kingdom. We're assailed from the north, the east and the south. We must prepare to defend every inch of land, the lives of our women and children, our abbeys and churches. Are you all with me?'

They were, more or less, though Edith detected that per-haps the Mercians were less enthusiastic. It occured to her that they might see a Norman invasion as an opportunity. They could press him from the north while the duke pushed up from the south. She suspected that Edwin had ambitions. He was, after all, distantly descended from the long line of kings who ruled Mercia before Alfred the Great became king of all the English. Such blood made men dangerous. It had been one of the causes of the old rivalry between the House of Leofric and the House of Godwin.

And, just as this thought came into her mind, Ældyth spoke for the first time, looking across the table at her brothers. 'I want you all to know that I'm expecting a child, an heir to the throne, with the blood of Earl Godwin and Earl Leofric running in his veins. Whatever your differences, you must all fight for his future.'

So, the new queen had a good mind, Edith thought. It seemed that for all her quietness she missed nothing.

Gyrth murmured in Edith's ear, 'But what if it's a girl?' She elbowed him in the ribs in a very unqueenly way and hoped that Ældyth hadn't heard.

Then the meeting was over and the archbishop said a prayer and blessed everyone and the chamber began to empty.

As Edith gathered up her cloak, the archbishop came to stand beside her. 'If I may, my Lady, I would like to talk to you about the late king.'

'Of course. Would you care to come to my chamber where we can be more private?'

After Stigand had left, after he had given her his blessing, Edith knelt wearily at her prie-dieu. She prayed for God to give her the humility she was supposed to have, and the strength to accept the situation she was in. If the court was to go to York, she would not be going with it for the first time since she married King Edward. Harold had told her last night that she would have to stay in London, sending him any news she received from Normandy. 'Leofwine will be in Kent, keeping watch, and Gyrth on the east coast, but I need someone in London who's used to handling the business of state,' he'd said. The queen was to go with him, but the Swan-neck was to remain, which was no comfort to Edith at all. The palace would be very empty when the court had gone. As empty as she herself felt now.

The archbishop's words were still going round in her head. He had sat in the chair beside the fire and said, 'King Edward was a saint, and should be declared as such.' Apparently, some woman had touched his tomb and recovered the sight in one of her eyes. There was also the matter of a vision that Edward was believed to have had during a dinner in hall. He claimed to have seen the Seven Sleepers in bed and that they had rolled over onto their left side – a sign of coming trouble. Edith had never believed in it. Edward was prone to seizures in his later years, episodes of absence that ended in confusion. But Stigand believed in the vision and the miracle and he was going to write to Rome.

That was something else that Edith had been praying about. Rumours of Edward's sainthood had been around the court and in the country for years, mainly based on his famous chastity and the visions. Edith wasn't sure that this alone was enough. She had always wondered whether Edward was chaste, not for saintliness, but in order to avoid the intimacy of women? There had been rumours, jokes about his relationship with Tostig. They had been dismissed, of course. She had heard the example of Jesus Christ cited as an excuse. After all Jesus had only men as his disciples. And did he not have a favourite among them – John, whom he loved as the king had loved Tostig? That was the argument that echoed in her head, the one she was expected to believe. Saint Edward with his beloved disciple. But then the counter-argument surfaced again. What about the women?

Where did she fit into this story? Even Jesus Christ had Mary and Martha as well as his disciples. When Edith had rubbed the king's feet as he lay dying, she had thought of the Magdalene washing Jesus' feet at the Last Supper. But then, she remembered Edward's revulsion on their wedding night, the way he had touched her and turned away from her as from something unclean. The truth was, Edith acknowledged reluctantly, that Edward was anything but saintly, though it seemed, from the archbishop's words, that they were determined to make him a saint and the church would have its own narrative. Her mind was still unquiet; praying had done nothing to banish her thoughts.

As she got up from the prie-dieu, her Lady of the Bedchamber, Mathilde, rose from the settle beside the fireplace and put down her needlework. They were as close to friends as any two women could be when one was a queen and the other a waiting maid. Mathilde had come to England with Edward's retinue from France – a highborn noblewoman from one of the northern abbeys – and had been handpicked by Edward's first archbishop, the Norman Robert of Jumièges, to be her Lady of the Bedchamber. She was the only maid that Edward had allowed Edith to take with her when she was banished from court. There was no part of the queen's life Mathilde didn't know. And now, she had guessed what was preoccupying Edith's mind.

'Have you thought of commissioning a brother in the scriptorium to write the history of your husband, my Lady?' Mathilde said. 'If he is to be a saint, someone must write it.'

'Why should I make my husband a saint when we both know he wasn't?'

'I was thinking of you, my lady.'

Edith looked at her, puzzled.

'In telling your husband's story, you will tell your own, just as Queen Emma did.'

Edith began to understand. Emma had commissioned

a scribe to write the history of her own life in order to tell a story that excused her treatment of her sons by Æthelred, and blame someone else for the murder of Edward's brother. It was an outrageous reworking of the facts to put herself forward as a blameless queen.

Mathilde went on, 'I have watched you these twenty years, maligned and spoken against falsely, and I think you should tell your own story. It makes no matter if people think he kept himself out of your bed for the good of his soul, so long as they know that you were not at fault.'

Could it be done? Was it possible to find a religious brother in the scriptorium who would write a history of her husband, not just because of his supposedly saintly life, but because it was the only way she herself could be remembered. Since Mathilde had put it in her mind, she thought of her mother-in-law's book – the *Enconium Emmae*. There was a copy, bound in a cover of gilded calf-skin, on her shelf.

On the prie-dieu, before she went to bed, Edith whispered her concerns to God. 'We are mere names in history – the wife of, daughter of, sister of, whenever a man is being talked of. Dear Lord, I don't want my life to be for nothing. I have no child to leave as a legacy. Is it vanity to want to be remembered?'

Edith sometimes wondered whether she should leave court and live in one of her own houses at Exeter or Winchester. There was a very pretty house in Winchester that had belonged to Queen Emma which Edith was very fond of. Not an abbey – never again an abbey, not even Wilton. But, for the moment, Harold needed her counsel, someone to counter the influence of the Mercians.

~ ~ ~

The king came to Eadgifu's room alone, wrapped in his fur cloak against the cold of the corridors, entering unannounced. Her maids had already retired and Eadgifu was sitting up in bed reading the evening prayers. Harold came and sat on the edge of the bed. 'I wanted to tell you myself, before anyone else does. Ældyth is having a child.'

Eadgifu took a deep breath. 'Your sister's already told me the news. Didn't take you long did it?'

'I'm sorry,' he said, 'for the pain I've caused you. But there was no other way.'

'It wasn't just for me, but for our children. What's to become of them? One moment they are æthelings – princes of the blood – the next they are nothing. Edwin of Mercia was very quick to tell me that his sister's child will take precedence over ours.'

'Would you have had me refuse the crown I've spent my life defending?'

Eadgifu said nothing. What could be said? She folded her book and put it to one side.

Harold took her hand. 'We were fortunate to marry for love and have such a long time together. It's something rarely given to kings and princes – or even earls,' he added with a wry smile. 'And our children won't suffer – I promise. They have as much right to the succession as any others I might have. It's the Witan that makes the choice.'

Eadgifu could feel her anger and resentment fading before his presence. She could smell the soap he had used to wash, the wood-smoke on his fur. No traces of the Welsh mare.

'The hardest thing to bear is that I'm also breeding again.'

Harold was very still. His grip on her hand tightened. 'How long have you known?'

'Since the beginning of January. I'd begun to suspect just before the old king died, but you were so busy, preoccupied . .. and then afterwards . . . I couldn't find the words – and I felt angry and humiliated.'

Harold opened his arms and held her very tight. 'I'm sorry. So sorry.' He kissed her, gently at first, and then with more passion. 'You will always be first with me, you can be sure of that. Everything else is duty.'

And pleasure, Eadgifu thought. What man could resist so beautiful a woman as Ældyth Queen of the Welsh, the thrill of that new, young body under his? That tight cunt, unstretched by the birth of five children? Eadgifu didn't say any of it and, in spite of those thoughts, she felt herself responding to his kisses. The comfort of his arms around her. The love she still felt for him couldn't be denied.

'Can I come into your bed?' he asked. He sounded so uncertain of his reception – this was not the king, but a man trying to seduce the woman he loved.

She turned back the covers and let him climb in, feeling his fingers on her skin, the warmth of his familiar body against hers. But it was hard to ignore the knowledge that *that*, so intimate a part of his anatomy, had been inside another woman – the one who had taken her place beside him. That he had fathered a child on another woman. A woman eighteen years younger than herself. As he entered her, Eadgifu had to suppress a shudder, before she surrendered, in spite of herself, out of long habit, to the pleasure of his embrace.

~ ~ ~

The palace is busy with preparations. Everyone knows that there will be a battle. All the young thegns are polishing their weapons, oiling their shields and their leathers, play-fighting with swords in the lower hall or the yard if it's fine weather.

I've always loved watching Arthur practising his sword play. He's lithe, nimble on his feet, quick to parry his opponents' blades and thrust his own under their guard. And when he takes off his shirt at the end, to wipe the sweat from his skin, I can feel a powerful shiver that is part pleasure, part fear, inside my body. I don't understand this, but I like to feel it. Occasionally he glances at me, between bouts, and he smiles when he sees me watching him.

This afternoon, as we walked away, Arthur put his arm round my shoulder, as many of the boys do in a companionable way, and one of the others shouted out, 'Have fun with your pretty little bum-boy, Arthur!' and the others all burst out laughing. They're crude, they think everything's about sex. But was that how they saw our innocent friendship? Their words went through me like a blade.

Arthur dropped his arm as though I had the plague and, as soon as we were in the corridor, he turned on me. As I looked up at him, in shock and distress, he pushed me roughly away, so that I fell against the wall.

'Get away from me!' he yelled. 'Get out!' He looked upset, bewildered. 'You're unnatural!'

I went, running down the corridor on legs that would barely hold me up. I slipped into the lower hall, which was almost empty at that time of day, and sat down on a bench next to the fire. I wanted to cry, but boy's don't cry – at least not often, not openly.

When I had stopped trembling, I took out my lyre and began to tune it. I started to play one of the Danish songs my mother used to sing at home, about a summer sun rising over the fells, fertile fields and a hall full of cheer. I couldn't trust my voice to sing the words, but the familiar tune comforted me. I have lost a good friend, my only friend since I came here.

Since then he's become wary of me, taking care not to glance in my direction. When I've stolen a look at him in hall, there's still that slightly bewildered expression in his eyes. I can't help that. I've told no one my story, not even the Lady Margaret. Only the gods know what would happen to me if they knew. I'll not be a nun, or any man's concubine.

~ ~ ~

Eadgifu had lain awake all night after Harold's visit – thinking, arguing with herself. Somewhere around dawn she made a decision. There was nothing to be gained from hostility. She had what the Mercian woman would never have – Harold's love, his youth – freely given to her. He was a care-worn king now; but once he had been just a young man, rich and privileged. She remembered their love-making when they were first together, carefree, athletic, fuelled by passion.

When she was dressed and breakfasted, she went along the corridor to Ældyth's rooms.

Harold's new wife seemed very surprised to see her when she was announced. After the formalities, Ældyth said; 'Harold was very pleased to see you in hall.'

'I wanted to see what you were like.'

Ældyth nodded. 'I understand. I've been curious about you too.'

Eadgifu felt uncomfortable, looking at her, aware of her own bulging stomach, sagging breasts, the lines she knew were beginning to thread her cheeks. This girl was young enough to be her daughter. 'I love my husband,' she said, 'and, since we're not divorced, I'm still his wife.'

Ældyth lowered her head as if in assent, but as she did so, Eadgifu saw her eyes blazing with anger. After a moment, she looked up and stared Eadgifu full in the face. 'But I am the queen.'

It was indisputable. Eadgifu laughed. 'Don't ever expect me to pay homage to you,' she said, as she waved away the refreshments one of the Welsh women was offering her. 'I just wanted you to know.'

Part Three

A Knowing Woman

'She dreamt that she was standing out in her herb-garden, and she took a thorn out of her shift; but while she was holding the thorn in her hand it grew so that it became a great tree, one end of which struck itself down into the earth, and it became firmly rooted; and the other end of the tree raised itself so high in the air that she could scarcely see over it, and it became also wonderfully thick. The under part of the tree was red with blood, but the stem upwards was beautifully green and the branches white as snow.'

'Ragnhild's Dream', Snorri Sturluson, *Helmskringla*

We've had a long and weary journey north. Edwin's steward found me a pony – a sturdy pie-bald thing, not good for speed, but as safe a seat as any fireside settle. The king made slow progress, stopping overnight at monasteries and the halls of any ealdorman rich enough to feed his train. I travelled in the van with the baggage and the stewards, sleeping in tents. The Mercian brothers have split up – Morcar to go north to his own earldom in case the Landwaster arrives, and Edwin to accompany the king to York. Arthur, on a beautiful black beast with a long stride, travels in the front with his brother whose carles are providing a guard for the king's wife. The queen hasn't travelled well. She is green as goose-shit. But the king insisted that she come so that the ealdormen and their thegns could swear an oath of loyalty to her and her unborn child at the same time.

Coming into York again made me feel sad to the core of my bones. Two years now since Tostig Godwinson brought me here as a gift from Harald the Landwaster; more than one since he sent me as a gift to his liege-lord, Edward, with secret messages. I was supposed to keep him informed of everything that went on at court, but every message I wrote was read by Queen Edith, and then, last year, Tostig was deposed and fled in fury to Flanders. I've thought often about Tostig and Harold and their rivalry. People at court refer to them as the 'cloud-born brothers' and they are, indeed, very handsome noblemen, both with that air of being destined for greatness, though in different ways. Tostig's features are more delicate, his hair a lighter colour, falling in fine waves. He's almost as tall as Harold, less muscular, but no less imposing. And whereas Harold has a quiet presence, Tostig is mercurial, quick with a jest or a jibe, an extravagant compliment to the ladies, but also quick to take offence, quick with his fists. He's not a man to trifle with.

So now we're in York, as the king and his people call it, though I've been told that it was the capital of the Norse kingdom here and still called Jorvik by the people who live in it. Here in the Northland I can smell the sea again, hear the waves, watch the boats sailing to and from my homeland and imagine being on one of them, returning from exile and servitude to whatever is left of my family.

'You're among your own people now,' the steward said with a grin, as he sent me off in the direction of the lodging house where all the servants were to sleep. And there was certainly something familiar about the low wooden houses with their turf roofs and the smell of peat smoke, rotting fish and mutton fat.

Our quarters are in a hayloft above the stables, warm but malodorous and comfortless. A young scop, a mere boy, and a slave at that, does not merit good lodgings or a comfortable bed. Now that Arthur is no longer my friend, I can no longer sleep in Edwin's hall. The Mercians and Northumbrians are occupying Morcar's palace, once Tostig's, which is much smaller than Edwin's palace in London, though stone built and better fortified. I haven't spoken to Arthur since we left. He keeps company with the inner circle of thegns who surround Edwin and sleeps at his brother's hearth. Once or twice, when we've been in attendance on the king, I've felt his eyes on me, but I've kept my own lowered. I can't forget his words; 'Stay away from me!' and the revulsion in his voice.

In the loft that first evening, I tried to find a sleeping place that had some privacy, but there was none. The floor was crowded with Edwin's carles and retainers – most of them older men. Unlike the palace there are fewer boys here.

'Too stuck up to sleep with the rest of us then?' one of the carles shouted. They were playing a board game for money, and drinking ale. I thought they wouldn't notice my search, but they did. I ignored them and curled up in a corner on a pile of straw, my lyre in its leather bag beside me. I made my bundle into a pillow and wrapped my cloak securely around me. It was a very long time before I drifted off to sleep, that old refrain, 'What will become of me? What will become of me?' rolling round and round in my head.

In the morning I was up early and walked along the river front before going up to the king's quarters in the abbey. The sun was just rising out of the mist drifting in up the river from the sea. *Haar*, we called it at home, *haar*. I could smell the salt in it and was gripped by such a pain in my stomach

I could hardly walk. What is to become of me? I can't live like this for much longer.

~ ~ ~

There was a strong smell of tallow and, occasionally, the sound of wax weeping onto the flagged floor from the many-branched candle holders suspended above the nave. Even with so much illumination, the far corners of the Minster were dark and full of flickering shadows. Ældyth could see the wall painting of the Virgin Mary in the side chapel, holding her child out as though offering him to supplicants. *We women are the peace-weavers – we seal treaties with our bodies,* Ældyth thought. She was sitting on a small wooden throne on her husband's left side, just below the altar of the minster, and was aware of her brother Edwin standing, just out of the light, watchful as ever. Her life was a bargain between those two men. Even wrapped in a fur cloak she could feel the dank cold of the church. These north-eastern climes seemed darker and more sombre than her native Mercia. Perhaps that was why her spirits had been low ever since they arrived. Ældyth watched Harold take the oaths of the Ealdormen of York, who kissed the ring of state on his finger, pressing their knees onto the cold stone of the minster floor, before rising to kneel at her feet, swearing loyalty to her and her unborn child – the union of Wessex and Mercia.

Harold's hands were beautifully manicured, but no one would ever mistake them for a woman's hands, or even a bishop's. They were broad and sinewy, with square ended fingers – trained to hold a sword or wield an axe. Ældyth could see the rippling muscles of his forearm through the fine fabric of his sleeve as he extended his hand to the rough-haired thegn kneeling at his feet. Ældyth felt a soft blush rising up her neck towards her face. She had expected to hate this man, perhaps at best to tolerate him. But, against all her instincts, she had begun to long for him to come to her bed and caress her. It was wrong; it was beyond all understanding. And he, after the first weeks of dutiful sex, had begun to spend more time, to stroke her skin, to try to give her pleasure. She had never known that with a man. But now ... It was impossible! She would not ... could not ... fall in love with this man. Looking down at her clenched hands she dragged her attention back to the queue of men waiting to pay homage to her husband.

Harold accepted it with supreme grace, as though he had been born to it. But he had been deputising for King Edward for so many years he was practised in the art of seeming kingly. Ældyth glanced across to where her brother stood, observing everything. Edwin's narrow face was inscrutable as he watched the men coming forward to bend their knees, looking, presumably, for any hint of reluctance. So far, they all seemed to be Harold's men. But then, these same men had once sworn fealty to Tostig before deposing him and appointing Morcar as their lord. She suspected that Tostig was on her husband's mind as he accepted their homage.

The night before they had left London, Ældyth had overheard a terrible argument between Harold and the Dowager Queen in Harold's private quarters. Edith was asking if he had written to Tostig asking him to come back.

'How can the breach be healed if you've not made the first move towards reconciliation?'

'I wasn't the one who threw all attempts at mediation in our faces.' Harold sounded very angry. 'It wasn't my conduct, or Edward's, that offended the Northumbrians. Tostig did that by himself!'

'But still,' Edith's voice was raised now, 'he believed that you did not do enough to intercede with the rebels on his behalf. Edward wanted you to take an army to Northumbria to save him, but you refused. You had your own brother outlawed!'

'Too right.' Ældyth heard Harold slam something down on a wooden surface. 'His behaviour was inexcusable. The Northumbrians were in the right. He murdered two of their envoys who'd been granted safe passage. But no one could ever tell Tostig anything! To have intervened would have been to start a civil war. He sealed his own fate. And now you want me to write begging letters to him.' Harold's voice changed into a falsetto imitation of his sister's; 'Come back, brother, all is forgiven!'

Then Edith was shouting, 'What did our mother tell you?'

A door slammed and the room had fallen silent.

Behind her brother Edwin, Ældyth could see Harold's eldest son Godwin, in his studded leathers, standing with Harold's hearth-carles as part of the king's guard of honour. He was nineteen, only a year short of Morcar. Godwin had Harold's face and bearing and, from his mother, the blood of King Æthelred in his veins. Nineteen years of privilege and ambition. If anything happened to Harold, the child in Ældyth's womb would count for nothing. Harold's sons would want the throne for themselves and Edwin and Morcar's support would be too little against the might of the Godwins. And she wouldn't trust them not to change their allegiances to what they perceived to be the winning side. Ældyth felt very vulnerable, seated on her throne, at the centre of things. She was surrounded by potential enemies. She couldn't even trust her own brothers. She would always be a gaming piece to play to their own advantage.

~ ~ ~

The days have fallen into a pattern. In the morning I go up to the abbey for breakfast, the lyre on my back usually enough to get me some food in the refectory, then to the king's hall among Edwin's men, where I play quietly in a corner, or perhaps listen to one of Harold's scops play before the evening meal and then – as late as possible – return to my uncomfortable lodgings. Sometimes, at night, the men goad me into playing for them, songs that remind them of their homes and their sweethearts – for all of them live a lonely life, sworn to follow their lord, seeing their families rarely. One of the younger men told me that his home was in Chester, but that since the middle of last year he has been with Edwin in London, Wales, the fenlands, and then Northumberland, travelling from manor to manor. He said that he had a babe almost a year old that he had never seen. Many of them come back from the hall the worse for drink and it gets very rowdy. There's fighting and swearing and a lot of lewd talk. One of the carles in Edwin's household, a dark, rough-haired man with broad shoulders and only half an ear on his left side, watches me when he thinks no one is looking, and I've become afraid.

Last night I prayed to Freyja to protect me. Was that sinful? I'm supposed to pray to Mary, the goddess of the Christians, but, frankly, I don't think she's of much use in this situation. She's supposed to be meek and mild, obedient, the perfect mother, the virgin bride. That's not what I need. Freyja, with her cloak of falcon feathers, is bold and vengeful, able to send her messengers to protect her own. If she does not protect me, I'm lost. He will catch me in some dark corner or other. If he knew I was a girl he would rape me, but since he has no notion of my true sex, will bugger me.

I put my face into the cloth I've spread over the straw and wept into it, breathing the musty dust of last year's summer. What is wrong with me? I never used to be so tearful.

In the morning things didn't seem so bad. I rolled up the cloth and stuffed it into my bag, slung the lyre over my shoulder and walked up to the king's quarters. There was a light dusting of snow, a late fall, on the moors above the town. But there were jonquils out in the grass under the trees, ragged and frost bitten, but small spots of colour promising spring.

After breakfast, I walked down to the quayside where the ships are offloaded. Many of them are fishing boats, their holds glittering silver with freshly caught fish, the air loud with seagulls and the voices of men arguing prices for the catch. Bigger vessels carry barrels of wine and oil from France, casks of salt, fine stone for carving, live animals, metal for smelting. They pile it all up on the quay ready to be carted away. Some of the boatmen speak in the languages of the North Lands, kingdoms of rock and ice, where darkness covers the earth for months in winter, where there are dragons in the old stories, and horses have wings and ships sail even without wind to fill their sails. Where I come from is not so far north and we speak differently, but still we can understand each other as if in some ancient time we had all spoken the same language. Listening to them makes me feel so homesick I could weep. I have wondered how easy it would be to creep onto one of their vessels after dark and hide among the bales and barrels of cargo on the deck? The longing is sometimes unbearable.

'Hey, girl!'

I heard a voice shouting out, but carried on walking, since it couldn't be for me.

'Hey, you – girl in the britches.'

I stopped and turned towards the voice.

A woman was crouching among the herring barrels, her back to the wall. She was wrapped in robes of coloured wool

– greens and blues and reds, and she was wearing a crystal pendant round her neck and thin bracelets of coloured beads. Her hair was dark and wild under her hood, her face the brown leather of tanned hide, but her eyes were a piercing turquoise blue. I was puzzled by her, but also fascinated.

The woman pressed herself up from the ground and stood upright with the aid of a stick of polished cherrywood.

'Come here,' the woman said, holding out a hand as brown and wrinkled as her face.

I was reluctant but felt compelled to move towards her.

The woman put her hand under my chin and tilted my head upwards so that she could look into my eyes. I tried to turn my head because her gaze was uncomfortable, as if she was looking straight into my mind, but she tightened her grip. And then she began to chant in a language I recognised;

> 'Song-singer, word-bringer,
> traveller by land and sea,
> two in one, son and daughter
> bird of war, you will fly far
> in foreign lands and then be free
> to serve a queen in great prosperity.'

'Who are you?' I asked in my own tongue.

'You know already, I think, my character if not my name. Merithien – soothsayer, a knowing-woman, servant of the old gods.' I stood unmoving, as if under a spell of enchantment. She touched my forehead with the crystal that hung round her neck and closed her eyes. 'You have a destiny,' she said 'You have seen terrible things and people you love have died a hard death. There will be more bloodshed before you are a grown woman, but you have the strength and the grace to survive. The gods have you in the palm of their hands and they will raise you up to a great height. Your spirit will fly like a raven and when that moment comes, you will know your fate and you will remember me.'

My throat was so constricted I could barely speak. 'Will I ever go home?' I managed to croak. It was the only fate I wanted to know about.

'Is there anything to go home for?' the woman said quietly. Her eyes held mine for a moment, full of compassion, and I knew that she was telling the truth.

~ ~ ~

Things, Edith thought, had not changed greatly since Edward's death. After Harold's departure for the north with his new queen, it had been much as it had been when Edward was away with her brothers. Robert the Staller came every morning for his instructions as to the household, and there would be letters to read and state papers to sign, accounts to scrutinise. There were also the reports to study. Harold had left orders for his brothers, Leofwine and Gyrth, to take control of the southern and eastern ports and set a watch for any movements on the coast of Normandy. Flanders too. Harold had not believed her when she had insisted that Tostig was not hostile, not to be feared.

But this morning was different, Robert the Staller hesitated after they had concluded their business, as if he had something else to say that he was reluctant to put into words.

'What is it?' Edith was impatient.

The Chief Steward primmed his mouth as if he had swallowed an unpleasant medicine. 'It's just that the king, before he left, asked me arrange something that I know you will not like.' Edith noticed that the hands that held the papers she had just given him were trembling.

'Go on.'

Robert coughed. 'He asked me to make sure that the queen's quarters would be empty by the time the king and queen come back from Northumbria. You do not wish to move, I know, but if the king wishes it . . .'

Edith opened her mouth to make a retort and then closed it. Why vent her anger on this old man, who was only carrying out an order. He had been Edward's steward before he became Harold's – a Norman official Edward had brought to England with him, immensely efficient and with long experience, but Edith knew as she watched his trembling hands that he was afraid that he would now be replaced if Harold was displeased with him. Cowardly Harold getting someone else to do his dirty work. 'Very well,' she said curtly. 'You have told me. You can go now.'

Robert bowed very low, with an expression of relief, and backed out of the room.

He can't make me, was Edith's first thought. *This has been my room since I married Edward. I will not give it up! I will not!* She moved around the room vigorously, her robe swirling round her feet as she walked. *What impertinence! Harold's my brother, not my lord.* But then, she caught sight of a volume lying on the table, one she had taken down from the bookcase only yesterday to read. The *Enconium Emmae*, the life of Emma, wife of Æthelred and then Cnut, mother of two kings, Harthacnut and Edward. Her turbulent mother-in-law, who had stayed in the queen's quarters after Edward's marriage until Edward had evicted her by sending his hearth-carles to remove her furniture.

All the breath went out of her as she looked at the leather binding with Emma's name on it. Edith sat down and opened the book at the frontispiece, which depicted Emma mounted on a throne, alone, receiving the book from the monk kneeling at her feet. Her three sons, Harthacnut, Edward and Alfred, peeped around the corners of her throne – clearly only secondary characters in the tale. Did she really want to be like Emma? Graceless and vindictive, clinging to power and position in the court? It was undignified. The stark reality was that there were now two women in front of her in Harold's favour, Queen Ældyth and the Swan-neck – three, possibly, because she had forgotten their mother Gytha and the power that she wielded over the family.

Edith looked around the room at the tapestries she'd woven, the icons that had been gifted by successions of bishops and archbishops. The jewellery box she'd been given as a child when her father Godwin had come back from a visit to Flanders. She had tricked herself into believing everything would go on the same. But everything was different and there were bitter choices to be made.

Her maid, Mathilde, came into the room. 'There is a young monk to see you, ma'am. He says his name is Goscelin. Will you receive him?'

Before he set off to accompany Harold to York, the archbishop had remembered their conversation about a saintly life of Edward and recommended a young Flemish Benedictine he had heard of. 'He's from the foundation at Saint-Omer, skilled in the lives of saints,' the archbishop had said. 'He is not attached, at the moment, to any foundation. The abbess at Wilton speaks highly of him. You could do no better.'

It had seemed a good choice. Edith's younger sister was abbess at Saint-Omer. So, Goscelin had been summoned and now, after being ushered in by Mathilde, was bending in front of her, making his obeisance – a short, brown man in a black habit, his tonsure the only pale thing about him. About twenty-five, Edith thought, and far too muscular for a monk who spent his life in a scriptorium.

'You wished to see me, my Lady,' he said in careful, heavily accented Anglo Saxon, as he sat down on the stool Edith had indicated.

She replied in French. 'I expect the archbishop told

you that I've been thinking about the need for a life of my sainted husband.'

He nodded submissively and she saw a look of relief pass over his face at the sound of his own language. When he raised his eyes, she saw just a flicker of humour in them as well as a vast intelligence. It startled her. She would need to be wary. He was not like any monk she had ever met.

Goscelin began to speak. 'And that would include a history of your illustrious family, my Lady, your brother the king, and yourself?'

The archbishop had obviously primed him well. 'There's a need for vindication – not just of my late husband's . . .' she hesitated, searching for the right words, 'famed celibacy', seemed the most suitable phrase. Then she went on, 'But also to dispel doubts about my father's loyalty to his king. You will have heard rumours of his involvement in the murder of Edward's brother, Alfred the Ætheling?'

Goscelin nodded, his face expressionless.

'Ridiculous of course.' Edith made her voice sound firm, as if there were no doubts. 'Earl Godwin merely carried out the orders of Harthacnut to arrest him. What happened afterwards was no fault of his. Alfred was blinded by his captors and died at Ely.'

But there was another narrative, one that involved Queen Emma, and Alfred's death was a grievance Edward never forgot, however well Godwin served him. Edith remembered the king saying to her father, one evening after a quarrel, "I will forgive you when Alfred stands in front of me, restored to life". But it was also true that Edward had been very quick to see how Alfred's death benefitted himself. A younger brother seeking to become king was conveniently removed. Godwin had put Edward on the throne by it, and he had willingly accepted the weregild Godwin paid.

The monk had bowed his head so that Edith couldn't see his face.

'And there's another truth that needs to be told, about

my brother Tostig.'

Goscelin was quiet for a moment, then raised his head and began slowly, as if feeling his way. 'May I speak freely, my Lady?'

Edith nodded her assent.

'There are rumours in Flanders, from Tostig's refuge at the court of Count Baldwin, that he thinks that, as King Edward's favourite, he should have been king in place of his brother Harold. Does that seem true to you?'

'I've heard those stories.' Edith's tone was terse. She wasn't pleased by the young monk's presumption in repeating the gossip. 'I know that Tostig bears a grudge against his brother for not giving him more support against the Northumbrian nobles when they took away his earldom. But if my husband had wanted Tostig to be king he would have named him on his deathbed. Not Harold.'

Edith was aware as she told Goscelin the story, that only Harold and the archbishop had heard the king's dying words. It was typical of Edward to have left the opportunity for an alternative tale – one that told of Harold Godwinson's vaunting ambition and determination to secure the throne for himself. Edith, from her place at the foot of Edward's bed, had heard no more than anyone.

Goscelin was speaking again. 'I see you are aware of your predecessor's *Encomium*?'

Edith followed his gaze towards Queen Emma's piece of sophistry, sitting on her table. How strange that he should mention it just when it had been so prominent in her own thoughts. She spoke with more asperity than she intended. 'I wouldn't wish to emulate my mother-in-law's manipulation of the truth. For that's what it is. My husband regarded her as a Medea who would murder her own children rather than relinquish power.'

There was a short silence. Then Edith said, 'Would you

be interested in the task if I asked you?'

'It would certainly be a delicate undertaking.' Goscelin's ink-stained fingers were pleating the wool of his habit across his knees. 'There are risks . . . The truth always has its detractors.'

Edith heard the slight change of tone on 'truth' and wasn't sure if he was speaking ironically. Was he mocking her? His face was perfectly serious, so perhaps she had imagined it. 'I would want a noble document, in vivid prose, perhaps ornamented with poetry. I'm told you are skilled in verse?'

'Thank you, my Lady, – I would do my very best with the skills God has seen fit to bestow on me. The archbishop will have told you that I am free to attempt the task, being, as it were, a bird of the wilderness.' His eyes suddenly glowed with humour and he bowed his head again.

'Good. Then I give you permission to set to work. And I expect to see you in hall tonight.'

Goscelin got up from the stool and bowed himself out.

When the curtains had rippled together across the doorway, Edith's maid stepped quietly out of the shadows at the back of the room.

'What do you make of him Mathilde?'

'He seems genuine enough. An earnest young man wanting to make his mark in the world. He did not feel able to refuse such an important commission, but I think he knows the dangerous path he must tread.'

'Dangerous?'

'*Certainement.* He must please the queen and the all-powerful Godwins while also keeping to the narrative of the church. He must make Edward a saint, while telling the story of his wife's family and their marriage. An impossible task, wouldn't you agree?'

~ ~ ~

Last night I was roused from sleep by a movement near me – the brushing of feet on the dusty floor, too quiet for any honest purpose. I could hear loud breathing, then, before I could decide what to do, he fell on me from behind, crushing me down onto the straw, his hand clamped over my mouth. I could feel his hot breath on my neck, smell the reek of him, but however I struggled, he was heavy and strong and pinned me to the floor.

But, as he began to fumble with my clothes, his grip slackened, and I found that my left hand was free. I slid my seax knife from under my bundle and, without thinking any further, twisted my body round as far as I could and stuck it into him. The sensation of blade slicing through flesh made me shudder. He made a noise like a stuck pig. Swiftly, before any of the men could wake, I grabbed my lyre and my bundle, pulled my cloak from under him and ran.

~ ~ ~

The messenger brought a letter from Harold in York, written in his own hand, the clear script Eadgifu knew so well. It was a mark of favour to receive a letter not dictated to a scribe, whose letters would invariably begin, 'The king sends his greetings . . .' This one began, 'My dearest Swan. I hope you are keeping well, and the infant. I miss your lively company and your wit. This northern court is a cold place in a bleak country. My brother hated it and I begin to have some sympathy for his feelings. But there is nothing lacking in the northerners' loyalty. I hope to bring them all with me in our coming troubles. Have you thought of leaving London and going into the country? Perhaps to our manor at Waltham? You are very precious to me and I would wish yourself and the younger children out of the way of any danger. But I will leave that decision to your excellent judgement. You will be glad to know that Godwin is acquitting himself as well as his namesake used to do, bidding fair both in diplomacy and his fighting skill. Write to me and give me news of his brothers and sisters, and of your dear self, whose presence I feel the want of every day. Your own H'.

It was difficult to feel anger and resentment in the face of such an expression of affection. Harold, for all his pride and power, loved deeply, passionately; his country, his children, his family and, presumably, Eadgifu thought with a smile, his common law wife. She re-read the letter, feeling – for the first time – sorry for his Mercian queen.

Yesterday she had had a visit from her mother-in-law, Gytha, who was still at court, much to the dowager queen's annoyance. Gytha couldn't resist meddling in anything where her children were concerned and she disapproved of her daughter's new project, the saintly biography. 'What does she want to go writing books for?' Gytha complained, after being placed in the most comfortable chair near the fire and wrapped in woolen stoles. Eadgifu ordered mead and the small, sweet cakes she liked.

But after she had grumbled and settled herself as she wished, Gytha turned her eyes on Eadgifu. 'What ails you, Swan-neck? You don't look happy. Is it the child?'

Eadgifu shook her head. 'My troubles are not anything that can be solved.'

'The Welsh queen, I presume.' Gytha nodded to her to go on.

'Not entirely. The biggest problem that I have to face is that, for the first time, I'm unequal to my husband. As his wife, Countess of Wessex, rich in my own right with my own lands and manors, almost as many as Harold, I was in no way inferior, nor in the practice of charity. I've endowed as many monasteries and abbeys as he has.'

Eadgifu paused, suddenly tearful. Gytha remained silent, waiting for her to speak again.

'And another woman has taken, not just my husband – but the place I would have occupied, seated beside him. I always expected to be queen. The idea that I might not had never occurred to me. I was Countess of Wessex, and now I'm nothing. I have no title, no place at court. I'm only the mother of his children. A secondary wife. No better than a concubine.'

Gytha nodded. 'Things are changing for women. I have observed it. And not for the better with these new French customs. If you marry, as they would have you do, in the Christian church, you lose many of the rights we have taken for granted. We cannot divorce a bad husband. We must promise to obey, even if he's an idiot. Unlike our own customs, women are to be shackled and fettered.'

She sounded quite angry. 'Don't envy the Welsh Mare, my dear. You have your lands, your children, and you still have your husband's affections. You are in a better place than her.'

Eadgifu had placed Harold's letter inside her tunic, between her linen shift and her skin. She involuntarily put her hand over it, pressing the paper against her breast. 'Harold thinks I should take the children into the country, in case of an invasion from Normandy. I'm loathe to leave London unless the need is urgent. What would you advise, Gytha?'

'Stay near your husband. I've never been one for scurrying away on a rumour. The children will be safe enough here. London is the best fortified town in the kingdom.'

'They are my own feelings. Thank you. Will you stay, or will you go back to Wessex?'

'I shall go as soon as the weather is a little better. If there's an invasion, I will take refuge with the nuns at Wilton. Who would want to harm an old woman in any case? If I survived as Godwin's wife, I will certainly survive as his widow!'

She laughed and Eadgifu felt comforted. But her mind was still uneasy and she spent the afternoon in the nursery

with the children, thinking of a problem that had preoccupied her since Edward's death – her relationship with her
sister-in-law, Edith. Before Edward died their positions
had been very clear – Harold's sister and Harold's wife,
Queen and Countess, both women of importance. Now,
it wasn't so easy. Edith was no longer queen and she
herself was no longer Harold's official wife. Since the day
when the Dowager had been so brutal to her about the
likelihood of his marriage, they had exchanged few words.
The Swan-neck still felt bruised by that encounter, but it
felt wrong to be at war with each other. There was already
an atmosphere in the palace; everything was in flux. It
was important for the family to be united in the face of
conflict. Edith was a difficult woman, but the breach must
be healed for Harold's sake.

~ ~ ~

I walked all night through the city, watching the dawn creep
up over the sea from the city walls. As far as I knew, no
one had pursued me, so perhaps he had not been mortally
wounded. Even so, I dared not go to the king's quarters, or
Edwin's hall, until I knew how things stood. As I walked,
exhausted and hungry, down a narrow street I hadn't explored before, I heard a woman talking in my birth-tongue
– so familiar that for a moment I wasn't aware of the words.
'*Bit theort elskin,*' she was saying, and I heard the child reply.
I stopped to listen, entranced to hear my native speech. Two
hounds ran up to sniff at my britches. The woman looked
up from the clothes she was washing in a stone trough and
smiled at me. I smiled back. '*God dag,*' I said.
     '*Hvaer er du fram?*' she asked.
     'Danmark, Nordjylland.' I answered in the same lan-
guage, and then, because some explanation seemed to be
required, went on, 'I was captured by the Landwaster.'

'Ah. Harald Hadrada! We know him. One of the reasons we came here from our homeland. But you, how did you come here?'

'He gave me as a slave to a Saxon earl, who gave me to the king and now I'm scop to the English court.'

'Where are you staying?'

I told her about the lodging house and the unpleasant men, that I was afraid, though I didn't mention the assault, and that I was looking for a new place to sleep. After a few moments' consideration she said, 'There are such places, but perhaps not the best, for one so young and gently born, if you don't mind my saying.' She was looking at me very carefully and after a pause said, 'We have room for one here, if you don't mind so small a dwelling.'

'I have no money to pay you. Earl Edwin's steward pays for the lodging house.'

She stood up and dried her hands on her skirt. She was tall and thin with her hair plaited down her back. 'No matter. It would be good to hear talk of my own country, and I see you have your lyre on your shoulder. Perhaps you could pay us with a tune or two?'

I nodded and followed her into the house, where I sat down on the ground near the fire as she indicated. My legs felt very weary. She gave me some ale and flat cakes baked on a stone. There were two small children playing in the ashes of the hearth. Her husband was a tanner, she said, working down by the river.

'My name is Ingrid,' she said, 'Ingrid Thorkilsdottir. What shall we call you?'

'I'm Hari Magnusd . . .' – my tongue stumbled and then recovered – 'Magnusson.' I replied and hoped she hadn't noticed the slip. It's so rarely I'm ever asked for my whole name and it's hard to change old habits.

'Welcome to my house Hari,' she said, looking at me rather strangely.

She went out, after I'd eaten, carrying a basket, and I agreed to mind the children while she went to market.

I've no experience with children and it was hard to tell whether they were boy or girl. They had long hair and were wearing tunics made from some rough fabric, ripped and muddied from their games. They sat in front of me with solemn, curious eyes as if waiting for me to do something. '*Was ist das?*' the older of the two asked at last, pointing to the bag that held my lyre.

I took it out. 'Would you like me to play something for you?'

They nodded. I began to play and to sing some of the Danish children's rhymes that I used to sing as a child. It was the strangest feeling. When I stopped, my cheeks were wet and the tears had dripped onto my tunic. I dried my eyes with the hem of it.

'More, more,' the children begged, jumping around with excitement. But I shook my head. I felt exhausted in body and spirit. When Ingrid came home from the market I curled up on the hearth and slept.

In the evening, when Ingrid's husband came in, it was clear he was a jovial man, as friendly as his wife, though he stank of his trade. The family seemed not to notice, and I wondered whether living so long in royal halls had made me fastidious. His name was Ansgar.

'And what name must I call you by?' he asked.

'She calls herself Hari,' Ingrid said, using the female pronoun.

I almost spilt my ale. But her husband seemed not to take any notice. He said, 'Welcome Hari,' and went out into the yard at the back.

After he had gone, I said, 'How did you know?'

She just smiled. 'I wasn't sure when I first saw you, but

when I asked your name you said, "Hari Magnusd. . ." and stopped as if you weren't sure what came next. Hari Magnusdottir is what you were going to say, I think, before you thought better of it?'

I nodded. 'My given name is Hannë, but I've been living as a boy at the court to avoid trouble.'

She looked at me as though assessing me. 'How old are you?'

'Fifteen now.'

Ingrid put a hand on my arm. She looked very serious. 'You won't be able to keep it a secret for ever, Hannë. There's something in the shape of your face, your voice, the way you move, that gives it away. I guessed it, and others will soon too. You can't stop yourself growing into a woman.'

Looking down into the ashes of the fire, I knew she spoke the truth. Before we quarrelled, Arthur had commented that I was growing fat, and it's true. Despite all my efforts to eat as little as possible, my body is filling out and a fuzz of downy hair has begun to grow under my arms and between my legs. I've also noticed that dogs have begun to sniff around me in a way that makes me uneasy.

'That's why I ran away,' I told her. 'One of the men attacked me while I slept. I stuck my knife into him to escape and I'm afraid of what might happen to me if he is dead or seriously wounded.' It felt better to tell someone.

Ingrid looked grave. 'So, you are a fugitive.' She thought for a moment. 'There will be no escaping it, if you have caused him serious harm. You will have to go back to the court and throw yourself on the mercy of the king.'

I nodded.

'You can stay here tonight, but tomorrow you must face what you have done, Hannë.'

Tomorrow was still hours away, and I decided that there was still enough time to work out a way of escape.

~ ~ ~

Goscelin was in a good humour. He said he had been thinking about the project and proposed writing a complete section of the biography on the rise of the Godwin family at the beginning. 'For it's necessary to establish your lineage and the great contribution you yourself have made to the kingdom by your wise counsel to the king, and that of your father before you.'

Edith didn't object.

'So, tell me something of your family, my Lady, your upbringing and education.'

'There were nine of us,' Edith said, remembering her mother perpetually breeding, nursing one infant after another.

'I was the third-born. Swein was the eldest, my father's favourite. He was always in trouble.' She pulled a face. 'No tree was too high for him to climb; no horse unrideable. And then when he was older, it was women. No woman was safe from him. You've heard of the Abbess of Leominster? A girl he believed had been promised to him in marriage by her father before she took refuge in the abbey. When he abducted her he believed that he was simply re-possessing his own.' She paused, as if choosing her words, before saying, 'In truth he was a gulping monster.'

Goscelin looked puzzled.

Edith sighed. 'He was greedy for everything, rash, swift to pick a fight, but also quick to regret it, and always genuinely sorry for his misdemeanours, until the next time. I like to think that he could have changed as he grew older, but he died on a pilgrimage, walking barefoot to Jerusalem to atone for his sins.'

'And how did he get on with his brothers?'

'Harold was a year or so younger and Swein largely

ignored him. They were very different – always arguing. Harold was the sensible one, practical, not getting into anything he didn't know his way out of.'

'Were you close?'

'Not so much as children. I was three years younger than Harold – a girl – and rather ignored. I was closest to Tostig, who was born barely a year after me. We were like twins. Tostig was my mother's favourite. We both looked to Harold to look after us.'

'Not Swein?'

Edith laughed. 'No! He had no interest in young children. He used to call Tostig 'the milkling', 'mother's boy' and names like that.'

'And what was Tostig like as a child?'

'Horse mad. Always in the stables. He loved hunting. My father gave him his first falcon when he was eight years old. But he was good, as good as Harold, when it came to sword play, though Harold was the better strategist. Harold fights as he plays chess – always several moves ahead of his opponent.'

'And what of your younger siblings?'

'When Leofwine and Gyrth were growing up I was already at Wilton, being educated by the nuns. I have a young brother Wulfnoth, currently a hostage in Normandy, and two younger sisters. You may have met one of them at Saint Omer? My father placed her there when we were exiled in '51 and she has chosen to stay cloistered.'

'I had heard that she was there, but I regret that I have not made her acquaintance.'

'Harold is very fond of Gunhilda. When he went to Rome, he brought back a holy relic, St Brigid's Stole, as a present for her.'

Goscelin dipped his pen again and took another sheet of parchment. 'Tell me about what happened when King Harthacnut died and your father had to pledge his loyalty to King Edward. That must have been a difficult time.' He looked up at her, expectantly. Edith thought she had never seen such fine eyes, a deep brown. She rebuked herself and looked away.

'My father, Godwin, rest in grace, gave to King Edward a great ship to prove his loyalty, when Edward came to his throne.' Edith paused. There were no sounds in the room beyond the crackle of the fire and the scratch, scratch of the monk's quill on parchment.

Goscelin looked up again and dipped the tip in his ink well, waiting for her next words. Edith avoided his eyes.

"It was necessary to make a grand gesture. It was well known that my father had given Cnut's son Harthacnut a ship on his coming back to England as king – a fitting tribute since my father had married my mother Gytha, Cnut's sister-in-law. So, when Cnut and his sons, Harold Harefoot and Harthacnut, were all dead, he needed to prove to Edward that he would be loyal to him and not to the Danes.'

Edith remembered her mother telling her about it – one of Gytha's favourite stories; a ship out of a legend. 'It was made of English oak, with a prow in the shape of a dragon and the stern post carved with a lion, both decorated with gold. And on the mast a golden weather vane in the shape of an eagle clutching a warrior in its claws. No one had seen such a ship. There was provision for eighty warriors, each oarsman's bench heaped with gold, and helmets, swords, shields and axes for every warrior. And in the centre was a raised throne for the king, decorated with gold. It was a magnificent sight!'

'The Earl's great ship is talked of even in France,' Goscelin murmured, writing furiously.

'But it was not enough for the king,' Edith went on. 'There were rumours – as we discussed at the beginning – that my father had murdered the king's brother Alfred on the orders of Harthacnut or his mother Emma. So, he pledged me to be the king's wife, as a mark of his undying loyalty.' The knowledge that she had been part of Godwin's weregild for the death of Alfred, was like acid in her stomach.

Her father, Edith marvelled, had been a master of diplomacy, for, on drawing up the marriage contract he had also placed his family perilously near the crown, to fall or prosper with Edward's fortunes. Godwin had served five kings – Æthelred, Cnut, Harold Harefoot, Harthacnut and Edward, each time increasing his land and fortune. Now she and her brothers had inherited his legacy, the highest reach of his ambition, more dangerous than he could ever have imagined.

Goscelin looked up. 'This is perhaps a delicate question, but one that is often asked. Do you know why King Edward had your family exiled in '51?'

Edith frowned. 'That has puzzled me ever since. I've thought and thought and still can't puzzle out just why he turned against us all so suddenly. The crisis happened on the eve of Tostig's marriage, a time of celebration. Edward became angry and unreasonable during the feast. He spent time closeted with the archbishop and in the morning, he gave the order. I've never seen him so angry. It was a shock to all of us. Tostig's wedding was ruined, and he was the one who could usually do no wrong.'

'Do your brothers have any theories about it?'

'Harold thinks it was partly the marriage, which went against Edward's wishes, and also what had happened to Edward's guest, Eustace of Boulogne, at Dover a few days before.'

Goscelin raised his eyebrows. 'Dover?'

'Yes. Eustace got into an argument with some of the burgers, after being refused accommodation, and a fight broke out. Two men were killed. Eustace demanded that Edward give him justice for the insult he felt he'd suffered.

My father refused to punish our own people. Dover was one of Godwin's manors and he had no truck with overbearing Normans. He said that Eustace had probably deserved whatever insults he'd been offered. Harold thinks that that was what annoyed Edward. Just another example of the Godwins ignoring his wishes – the last drop of water that sunk the ship. But I still don't think that's the whole story.'

Goscelin was still writing. She watched him dipping the quill into the ink with a practised rhythm. The way his broad fingers moved over the parchment. His inscrutable face. What sort of man was he, she wondered?

These thoughts were not ones she wanted to entertain. Despite the cushions, carefully arranged by Mathilde, Edith was becoming uncomfortable, aware of a profound tiredness. 'I think that's enough for today,' she said with a weary sigh. 'Perhaps tomorrow?'

Goscelin packed away his quill and parchment, his movements quick and neat. 'A short prayer before I go, my lady?'

Kneeling beside him at the prie-dieu, listening to the Latin words of the prayer for the hour of None, Edith could smell the warm, masculine scent of him and felt a flush of shame that no prayer could atone for.

~ ~ ~

I got up in the early morning and went up onto the old walls of the city. There are some who say they are the work of giants, but one of the monks had told me, when I was at Tostig's palace here, that they were built by the ancient Romans when one of their emperors conquered England a very long time ago. The facts of it are written down in Latin, he explained, and so not generally known.

The walls are crumbling in places now, but still the views

are beautiful, extending out across the countryside, meadow and woodland and to the river as it meanders down from the moors, growing in strength, almost as if its spirit was eager to flow into the sea. The English no longer believe that each thing has its own spirit, that each tree or rock or stream is alive and has its own character; that they talk to each other and can speak to you if you are quiet and know how to listen. It grieves me that, while I was living at Tostig's court, I didn't often get the chance to go out into the country as I used to do, and in London it's impossible for a slave to leave the court without permission. It's a long time since I lay under a tree, dreaming, or dabbled my hands in a stream.

I've lain awake all night worrying about what I should do about the carle I wounded – or worse. I've even considered fleeing on one of the ships for a new destination, a new identity. But, up here on the walls, in the peaceful, early morning air, I realised that Ingrid was right when she told me that I must face up to it or I will never have any rest.

In the end I didn't have a choice. Coming down from the wall, through the narrow streets towards the minster, in a throng of people going to market, or about their business, I was suddenly seized by the hair and yanked back. I knew by the smell of him who it was.

'You bastard boy! Now I have you! And you will pay for what you did.' His angry face was in mine, his putrid breath in my nostrils.

I could see that one of his arms was bound up, his right arm, his sword arm.

'You deserved it!' I said, determined not to be cowed. 'If I told the priests what you were going to do to me . . .'

He began to laugh, but in a threatening manner. 'The priests are the worst. What are they going to say? Whose word would they believe?' He shook me, almost pulling my hair out by the roots.

'You little sod! You stuck me in my sword arm, and what

use is a warrior who can't lift a sword. Tell me!' He shook me again.

I screamed with the pain and one of the passing men stopped beside us. 'Let me go,' I cried.

'What's going on here?' the man asked, and my attacker slackened his grip a little, involuntarily, hampered by his wounded arm, as he turned to reply. I seized the moment and tore myself free and ran. The streets were familiar, often explored, better known to me than to my assailant. I reached the minster and ran through the side door into the quiet interior and the darkness and shadows of the aisles. Surely he would not attack me here? At least the man was alive and had not suffered a mortal wound. But that thought was not as comforting as it should have been. He could still do me great harm, and there was the question of weregild for injuring a man. Earl Edwin would be certain to demand it. How could I ever pay such a fine? I needed someone who could help me. My thoughts went straight to Arthur. In the old days of our friendship, there would have been no hesitation. But I've seen so little of him here. We've been avoiding each other.

I went in search of him in the king's lodgings, slipping in and out of rooms unchallenged, as the young scop who played often in hall, known to everyone, welcomed by all. Arthur was at breakfast, his sword on the bench beside him. He looked up in surprise. 'Hari! Were you looking for me?'

I nodded, suddenly frozen into silence by the sight of him. How could I possibly explain. But I had to try. 'I've found myself in a terrible situation and I need your advice,' I said in the end. Arthur nodded and went on eating his slice of beef and bread. 'Can we talk alone?' He looked surprised but nodded again. When he had finished eating, he took me to a corner of the hall which had been vacated by a group of carles after their own meal.

'What is it that's so important?' Arthur asked. He was friendly towards me, but distant, the old friendship gone.

I told him about the carle who had attacked me in the night and how I had stabbed him in order to escape and how the man had accosted me again and threatened to kill me. What was I to do?

'You are very attractive to a man of a certain kind, Hari, surely you must know that?' He said it in a cold, level sort of voice.

I looked up at him. 'Arthur, I cannot tell you why, or what my circumstances are, but I must tell you that I am not of their kind, nor ever could be.' I forced myself to look him directly in the eye. 'I am fifteen and innocent and I do not know how I am to go on hiding and living without protection except for my knife. And you can see what trouble that has put me in.'

He was looking at me very closely, his eyes narrowed. As his eyes met mine, I saw, first puzzlement and then a gleam of understanding flash between his eyelashes. At length he said, 'You're right. You need protection. Sleeping among my brother's carles is too much danger for one as young as you.' He spoke as though he was many years older than me and not rather less than two.

Arthur smiled suddenly. 'It is a terrible thing to be lord-less, to have no one to feed you or defend you.'

'And to be a slave is not a fate to welcome either.'

'No, I imagine not. Though I have never thought of you as a slave. You aren't like any slave I've ever known.'

He spoke so kindly, so like the old Arthur, that I decided to risk giving him at least some of my history. 'Perhaps because I was once the child of a noble family, as you are, petted and spoilt, and with a future in my father's gift. Until Harald the Landwaster arrived in his ships, bringing bloodshed and plunder, seizing anything of value, including the children of the town to sell to the highest bidder. Being educated in song and story, I was worth a great deal to him.'

Arthur looked surprised. 'And then?'

'Harald the Viking gave me as a gift to Tostig Godwin-son, who then gave me to King Edward. That is my history.'

'Or some of it.' Arthur was looking at me with a very serious expression. 'There is a lot more to tell – am I right?'

I nodded but said nothing. It had cost me a great deal to give him the details that I had.

'Very well.' He turned away and then turned back, with a look I remembered. 'I will speak to my brother about your assailant. You have nothing to fear.' And then he left.

~ ~ ~

Ældyth thought that she should be happier than she was. Even Harold had noticed her mood. Two nights ago he had come to bid her goodnight and sat on the edge of the bed and asked her what was wrong. It was difficult to know what to answer. 'I miss my daughter, Nest,' she had said, unable to put into words the emotions that were swirling around in her head.

'That's easily put right,' Harold said. 'Tell your brother to have her brought to London, so that she's there to meet you when we go back. You should have spoken earlier. There was no reason not to have her at court.'

And so, the order had been given. The king was eager that everything should be done for her comfort and happiness. His queen should lack nothing. And yet, she felt utterly miserable.

Recently, she had been sleeping badly and having strange dreams – the kind of dreams, which, in the old religion which Gruffyth had adhered to, would have been given significant meanings. Last night she had dreamt, for the second time, that she walked in a garden under a great tree with branching boughs, where two ravens sat, uttering their strange cries. Listening to them, she had wept, and her tears had turned into white flowers where they dropped onto the grass. The night before she had dreamed of the same garden and how she had caught her cloak in a thornbush as she walked and how, as she pulled it free, the thorn had dropped to the ground and grown suddenly into a beautiful bush covered in the same white flowers. The dreams nagged at her during the day, filling her with apprehension. What did they mean? Or did they mean nothing at all? The priests would have dismissed them, she knew. Her chaplain was an old man, steeped in the new Christianity. Ældyth and her brothers had been tutored by a monk from Lindisfarne, in that blend of Christian and Celtic faith that recognised the old mysticism.

Merwenne, noticing her sombre spirits at breakfast, suggested that music might cheer her. 'We could all do with something cheerful in this dark weather.' She looked at Margaret, 'Where is that young bard you talk to sometimes? The one I've seen playing in hall?'

'You mean Hari? The Danish boy? The one who is scop to Earl Edwin?'

'Yes. Do you think you could find him and bring him to my Lady?'

It took very little time to find him in the refectory, where Margaret had seen him sitting earlier in the day. Margaret brought him in and, when he stood in front of her, Ældyth thought he looked very young and underfed, his blond hair roughly cut, wearing an old tunic that had seen more prosperous days. But when he took out his lyre and tuned it, he played and sang very sweetly with a voice that was unbroken.

'I will ask my brother if he can spare you,' Ældyth said. 'For I miss music and you play very well. It would be good for me to have my own scop, as I did at the Welsh court. You are Danish, I think?'

He bowed his head. 'I was captured and brought as a slave from my father's court.'

'So you are noble-born?' Ældyth felt no surprise. There was something in his bearing, the intelligence in his face, that did not belong to the peasantry. And where would that musical skill come from, if not from a courtly education?

'If you are to play for me, you must be properly clad,' Ældyth said. 'I cannot have one of my attendants dressed in rags. Merwenne, can you ask one of the servants to find suitable clothes for my scop?'

Merwenne was right. What was lacking was music.

~ ~ ~

'How did you come to be a monk, Brother Goscelin', Edith asked, allowing herself to use his name. Recently they had begun to talk about ordinary things in a friendly way when he arrived, sometimes for more than half the time before they returned to the subject of her husband's life.

'My father was a ploughman on the abbey's land. I would have had no education, like my older brothers, but the steward of the monastery, out one day surveying the land, overheard me singing while I lead the horses – a hymn I had heard in the abbey church.' He blushed. 'I have always had a quick memory for words and tunes.' He paused as if not sure how much she wanted him to tell.

'And then?'

'He spoke to the abbot who talked to my father and asked me to sing for him and afterwards I was admitted into the abbey with the other boys to learn my lessons and sing in the choir.'

'So it was not religious fervour that brought you to the monastic life?'

'No, my Lady. Not a vocation. But it lifted me out of a life of ignorance and gave me opportunities I could never have dreamt of.' He paused and smiled. 'Unfortunately, when I was about fourteen my voice broke and afterwards I could not sing so well.' His smile broadened. 'I could have left and gone back to the land, but by then I had begun to be useful in the scriptorium. So I stayed and took my vows.'

'You have found your place.'

'Indeed. By the Grace of God, who knows best what is good for us.' He bowed his head in an attitude of meekness, but Edith thought that he was not a naturally meek man. Goscelin had an air of self-containment and confidence that was attractive.

'Do you still see your mother and father?'

'They are sadly no longer in this world, God rest their souls. I write to the priest of the parish for news of my siblings, but as they cannot read or write, I cannot have any dialogue with them directly. There are five of them, three girls and two boys. The boys work on the land and the girls are all married, all fortunately placed.'

He seemed uneasy talking about himself and took up his pen, rearranging the parchment in front of him. 'Can we talk about your marriage to the king, my lady? Another delicate subject, but one I must have clear if I'm to write this work.'

Edith sighed. A shadow passed over her face. This was the subject she had been avoiding. She took a breath and paused for a moment before beginning. 'It was a *mariage blanc.*'

Goscelin nodded, as if this was something he already knew.

Edith went on, with some difficulty. 'He never touched me once, you know. Not once. Earl Godwin sold me to him for rank and position, to make himself the father of the queen. It was as near the throne as he was ever going to be. But in doing so he deprived me of everything worth having – human love, children . . .' Edith's voice cracked on the word, and she paused to regain control of herself. 'I have often wondered if Godwin knew what Edward was before he agreed to the marriage and, if he did, how he could be so cruel to his daughter.'

'Did the king ever talk to you of it? Did he mention that he had taken a vow of chastity, for instance?'

Edith shook her head.

Goscelin put down his pen. 'I have been pondering how to bring this matter forward in the book. There is a word in Latin, ambiguous in meaning. *Caelebs*, which can mean chaste as in fidelity, unmarried, but also celibate. The king's abstinence could be described as such, I think.'

'Celibate, yes, as to women.' There was an edge to Edith's voice. She was surprised at the strength of the venom that she felt. 'I can say that out loud between us, though you cannot put it in the book.' Edith glanced at him briefly. Goscelin's expression betrayed nothing, but Edith was sure he understood. 'But it condemned me also to celibacy. And you must know the torments of that.'

Goscelin's pen hesitated briefly, and he nodded an acknowledgment without looking up.

Edith went on. 'You had the choice, you chose to renounce those things of your own free will, but I was never asked. It was taken from me. And there are times, God help me, when I cannot bear it!'

Edith felt the tears running down her cheeks and was powerless to stop them. She heard herself sobbing, which alarmed her, for she never allowed herself to cry. Never. But here she was weeping wildly, and the holy brother, much discomfited, came and put his hand on her head to comfort her. His hand was warm on her hair; the pressure, like a caress, before he called her waiting women to come in.

~ ~ ~

This morning, I went straight into the queen's chambers after I'd eaten in the refectory. It's a good feeling to know that I have a place. When I go back to Ingrid's house to sleep in the evening I'm among friends, and I'm welcomed among the queen's women during the day. I play to them while they sew and the queen reads. They chatter among themselves a great deal and it's just the sort of comfortable small talk and gossip I knew in my father's hall. It's the nearest to 'home' that I have felt in more than three years.

But today, there was some disquiet among the women when I entered the room and the queen looked upset.

'She has had another dream,' the Lady Margaret said to me quietly, as I took my place on a stool beside the fire.

'What kind of dream?'

'One that keeps returning, a disturbing dream which she doesn't understand.'

The queen's Welsh maid was saying, 'These dreams shouldn't be ignored, my Lady. There must be someone who can tell us their meaning.'

One of the Godwin sisters, Hilde I think, said brusquely, 'That's all superstition! These dreams are caused by something you've eaten that doesn't agree with you.'

'No!' The queen sounded angry. 'I'm sure the dreams have been sent to tell me something important. When I first dreamt of the tree there were two ravens in it, but last night there was only one and the grass at the foot of the tree was stained with blood. It was so real, like a vision. I've become afraid.'

'We need a seer,' Merwenne said. 'An interpreter of dreams. But where do we find such a person here?'

There was a silence. Eventually I said, 'By your leave, my Lady, I might know of one, a woman of my own people, what we call a 'knowing woman', skilled in the ancient lore.'

'But that is a heathen thing,' Lady Margaret said sharply. 'We are a Christian people.'

'In the bible, God allowed Joseph to interpret dreams, did he not?' It was the queen who spoke. She turned her head towards me. 'Could you find your seer, Hari? Do you know where she is to be found?'

'I'm not sure.' Would Merithien still be there? Had she been sent to me by the gods and would now be somewhere else on another errand? 'I will try, my Lady.' I wasn't confident that I could find her – such people can't be summoned at will.

~ ~ ~

In the interval between the afternoon prayers and the evening meal in hall, Eadgifu walked down the corridor towards the royal apartments. It was already dark, the long winter nights only beginning to recede towards summer and the torches were lit on the walls. She knocked on the Dowager's door and, after an interval, the Norman maid opened it and bowed her in.

The Lady Edith was sitting by the fire, sewing a tapestry. She looked surprised to see her sister-in-law but waved her to a chair on the other side of the fire. 'This is a rare privilege!' There was a slight edge to her voice.

The Swan-neck tried to remember the speech she'd prepared earlier in the afternoon, but the words evaporated. 'I know you'll be surprised at my visit,' she began, more hesitantly than she'd planned. 'In the past we haven't always got along.' That was an understatement, a voice said in her inner ear. They had always irritated each other. The fact that she had children was almost more than Edith could bear. She was, like all the Godwins, proud, autocratic, used to getting her own way, quick to take offence. The only exception to the latter was Harold, who was remarkably even tempered and able to keep his own counsel. *I must try harder with his sister*, the Swan-neck told herself and began to speak again.

'Recently, I've been very unhappy, my position at court usurped by Ælddyth of Mercia, as you predicted,' Eadgifu glanced at the Dowager, 'and my titles and courtesies lost by Harold's marriage to her. It hasn't been easy, and I've kept myself to myself because of the hurt and the shame of it.' Something the Dowager had been quick to criticise in the past, Eadgifu thought. But she must put all these thoughts out of her mind.

'It occurred to me, when I was talking to your mother earlier – and please don't take offence – that you're in the same position, having been supplanted by the Mercian queen and no longer first in the court.'

'And this is supposed to comfort me?' the Dowager's face showed a flash of anger. The tone of her words was bitter.

'No, that was not my object. I just thought that, here we are, two women of the same family, both suffering from the same cause, and that we should be friends. We're living in a time of much anxiety, facing a possible war. Can we not be allies at the least? Harold needs all our support.'

Edith's face softened, but her voice was still hard. 'He does. But we're very different people. I'm not sure we can ever be properly friends. Allies?' She paused as if considering the question. 'Yes, perhaps. The court's a lonely place when one no longer has a distinct role to play. Did Gytha tell you that Harold has told me to move my quarters?'

'No. Has he?'

'Through Robert the Staller. So, like you, I must translate myself to new apartments. And, as Harold will want you near him as well as the new queen, I will have to find lodgings further away from the centre of power. I've had much heart-searching over this, not wanting to be like my own mother-in-law, Emma. And I'm wondering what to do with my life. I'm still a young woman. You have Harold and you have your children. I have no husband and no children.

What am I to do when Harold returns from the north with his queen and takes whatever is left of the reins of state from me? I haven't answered that question yet, but I don't intend to let them go easily.'

Eadgifu Swan-neck saw, for the first time, a vulnerable woman sitting opposite her. The Dowager's position, as she had described it, was unenviable, and certainly worse than her own.

'We have a joint enemy, my Lady.' The Dowager looked up in surprise as Eadgifu spoke. 'Perhaps enemy is too hard a word, but she's taken something from each of us.'

'What do you propose to do?' Edith's voice was flat, emotionless.

'I don't know. But I think we must make more effort to support each other in the new lives we have to make. We're both wealthy, and there's a great deal of charitable work to be done. I'm not political, like you. I've always confined myself to family life, the ordering of my own estates. But I sense that there's a change coming. I've asked my stewards to make sure that every man on my manors is prepared to fight for Harold when the time comes.'

'I pray that day won't come,' the Dowager said. 'William may decide that the price of an attempt on the English throne is too great. And I can't believe that the Norse Viking who bears Harold's name, could mount a serious attempt. He has no claim to the throne at all.'

'I hope you're right. Harold's not so confident, but then he has a prudent disposition.'

The Dowager smiled for the first time. 'He's like his mother. He has the Danish attitude to trouble. Hope for sunlight, prepare for snow.'

'It's served him well.' Eadgifu smiled back at her sister-in-law. 'Do you dine in hall tonight?'

'I was undecided, but if you're going, then I'll join you.'

For the first time, the two women walked into hall

together, the Dowager slightly in front of her, as befitted her status. But Eadgifu, for once, didn't mind. It seemed they had achieved a truce in hostilities.

~ ~ ~

As if the gods knew that she was wanted, a few days later Merithien was there on the quayside, with her cherrywood stick and her swirling cloak, talking to one of the boat captains. She turned when she saw me and smiled.

'Come to ask me another question Hari?'

'How do you know my name? I never gave it to you!'

'I am not called a "knowing woman" for nothing. What do you want from me?'

'It isn't me, it's the queen. She's been having strange dreams, like Ragnhild the Mighty in the old stories, and is anxious to know what they mean. There are ravens and trees and white flowers and blood. You will understand, I think. Will you come?'

She stood for a moment, tapping her stick on the ground thoughtfully. Then she said, 'I will, but I'm not sure she will want to hear what I have to say.'

'Perhaps not, but at present she's so disturbed she's afraid to sleep. At least she will know, even if she doesn't like it.'

We made a strange pair as we entered the royal quarters. Merithien is tall and with her wild hair and her brightly coloured clothes she draws every eye. Beside her I feel like an elven creature, small and thin and fair as she is dark. I was a little apprehensive about presenting her to the queen, but Merithien bowed very low. I noticed that she and Merwenne exchanged looks, as if they knew each other, which would be impossible, so perhaps they simply recognised some quality they shared.

'Your scop tells me that you are having strange dreams,

my Lady.' Merithien said, in the Saxon tongue. 'Could you tell me the nature of them?'

The queen told her of the garden, the tears and the white flowers and the thorn that grew into a bush, of the tree with the two ravens that became a tree with only one, standing in bloodstained earth.

'The tree is easy,' Merithien began. 'In the old stories it is Yggdrasil, the tree of life, and so it is in the Christian stories – a tree of death that yet brings forth life. The Christians would tell you that the thorn bush was the very one that grew in the Garden of Gethsemane, a sprig of which, Joseph, a friend of the man Jesus, brought to Glastonbury to grow in English soil. The ravens are easy too. They are messengers. A raven sat on each of Odin's shoulders in my own religion and they were the friends of Bran in the religion of the Welsh – you will have heard of them,' she nodded to Merwenne. 'Birds of war and guardians of peace.'

Merwenne nodded back.

'But what does it all mean?' The queen asked. 'I understand the symbols, but not what they're telling me. I have this terrible feeling of foreboding.'

'That is not easy to interpret, even for one of my skill.' Merithien rested with both hands on her stick, her head bent forward for a moment. Then she raised it. 'There will be war. Blood at the foot of the tree. That is what it means. And someone will die – the two ravens who become one. In the Christian stories there are two brothers Cain and Abel, and one kills the other. I fear bloodshed. Fratricide. A curse on the one who commits it.'

There was a sharp intake of breath in the room. Merithien paused and then went on, 'You must not think that this dream is wholly about loss. You described the sun shining on the upper branches of the tree, the tears that spring up into white flowers, and that must mean that something good will grow from the darkness.'

She paused again, and I could see her hesitate before she

spoke. 'I have been reluctant to tell you this, but there is another message in this dream. You are not safe, even in your own garden. Be careful who you trust. We have a saying, where I come from, that is important for you to remember when you look at those close to you. "No one is so good as to be free from all evil; nor so bad as to be worth nothing."'

She waited for a moment, as if to let the full meaning of it sink in. Then she bowed and began to back away.

The queen looked sombre, but she said, 'I thank you for your words. I think I understand it better now.' Then she turned to her ladies and said, 'Merwenne, take the seer away and see that she has refreshments and suitable reward for her advice.'

As she passed me, Merithien turned her face in my direction and said softly, 'Goodbye, Hari the shape-shifter. I think we will not see each other again.' And then Merwenne led her out of the room.

'Why did she call you "shape-shifter"?' Lady Margaret said in my ear.

I shook my head, without turning to look at her.

'You aren't always what you seem, are you Hari?'

Ingrid is right. People are beginning to suspect something. But I'm not ready to explain to Margaret yet.

When the queen had retired to lie down, the ladies were very free with their comments. The Godwin sister said, 'Which brothers do you think she meant? There are two pairs to choose from.'

'It's all pagan nonsense,' Lady Margaret was still angry. 'I hope that the king and the court don't get to hear of the queen consulting with a heathen shaman.'

Merwenne came back into the room in time to hear her. 'Oh, and would a heathen have quoted so much of the bible do you think?' Her voice was fierce. 'Her words have calmed the queen and for that we should be glad. Being with child, and such an important child, is an anxious time for a woman and brings much superstition. Let it rest.'

Margaret sighed, but she said nothing further.

I tuned my lyre and began to play.

~ ~ ~

The Benedictine brothers of York had made it as difficult as possible for the king to visit the queen at night, by placing their quarters as far apart down the icy stone corridors as possible. But Harold came. Ældyth felt his warm presence beside her, his cold feet against hers. She turned over, glad to feel his fingers on her skin, caressing her with practised ease. Not at all like Gruffyth, who came, took his pleasure and then fell asleep, snoring like an old boar. She was only an empty vessel for his seed. Not so Harold. He stroked her swollen, painful breasts with gentle hands, as though he understood what pregnancy did to a woman, and when she shuddered with pleasure in that final paroxysm of joy, it was like an epiphany. Why had no one ever told her that love-making could be like this?

Lying awake, still tingling with the aftermath, as though her skin remembered every touch of his fingers, she listened to Harold breathing deeply in his sleep and gave a prayer of thanks for the gift of a husband she could regard with affection. When she was with him she felt that she was not just a peace-weaver doing her duty, but one of a pair of lovers.

Gazing up into the darkness of the bed's canopy, her mind strayed to the events of the day. Ældyth went over all the things the seer had told her, the interpretations of the dreams she'd been having, particularly the killing of one brother by the other. Could this be her own brothers, Edwin and Morcar? There was certainly rivalry between them, and she knew that they both coveted the crown if they could see any way to get it. And then there was Harold and his brother Tostig. No love lost there either and Tostig aggrieved that he hadn't been given the throne by the old king. '*Can there never be peace in such families as ours?*' Ældyth thought. And she knew that what the seer had said, about not being safe in her own garden, was true. Until she had a son who could unite the factions and claim the throne for both the earldoms of Mercia and Wessex, there would be no safety. Before she went to sleep she sent up silent prayers to the Virgin to give her a son, placing her hands on her already swollen belly, willing the child within to grow strong and healthy, as her daughter Nest had done.

~ ~ ~

We are to return to London, by stages, just as we journeyed up. I am to travel with the queen, which means that I will see Arthur often, since he is among the carles taxed with her protection. I have a new tunic of green linen with a neck binding of blue, the queen's colour, and I think it looks very handsome. Ingrid certainly thought so when I took my leave of her. 'I'll miss you Hannë,' she said, straightening the fabric across my shoulders. 'It's been wonderful to have one of my kinswomen to talk to.' I didn't tell her that it had been equally wonderful to be treated as a girl again, to be called by my given name. It made me feel like a whole person, not the imposter I know, every day, that I am. It was also disturbing, because it has made me feel dissatisfied with my disguise and the need for it. I want to be what I am, a girl, an ordinary girl. Will it ever be possible?

Before I left, Ingrid took me aside and asked if I knew what happened to girls when they became women. 'Has anyone talked to you about your moon-courses?'

I blushed with embarrassment. 'I had sisters at home, so I know something.'

'Do you know what to do?'

I shook my head. This was a subject that had begun to worry me.

Ingrid took my arm and led me away from the children, to a chest at the back of the room. She opened the lid and took out some fabric.

'Do you have one of these?' She held up an oblong piece of linen with a long tie at each corner. I shook my head again.

'You will need one to tie between your legs. Then you will need napkins to fold and put inside it to catch the blood.' She took another piece of fabric out of the chest and held both pieces of cloth out to me. 'Take these. They are all I can spare but will do for the present. Now you must make your own, to be prepared.'

I could hardly speak for embarrassment, but I took the gifts, knowing how ill she could spare them. This family had so little.

'You have been like a mother to me,' I managed to whisper. 'Thank you, thank you.'

She gave me a hug, a tight embrace that made my eyes fill with tears. I know that I will never see her again. Yet another person who will disappear from my itinerant life as if from a dream.

When I left the house for the last time, carrying my bundle and my lyre on my back, I left the silver cup given me by Edwin tucked inside the chest, so that when Ingrid opens it again she will find it and know how much her hospitality has meant to me.

Part Four

The Long-haired Wyrme

'At that time, throughout all England, a portent such as men had never seen before was seen in the heavens. Some declared that the star was a comet, which some call 'the long-haired star': it first appeared on the eve of the festival of Letania Maior, that is on 24 April, and shone every night for a week.'

The Anglo-Saxon Chronicle

As we approached London, one of the men pointed out a particularly bright star in the sky to the west. 'That's new,' he said.

'You know about stars?'

'My father was a captain of the king's ships under the last king. He taught me how to steer by the stars. That's one I haven't seen before. An omen perhaps.'

Not all the omens are to be feared. Some of them are portents of a new order, of great happenings, like the star the Christian priests say appeared at the birth of the Christ. I wonder what this omen will mean?

Before we left York, Arthur sought me out and suggested

113

that I should sleep in the queen's lodgings as we travelled, rather than in the tents with the less important carles and retainers. He is also sleeping in the queen's lodgings being part of the guard that Edwin is providing for his sister. Arthur takes care not to sleep near me, but I can see him watching me and it's comforting to know that I have some protection now.

He suspects something, I know. The afternoon before we left York he came into the queen's quarters with a message from Earl Edwin. I was playing my lyre beside the fire, while Ældyth's ladies were packing her belongings into chests for the journey. Afterwards, before he took his final leave, he came over to the fireside as if to warm himself and listened for a while to what I was playing. I became aware that he was watching me intently. He moved closer and I stopped playing.

'Carry on,' he said. His voice was shaking oddly. 'I haven't heard you play that before.'

'It's a tune I learned in my homeland. I find it comforting.' I began playing again, trying to ignore that every part of my body was aware of his presence.

He was watching my fingers on the strings. And then, very quietly, he said, 'You have the hands of a girl, Hari.'

I said nothing. But my fingers faltered and I stumbled over the notes.

'Who are you, Hari?'

I still said nothing, though I longed to tell him everything.

'I'm sorry,' he said in a softer voice. 'I wish we could be friends.'

I turned my head a little so that he couldn't see the tear making its way down my left cheek and waited until he'd gone.

~ ~ ~

Harold came in carrying little Gytha, with Magnus at his heels. He was tossing Gytha and making her laugh making bear-like noises and threatening to bite her feet.

'Are you well, my Swan?' he asked Eadgifu, as he fended off Magnus' demands to watch how well he could now wield his wooden sword.

Eadgifu was aware of a constraint in Harold's manner towards her – nothing obvious, just a slight reserve that no one but a wife of twenty years would notice. He put Gytha down and kissed Eadgifu on the cheek before giving his attention to Magnus. 'You've grown!' he told him. 'You're too big for that toy – I'll have to have a half-sword forged for you.'

'Can we play, father?'

'I'm afraid not, little one.'

He turned apologetically to Eadgifu, 'There's a Council meeting in less than an hour and I must see a few people before that.' He smiled his disarming grin that usually lit up his eyes, though not today.

Eadgifu smiled back, even as something sank inside her.

'Will I see you in hall?' he asked.

'Your sister and I will be there. You'll be glad to know that we've declared a truce since you left for York.'

'Good. I want all my family to be on good terms with each other.' He turned to take his leave of the children, bent down and took something out of the pouch that hung from his belt. There was a flash of silver. 'Hold out your hands,' he said to Gytha and Magnus. 'Here's a present for you.' And he put a coin into each palm. Standing up he turned to Eadgifu, smiling. 'They're the first out of the mint with my face on.' Then he was gone with a flash of his cloak.

Something had changed, Eadgifu was sure, but what it was, she dared not think.

~ ~ ~

It was a long, weary journey and Ælðyth had been so sick with the jolting and bumping of the horse under her that she had feared to lose the child inside her. But there, in her chamber as she entered it at last, was Nest, waiting with her nurse. Nest ran to her the moment she came into the room, still in her travelling cloak, still nauseous from the journey. But her daughter's smile, her cry of 'Mummy!', the feel of her warm, familiar body in her arms, felt like a cure for all ills.

'Oh, mummy, how I've wanted you,' Nest said, burying her face in Ælðyth's neck. She held her daughter tightly. Harold had kept his promise. He was a good man. He had also arranged for her to occupy the Queen's chambers next to his own. Ælðyth wondered how the Dowager had felt about being moved out of her quarters.

Her next visitor, a few hours later, was less welcome. Harold's mother, the dowager Countess of Wessex, despite her spoken intention to return to her own manor, had remained at the palace while Harold was away, to the annoyance of her daughter. Ælðyth was reading to Nest on the settle in the window when Angharad announced the Countess. She came through the door in a flurry of linen and expensive eastern velvet, a grey veil held in place by a thin gold band over her hair, which was still dark, with one white streak from her forehead to her crown. Although Ælðyth had met Gytha on a few occasions before, it was the first time she had been alone with her.

'They tell me,' Gytha said without preamble, 'that you are as sick now as you were at the beginning. Is it true?'

'It is,' Ælðyth said. She was beginning to get used to the fact that, since two of her waiting women were Godwins, every detail of her life was public knowledge. 'I was never like that with my daughter, so it has surprised me.'

'It will be a boy, certainly,' Gytha said as she settled herself among the cushions Angharad was arranging on the carved wooden chair near the fire for her comfort. 'It was so with me. Daughters gave me no trouble in carrying, but my sons made me sick as a dog.'

'I hope it's a son,' Ældyth said, putting one hand protectively on her swelling belly. 'There's a great deal at stake if it isn't.'

'No matter,' Gytha said. 'You'll have a boy the next time. Harold won't mind. He likes children.'

And, Ældyth thought, *he has male heirs already. It's my brothers who will be displeased.*

She wondered why Gytha had come. The Countess was not a woman for small talk and social visits. 'I thought you would be in Wessex at this time? Harold said that you usually spend the summer at Bosham?'

'It was my intention. But I've had troublesome news I didn't want to pass on to Harold while he was in York. So, I stayed to talk to him in person before the meeting of the Council, when his brothers would be there and the archbishop.'

'News?'

Gytha sighed. 'From my daughter, Gunhilda, who is cloistered at St Omer in Flanders. She wrote me a letter which I don't know whether or not to believe.'

'Have you shown it to Queen Edith?' As regent in Harold's absence, she was the rightful person to deal with it.

'I did. Edith thinks it's a false rumour. But Harold takes a different view. Gunhilda thinks her brother Tostig has plans, not just for claiming back his lost territory, but also for seizing the throne, encouraged by his cousin-in-law, William of Normandy. Their wives are blood relatives, you know.'

Ældyth nodded.

'According to Gunhilda, Tostig has been staying at St

Omer and from there he went to visit William. Why would he do that if not to foment trouble?'

Ældyth felt a prick of alarm. 'Edith always dismisses the idea that Tostig could be a traitor and I, too, find it difficult to believe. Harold was crowned and anointed by the archbishop as the rightful king. How could Tostig think of doing such harm to his own brother?'

'You don't know my sons!' Gytha shifted in her chair. 'Three of them are like Harold, straight as a willow wand and reliable as oak. But the other two!' She grimaced. 'Swein and Tostig. The devil must have been present when they were conceived. But there's no use complaining. You know that Swein put about the rumour that he was not Godwin's son, but Cnut's? My own brother-in-law! I had to swear an oath in front of an assembly of noblewomen. I still remember the humiliation. Swein caused a great deal of trouble for our family and Tostig will do the same.'

Ældyth thought Gytha looked suddenly sad and old and rather frail.

'Tostig was my favourite, you know. He used to like to sit with me and talk while I sewed. And he was fonder of my company than his father's. Godwin could be harsh with the boys, especially Tostig. He wanted him to be like himself.' Gytha gave a dry laugh. 'Godwin would fuck anything that moved – easy to see where Swein got it from. Any number of cuckoos he planted in other men's nests. How he got away with it I don't know. You must be glad that Harold's not the same.'

Ældyth was glad that, just at this moment, Angharad came in with mead and cakes for the dowager Countess so that she didn't have to answer. Angharad also brought a welcome cup of water for Ældyth.

'Have you tried an infusion of peppermint and fennel?' Gytha asked. 'You should talk to your sister-wife, the Swan-neck. There's nothing she doesn't know about child-bearing. And, like you, she's suffering the same affliction.'

'She's also with child?' Ældyth felt as though she'd been struck.

'Why should you think it strange?' Gytha said. 'You are both his wives.'

'But ...' Ældyth found it difficult to breathe for a moment. 'He's a Christian. He can't have two wives. She was put aside when he married me. My brothers assured me.'

Gytha smiled, but to Ældyth it seemed as though it held malice. 'You are an intelligent woman.' Gytha said. 'You must know that he married you to gain a throne, but his enduring love is for the Swan-neck. Why should he leave her bed entirely for yours?'

Inside her head Ældyth felt a tumbling sensation. Why had she imagined that Harold felt anything more for her than the desire of an older man for a young girl? She had grown to love him, had thought that he felt some affection for her, but she was obviously mistaken. On the nights he wasn't with her, he was in bed with the Swan-neck and had got her with child too. Ældyth realised she was going to vomit and hurried out in the ante-room to throw up into the wash bowl.

Gytha came to the door. When she spoke it was to her daughter-in-law Hilde. 'Take care of her. Peppermint tea will help and afterwards the queen should rest.' And with that she left.

Ældyth felt a great gladness that Gytha was gone. She had been warned that her mother-in-law, like her daughter Edith, had a spiteful tongue. Living among the Godwin women was little better than camping near a hornet's nest. And then she remembered the Swan-neck saying, when she had come to her room in those first weeks; 'I am still his wife.' So that was what she had meant. It was difficult to accept that Eadgifu still shared his bed and his counsel. For someone who had contracted a Christian marriage, it was adultery, even if he was the king.

After Merwenne and Hilde had put Ældyth to bed she cried.

'I'll take Nest to play with her siblings,' Hilde said, which made her feel even worse. When they had gone, Merwenne drew the curtains round the bed and Ældyth heard her cross the room and sit down in the chair by the fire.

'Merwenne?'

'Yes, my Lady.'

'Can you find my little scop? Some music would help me sleep, I think.' Anything but this silence full of difficult thoughts.

Merwenne must have been successful because, not long after, a soft melody began to float across the room; music that seemed to talk about the sea softly shushing on a sandy shore, wind in the trees, and the sweet voice of the scop, a clear treble soaring like a bird, singing in a strange language that somehow needed no translation.

~ ~ ~

All the talk was of the star that had grown huge and now sported a burning tail. No one, not even the oldest man in the court, had seen anything like it. In the evening Edith and the Swan-neck and most of the court went out into the fields beyond the city gates to see it. The night was mild and cloudless and there in the blackness was the portent, what some were calling the 'long-haired wyrme' as if it was something out of the old fables.

It was larger than any other star in the heavens, moon-bright and glowing with a long, fiery dragon's tail that stretched across the horizon. A shiver of awe, something approaching fear, went down Edith's spine as she watched it. Goscelin had told her that it was a comet, a sky-wanderer, and would soon travel on out into the blackness beyond the sun. But Edith couldn't shake off the feeling that the star was some kind of omen. Her mother Gytha, with all the superstition of one reared in a semi-pagan family, certainly thought so. 'These are turbulent times,' she had said at dinner. 'We must all be ready for what is coming.' But, when pressed, she couldn't say what she thought might be coming, for good or evil. No one mentioned Gunhilda's letter about Tostig. In Council the broad opinion was that he had been to Normandy to find out whether William would return his earldom if he successfully invaded England. That William intended to do it seemed obvious.

As Edith took off her fur robe and allowed Mathilde to undress her, she tried not to think of her brother Harold and the threat across the water; William of Normandy, spreading propaganda about how Edward had promised the throne to him. There was a logic to it; after all, Edward's mother Emma was Norman and he had spent thirty years of his life at the Duke of Normandy's court. But more damaging, William was spreading the rumour that Harold had sworn a sacred oath to support his claim, with his hand on holy relics. That Harold had been effectively his prisoner at the time and unable to refuse at risk of his life, was beside the point. And Edith was aware that Harold could well have done so, knowing that the choice of the next king rested with the earls and bishops who formed the Witan, and that the oath would be void because it was under duress. She knew that he had spent a long time closeted with the archbishop on his return from Normandy.

'You're shivering, my Lady,' Mathilde said, arranging a woollen wrap over her shoulders.

'It was cold out there under the stars,' Edith replied. But she knew it wasn't the cold. Her mother was right. Something was coming towards them out of the dark, heralded by its own star, blazing like a battle banner across the horizon.

At the prie-dieu she begged fervently, aloud, for guidance

and protection. And then, shame-faced, aware of Matthilde waiting to put her to bed, she prayed silently that she might think less of Goscelin. *Guard thou my thoughts,* she asked, *and keep them pure.*

But it was no use. As soon as she closed her eyes and pulled up the covers he was there in front of her; the muscular arms, the male scent of him, the way his hair curled round his ears, one tendril escaping onto his temple. Her fingers moved instinctively down to the warm, comforting place between her legs, giving herself over to pleasure, until her whole body shuddered with it, stifling the cum-cry into her pillow. Then, breathless, dazed, guilty, she turned over in the bed, able to sleep at last.

~ ~ ~

The king sent for me just after breakfast. Brynn, the most senior of his hearth-carles, came for me as I was tuning my lyre at the table ready to play for the queen.

'Well, rapscallion,' Brynn said, with mock severity, as he caught me by the shoulder. 'What have you been up to that the king's scouring the palace for you?'

I felt a shiver of alarm and shook my head. 'I don't know why he wants me.' But in my mind I wondered whether he had heard of the stabbing of Edwin's carle, something I had thought was already settled. My stomach turned over.

Harold was in his receiving room, seated at a table with his chaplain and his brothers, Gyrth and Leofwine. He looked angry and there was an unsettled atmosphere in the room as if words had been spoken before I arrived. Brynn brought me to stand in front of him and the brothers at the table. They were all looking at me, curiously, as if they had never noticed me before.

The king surprised me by speaking in Danish. 'Your name's Hari, I believe.'

I nodded, my mouth too dry to speak.

'Where do you come from Hari?'

That was an odd question. As he was speaking my native language he must already know. I swallowed and my tongue detached itself from the roof of my mouth. 'From Denmark, Sir. Nordjylland.'

'And how did you get here. Your full history. I want to hear all of it.' Harold's voice was stern.

'I was taken as a slave from my father's court when the town was sacked by Harald of Norway.'

'Your father's court?' He seized on the word immediately, and his tone was accusatory.

'Earl Magnus Magnusson.' There was something in the king's piercing blue eyes that demanded truth.

There was a murmur round the table.

'Your father was the son of Magnus of Denmark?' Harold sounded surprised.

I nodded.

'Magnus was no friend of ours. You'd better tell me your lineage!' It was an order.

Perhaps it was time to come out of hiding. Would it make me more or less vulnerable to tell the king my parentage? I was tired of being in disguise, and there was a sort of perverse pride in telling them who I was – or rather who I had been. 'My father was only his son by a secondary wife, but my mother was Astrid the Fair, the grand-daughter of Sweyn Forkbeard.' I wondered just how dangerous the knowledge was. If I was indeed a boy, I would have a claim – a remote claim – to the Danish throne and, through Sweyn and his son Cnut, also to those of Norway and England.

Harold sat back in his chair as if considering what I'd said. 'So, you are a cousin of Harald of Norway?'

'Of sorts. At least my parents were. But he didn't know it. If he had, he wouldn't have allowed me to live.'

'That's true enough.' Harold smiled, though his eyes

remained cold. 'I'm told by my sister that you were at Harald's court during a visit by my brother, Earl Tostig.'

So that was it. 'Yes, Sir, I was. Earl Tostig was there and also the Earl of Orkney.'

'Do you know the purpose of that visit? What was discussed?'

'As to the former, Earl Tostig has two sons by a girl he kept as a concubine when he was very young. If I remember right, I think they're called Skuli and Ketil, both rather older than myself. They're fostered at the Norwegian court and good friends with Harald's son Olav. I presumed he was there to see his sons.'

'And the discussions?'

I felt Brynn's hand tighten on my shoulder. 'When they spoke in the Norse tongue, I could understand well enough, but my English was at that time imperfect, so I can't tell you all.'

I tried to remember what I could. In my mind's eye I could see the vast hall, the wooden seats softened by down pillows and fur throws, the serving women with wine and beer. I remembered the smell of woodsmoke and sweat, the murmur of voices. 'I know there was talk of Harald providing men to fight for Tostig in Northumbria, where he feared an uprising.'

'Go on, child.' The king's voice was silky with encouragement.

'The three men seemed very friendly, joking together, clapping each other on the back. King Edward's name was mentioned often and I think his health enquired for, but more than that I can't tell you with any certainty.'

'And what happened after?'

'Harald gave me as a parting gift to Earl Tostig, though he had little taste for poetry and music, as you probably know. He brought me back to Northumbria, where I learned the English tongue. Then the earl sent me to the king's court with private letters for Edward, making a gift of me to him. I'm a slave, after all.' I tried to keep bitterness out of my voice.

Harold nodded. 'And, if what my sister Edith says is true, Tostig asked you to gather information for him in the English court, knowing that you could read and write.'

Looking at Harold's face, I knew I must tell him everything. 'He did. But Queen Edith saw all my letters to the earl and shortly afterwards, what he feared came true and he was banished.'

Harold leaned forward, his eyes fixed on my face. 'Have you had any further communication with my brother since then?'

I met his eyes without flinching. 'None. After the king's death I became scop to Earl Edwin and then to his sister the queen. I swear that my allegiance is to her and to you as king.'

His chaplain came forward. Harold said, 'Would you swear that on the bible?' The priest held out a large volume bound in leather with a gold hasp studded with gems. I put my hand on it and said clearly, though my voice shook with fear, 'I swear that everything I have told you is the truth. I have not had any communication with Earl Tostig since he left England and my loyalty is to King Harold.'

The chaplain stepped back. I heard Gyrth give a small laugh and say in an audible whisper. 'Let's hope he's not a little pagan!'

I felt a flash of anger and looked at Harold, who was smiling at Gyrth's comments. 'I'm not a spy. As a slave I have to obey the orders of those who own me at risk of punishment if I don't, but let me assure you, I have no loyalty to the man who killed my family, or to his friend who gifted me, as carelessly as one would gift a dog, to a stranger.'

Harold looked startled, but he nodded and glanced around the table with his eyebrows raised. Then he signalled to Brynn to take me away. 'So', he said, turning towards Leofwine and switching into English. 'Tostig has friends in Norway, who were willing to back his cause.'

As Brynn escorted me out of the room I heard Leofwine reply, 'I couldn't quite believe it, but, after what we heard in Council, I fear the worst.'

When Brynn let me go to return to the queen's quarters, I was shaking so much I could barely walk. I can't stop wondering, now that they know who I am, believing me to be a boy, will they see me as a threat? Perhaps I would be safer as a girl after all. But then I would be condemned to a future, either as concubine to some man or other, or as a waiting maid to a lady less noble than those of my own family. Having no kin, and no dowry, no man worth having would marry me. Over the last three years I've begun to realise that – even as a slave – I have more freedom as a boy that I had as a girl. And then I think of Arthur and I'm not sure any more.

~ ~ ~

Since they came back from York, Harold hadn't been to Ældyth's bed at all, except to kiss her cheek and wish her a good night's sleep. Ældyth had been glad of it, since she learned of the Swan-neck's pregnancy. Edwin had come down to London for the meeting of the Council, which Harold had called, and she had told him, laying out her hurt and grievance. Edwin had laughed. 'Why should you expect anything else, sister?' he'd said. 'It's not a love match. And the king has the right to sleep with whoever he pleases.' Ældyth had realised that she must swallow down her disappointment like bile. She had thought Harold a better man than that, but then she remembered what the Seer had said in York; words to the effect that 'No one is entirely good or entirely bad'.

Tonight, Harold sat down on the edge of the bed and seemed to want to talk. 'Your little scop,' he said, 'has revealed himself to be of the royal line of Denmark. A grandson of Magnus of Denmark. Did you know?'

Ælduth was not surprised. 'I knew he was of noble birth. That much he told us. But why should it be a matter of concern?'

Harold ran his hand over his chin. 'It shouldn't be – he's too minor a figure to be a threat. But my brother Tostig sent him to the court to spy on us – I want him watched.'

'How?'

'I'll find one of Edmund's young friends to shadow him. But you must let me know if there's anything you notice that could be important.' Harold sighed. 'He says he's loyal to us and I've no reason to doubt it, but these are dangerous times. We can't be too careful.'

He looked as if he was rising to go, but Ælduth put out her hand. 'Don't go yet. I wanted to ask you what festivities were planned for the first day of summer.'

Harold looked startled. 'We don't normally celebrate it, except as part of Rogationtide after Easter.'

'Oh.' Ælduth was disappointed. 'We always had a bonfire in Wales, and at Chester, after I came back, we had a bonfire and also a feast to celebrate the coming of summer. It seems to me that everyone is so gloomy now, we need something joyful to raise our spirits.'

Harold smiled. The worry lines on his face relaxed a little. 'Well, then there had better be a feast and whatever celebrations you deem suitable. Arrange it with Robert the Staller – he'll see to it.' He got to his feet slowly, as if very tired. 'Let's have a celebration while we still can.' He called to the men outside the door and was gone.

Ælduth looked carefully at her scop when he came into the room the next day, but he looked just as usual; a mere boy with roughly cut hair around his ears and very blue eyes – a lot cleaner now that he was properly dressed. There was nothing furtive in his bearing and his face had a curious innocence. Ældyth wondered how it must feel to be born into such wealth and privilege as he must have been and then to lose it all, to be enslaved at such a young age.

She called her ladies together. 'Harold's given me permission to celebrate the coming of summer. I'm planning to have a bonfire on the eve as we did when I was at home.' Merwenne and Angharad clapped their hands and Ældyth smiled. 'And the next day, all the people used to go out into the fields and there was dancing and feasting and much merriment. What do you think of doing something like that?'

'In my country,' Margaret said, 'the first day of summer is the feast of St Walpurga. On the eve, we too light bonfires to ward off evil spirits. The next day we have a procession to the church chanting her prayers. Would there also be a procession?'

'I don't see why not.' Ældyth said. 'It's a religious feast, after all.'

'The feast of St John and St James here,' Hilde said, 'all part of Rogationtide, the Sundays after Easter – what we used to call 'the Gang days', or 'the Goings' because everyone was going out into the fields to make merry.'

Ældyth laughed. 'That was what my grandfather Leofric used to call them, the Gang days. I'm sorry it's fallen so much out of fashion. We had such fun.'

Hari was sitting quietly listening, but Ældyth saw him smile. 'And, my little scop, can you produce some music for the occasion? There's no merriment without music.'

He stood up and bowed low. 'I'll do my best, my Lady.'

Ældyth turned to Angharad, 'Can you find Robert the Staller? There are arrangements to be made.'

~ ~ ~

It was the evening of the bonfire and the feast. When we were all dressed and before we went into the hall, the Lady Margaret asked if she could read the prayer of St Walpurga. The queen agreed and we all bowed our heads while Margaret recited the words.

> *"St. Walburga, by thy blessed life of love, God blessed thee with the power to heal, to make whole the soul as well as the body. Beg for us what we cannot obtain for ourselves, and heal our world of sickness and sorrow. By your compassionate heart and intercession, free us from the pains that oppress us, and from the troubles that afflict our souls."*

I'm not a Christian, except for convenience, yet the words moved me to tears. I've never had greater need for healing than I do now, and for someone to talk to about my troubles. Perhaps Walpurga, like the old gods of my childhood, could be prayed to for comfort. Lady Margaret glanced up, as she ended her prayer, and saw my face as I blinked back the tears. She, too, has lost a homeland and a position in the world, so perhaps she understands.

The hall of the palace was more cheerful than it had been for Harold's coronation or his wedding, both coming so close after the old king's funeral. Now, it was decorated with wreaths of wild flowers braided with leaves. Candles burned in every corner sending shadows dancing up the walls. Food was piled high on the tables, beer and wine in abundance. Harold's two older scops were there as well as some itinerant musicians. The music and singing hardly stopped, and members of the court were dancing among the tables to the merrier tunes. Harold's oldest scop, white-haired and venerable, his swollen, arthritic fingers no longer nimble on the harp, recited the feast scene from Beowulf where the thegns make boasts to each other about the heroic deeds they've done. That always makes people smile because it still happens when a carle is in his cups and reminiscing about past battles. The other scop told a tale of King Arthur, which he knows the king likes very much. Perhaps Harold privately sees himself as a new King Arthur.

Then one of the carles took hold of me, hoisted me up onto a table with my lyre and told me to play. I've been composing a piece for several days, something of my own and I suddenly felt very loathe to perform it. Playing for the queen in her private quarters is one thing, but I was afraid that, among so many important people, my petty composition would be booed out of the hall. Not a story, or a riddle, a poem this time; something I've called 'Wanderer'. I choked down my fears and began.

> Pity me, whose light blazes
> in battle-glory so briefly before you,
> for I have left the warm embrace
> of wife and home-hearth to travel
> endlessly in search of favour, honour
> and the rewards of the ring-giver
> for this is my story, my journey
> and you, fast by your lord's fireside,
> must come with one who is friendless
> and lordless, to my story's end ...

The hall fell silent when I began and when I finished was still silent. I thought I had made a mistake and exposed myself in front of the whole court. But then I saw an old thegn at one of the lower tables wiping away a tear and the applause began, slowly at first and then more loudly, people banging their cups on the table and stamping their feet. I was allowed down from the table and the king looked at me across the hall and nodded his head in approval. The steward pushed a small purse of silver into my shaking hand.

The bonfire was good, though there hadn't been time to build so big a fire as we had at home, but the wood was dry and it burned white at the centre, sending sparks up into the sky like so many stars. The king was there with both his wives and his family. Then I saw Arthur watching it with some of the other young thegns. They were laughing and play-fighting with burning brands they'd plucked from the fire. The king's son Edmund was among them.

I moved away and sat on a bench near to some of the young girls of the court. After a while, as the fire burned lower and people began to go back to the warmth of the halls, Arthur came and sat beside me.

'I liked what you sang at the feast,' he said. 'I'd never heard that before.'

'It was my own composition,' I told him. 'About the sky-wanderer. But also about people like me.' It was something I'd written during a particularly bad night when I'd been desperately homesick, and I'd wondered whether the star had ever wanted to remain in one place. Maybe it, too, had been displaced by great events and sent on its erratic course.

'The Wanderer, you called it, didn't you? The carles all liked it. They're mostly wanderers, following their lords, particularly the mercenaries.'

'There are mercenaries?'

'A few. Edward paid professional warriors from other countries to make up the numbers of his carles and Harold hasn't sent them back. They're mostly Saxons, a few Swedes and a couple of Franks. Getting older now, but good fighters,' he paused and then said, 'providing they're well paid.' There was a disparaging note in his voice. 'Proper loyalty can't be bought.'

'Your brothers have gone home?'

He nodded. 'They both have lands to protect. Morcar has constant trouble from the Scots; Edwin from Strathclyde to the north and the Welsh to the west.'

'Will there ever be peace, do you think?'

'Compared to what used to be, we have it. My grandfather Leofric used to tell of the battles that were fought between the different earldoms and the supporters of rival kings. One month it was Æthelred, another it was Cnut, or Sweyn Forkbeard, and then their children came and went one after another. That's the good thing about Edward and now Harold, England is peaceful and with peace comes wealth. War's expensive. That's what Edwin says anyway.'

'So that's why both Harald of Norway and William of Normandy want England. Because it's wealthy?'

'Probably. But they're both power-hungry and ruthless. My brother met William once, when he came to visit Edward – I think it was when the Godwins were in exile.'

'What was he like?'

'It must have been fifteen years ago, so Edwin can only have been a child, but even so the Norman bastard made an impression. Edwin was surprised how young William was, but he compared him to a weasel – pinch-faced and hard-eyed. Shifty.' Arthur was silent for a while and then he asked, 'What did the king want with you the other day?' He paused and then said, 'Forgive me, there are rumours.'

'He wanted to know who my parents were and whether I was spying for Tostig Godwinson.'

'What did you tell him?'

'The truth. I'm no danger to the court that shelters me.' I couldn't resist adding, 'Do you think that loyalty that's bought is always suspect?'

'I'm sorry,' Arthur said. 'I didn't mean to question you like that.'

'It's all right. I know it's difficult to trust strangers.' I gave a small, wry laugh. 'Just like the strange star, earth wanderers are also distrusted!'

Arthur laughed too but then was suddenly serious. 'Are you ever lonely Hari? Not having any family here?'

After a moment, I nodded. I couldn't trust myself to speak.

He put his hand on my shoulder as if to comfort me, but it was an awkward gesture. Then, looking at the group of young thegns he'd left, he said:

'Tonight, Edmund's celebrating bedding his first girl.'

'Who is she?'

'One of his aunt's maids. He's come late to it – being the king's son he has to be careful.'

'Why?'

'She'll expect a great deal – to be the concubine of the king's son is important. He'll have to pay the price of a maidenhead.'

'Is it the same as in my home country? That a man could bed any woman so long as he took care of her and any children they might have afterwards?'

Arthur laughed. 'It used to be. But the Christian church doesn't like our customs. It wants to control us all. You're supposed to be married before you bed a woman.'

He glanced sideways at me. 'Still, it'll be a while before you're ready to bed anyone Hari. Your voice hasn't even broken.'

I said nothing for a moment and then asked. 'And have you bedded a maid yet?'

His face went a fiery red in the glow from the fire and he looked away. Then, before I could say anything, he got up and walked towards the hall.

~ ~ ~

Edith thought that the palace smelt like a still room. The young ones had been out collecting blossoms and flowers and the sweet leaves of herbs. Every corner, every window, even the floors had been festooned and petalled to celebrate the coming of summer. For Edith, it smacked of the old religion but was also a welcome change from the darkness of winter and the strange tensions of the past few months – sun-bright days, bird-song, warm air on her skin. Edith's heart already felt lighter.

Harold's wife – Edith still couldn't bring herself to think of Ælfgyth as 'the queen' – had organised a bonfire to be lit in the field beyond the city gates and it burned furiously – a fierce blaze against the blackness of the sky, which seemed doubly dark since the sky-wanderer departed. The younger people, servants, thegns, had all danced, making merry with ale and some of the most intrepid leaping the bonfire as it began to burn lower. Quite a few had their britches singed and had to be rolled in the grass to put out the flames. It had all been rather vulgar and unseemly, but also light-hearted and carefree.

At the feast, Ælfgyth looked more cheerful than she had seemed of late. Gytha had told Edith that the knowledge of the Swan-neck's pregnancy had hit her hard. Silly girl. Did she expect anything from Harold but a man's selfish pleasure taking? Not, she told herself sternly, that she knew anything of such things except by observation. She felt her stomach knot in a bitter contraction at the thought as she looked up at Ælfgyth on the high table.

After the food had been served, the hall echoed with the music of all the scops playing in turn. There were lyres and harps and goat-skin drums. Sometimes a scop passed his instrument to a member of the court. One of Edwin's Welsh thegns had sung a most beautiful song in his own language, and Ælfgyth's boy-child had also acquitted himself well. Harold, who had a fine voice when he felt like it, declined a turn and sat back with his cup of wine, smiling at everyone's enjoyment.

At the bottom of the table, with two of the chaplains, sat Goscelin, very merry, exchanging jokes with the men on either side of him. Edith ached as she watched his face. This was a new pain that no syrup of poppy could remove.

~ ~ ~

Eadgifu couldn't sleep after the feast, even propped upright on a bank of pillows. A particularly succulent piglet had tempted her to eat more than she knew she should. She'd forgotten the misery of craving foods that made the stomach churn. And there were another four months to go before she would get relief.

There was a commotion outside the door and then the curtains parted and Harold came in, throwing a command over his shoulder as he did so. He had brought his hearth-carles with him.

'Is this an official visit?' Eadgifu asked tartly.

'Does it still rankle, Swan?' He tossed his robe to the foot of the bed.

'Yes.'

'I'm sorry. It's hard, isn't it? But there's no comparison between you. No ease. I can't talk to her, you know, not the way we talk. And she doesn't know me as a man, only the king.'

'She's in love with you.'

'Don't be ridiculous. She does her duty.'

'I've seen the way she looks at you.'

'Oh, God.' Harold put his head in his hands. 'When I look at her I see the shadow of Gruffyth.'

Eadgifu felt that hard knot of sadness inside her gradually relax. She smiled a wry smile. 'Did you come expecting to bed me? If so, your fortunes are out – I ate too much at the feast.'

Harold laughed. He sounded weary. 'Can't we just talk – in the warm?'

Eadgifu made room for him in the bed. 'I see you brought your bodyguard. Did you think I would have a knife under the pillows?'

He laughed again. 'These are strange times, Swan. Tostig, it seems, may be in league with William. He's put at least one spy in the court. Who knows what other treachery's afoot.' He paused and then went on, 'I keep thinking of Cynewulf of Wessex in the stories my grandfather used to tell, who was murdered by his nephew while visiting his mistress.'

'Is Edith still defending Tostig?'

'She's keeping very quiet on that subject at the moment.'

Eadgifu turned on her side and ran her fingers through Harold's curly hair. There was more grey in it than there used to be.

'Are you afraid, Harold?'

He frowned, caught hold of her hand and kissed it. 'Not afraid, no, but worried. I can deal with Tostig – god knows I've had to deal with him all my life. But I worry about what else he's fomenting across the channel. There've been visits to Harald of Norway and William the Bastard and talk of them giving him support. He's certainly been asking for it. The only good thing is that, so long as this northerly wind blows, we're unlikely to have any trouble from Normandy.'

He released her hand and leaned over to kiss her stomach. 'What are you going to give me this time, Swan?'

'Gytha says it has to be another boy.'

'If it is, shall we call him Ulf, after my Danish uncle?'

'Gytha's brother?'

Harold nodded.

'Ulf.' Eadgifu considered it. 'A good name. Ulf Harold-son. But what if it's a girl?'

'I heard the name Astrid today – Gytha's sister-in-law, grandmother to Ældyth's little scop.'

'That makes him your ... some kind of cousin, doesn't it?'

'It does.' Harold was silent for a few moments. 'Tostig sent him to spy on Edward and myself. He speaks Danish and English fluently and as a scop, slips quietly in and out everywhere in the court without question.'

'Are you going to send him away?'

Harold shook his head. 'Gyrth and Leofwine agree that we could make use of him if the opportunity comes.'

Harold's arms crept round her and he put his head on her breasts. 'I'm too tired for love-making, but it would be good to sleep together in the old way.'

Eadgifu said nothing, but she released one arm from his shoulders and snuffed out the candle on her bedside table.

Why had she worried about the Welsh Mare? What she and Harold had could not be broken so easily. Friendship and children and love and that knowledge of each other from youth to middle age – a bond as strong as the roots of a tree, growing down into bedrock. That's what she told herself as she settled down to sleep. But there was still a nagging worry deep inside her. He had used the word 'mistress'.

~ ~ ~

For a week there was merriment, music in hall, food and wine in plenty and a kind of holiday atmosphere around the court. Ældyth played with her daughter and, if only Harold had returned to her bed, would have been happier than she had ever been since her marriage.

On the Thursday after the summer's eve festivities the Dowager unexpectedly came to her rooms, accompanied by her Norman maid-in-waiting. Ældyth asked Hilde to take Nest to the nursery and gave her attention to making

Edith welcome. She felt wary, as she always was when in the company of the former queen.

Edith waved all her pleasantries away, as well as the offers of wine and cakes. 'I want to talk to you about court business,' she said abruptly.

Ældyth looked puzzled.

'As the king's wife, it's been my responsibility to manage the court, to see Robert the Staller every morning, to arrange feasts, guests, go over the accounts and oversee all the other business of the household. Now, as the new king's wife, it should rightfully be yours.'

Ældyth felt that she had been rebuked. 'I didn't know that I had to do all those things now. Why has no one told me?'

'Do you want to take on this responsibility?'

'If I'm expected to then I suppose I must. But I would need to be shown what to do. I've never managed such a large establishment as this.' Ældyth felt dismayed and stupid. She should have known. She should have realised that being the queen was more than just receiving guests, presiding at the king's table (and warming his bed) as well as attending Council meetings.

Edith was looking at her with a hard, direct stare, but her expression was inscrutable. She reminded Ældyth of a snake she had seen once in Wales when walking out in what passed for a garden at Gruffydd's palace. A viper, lazily sunning itself on a rock, that had raised its head at her approach and looked straight at her before slithering off into the bushes. Edith went on, her voice smooth. 'It would seem unwise, would it not, for the reins of the royal household to pass from one who has handled them for twenty years to one totally inexperienced. Besides, I thought you might find it convenient to leave things as they are. After all, you have one child and are breeding again and your time will be taken by your children.'

The way she put it, that sounded entirely plausible. Edith would handle Robert the Staller, the accounts, the oversight of servants, while she spent her time with her family and on more pleasurable pursuits. And, Ældyth thought, I've always hated domestic affairs. Political affairs interested her much more. Perhaps she took after her grandmother, Lady Godiva, who had threatened to ride naked through Coventry if Leofric didn't reduce the taxation of his tenants. She smiled at the thought and Edith saw it.

'The idea finds favour with you?'

'The argument you make is very practical. You know everyone here, you know the ways of the court.' And, Ældyth thought wryly, many of them are your own family. 'So,' she went on, 'yes, if you are willing to continue. I'd thought, and Harold had thought, that you might wish to retire to your own lands.'

The flash of anger in Edith's eyes was unmistakeable. 'I've been Queen of England for twenty years and, in recent years, my brother and I have ruled as regents, equally. Why would I wish to leave the court that's been my home, my life, simply because my husband's dead?'

'Forgive me,' Ældyth said gently, aware that Edith's sister-in-law, Gyrth's wife Theo, was in the ante-room. 'I didn't mean to infer . . . I know I can't take your place and fill it with the kind of grace that you have done. But I am Harold's queen, in spite of that.' The ghost of Eadgifu Swan-neck floated through her mind in a moment of bitterness.

Ældyth looked at the woman in front of her and felt pity. Edith had no children of her own, no husband, no clear position at court. She was the Dowager. Ældyth wondered if Edith had been put out by her own organisation of the bonfire and the summer feast. Was she fearing to be usurped? Quickly, intuitively, Ældyth saw that Edith had come as a supplicant, something that must have come very hard to a woman as proud as she was. A single word would make the

difference between peace and estrangement. She also saw
that if she accepted Edith's offer to carry on managing the
court, it would be her gift. Edith would be in her power, not
the other way round.

'If you wish to carry on,' she said carefully, 'I would be
grateful, since I've no talent for domestic affairs and you do
it well from long experience.' She paused, thinking hard.
'But I would ask that if any changes are to be made, I am
consulted. Will you accept?'

Edith bowed her head in acknowledgement and smiled
as if she had won a victory.

When Edith had gone Theo said, 'You shouldn't have let
her get away with that. It's your right to manage things. As
the queen, you're in charge of everything, she just doesn't
want to give it up.'

Ældyth smiled. 'But if I'd refused, I'd have had an enemy,
ready to criticise my every mistake.'

Theo smiled back. 'Better to have Edith as a friend than
an enemy! We're all a little wary of her. Gyrth says she's
always been like that since she was a girl. Bossy. Wanting to
be in charge.'

'She's good at it. And now I'm free to do all the pleasant
things I want to do.'

Ældyth woke to the sound of feet running in the corridor.
Feet and then more feet. Someone was shouting. She sat up
in bed. There were voices coming from Harold's room. A
loud conversation. More footsteps. She got up and reached
for her robe and then went quickly through into Harold's
bedchamber.

Leofwine was standing there, his britches stained with
mud. He was sweating and looked exhausted. What was he
doing here so soon after leaving for Kent after the festivities?
Harold was struggling out of bed, his manservant pulling a

cloak around him. Leofwine hardly looked at Ældyth, he was talking urgently to Harold.

'We need to call the Council immediately. I've sent a messenger to Gyrth. My own men will try to contain him until we can send sufficient force.' Leofwine was choking with anger as he faced Harold.

Ældyth felt a chill in her stomach. Had William of Normandy finally landed? 'What is it?'

Harold turned at the sound of her words. He looked dazed but also furious. 'Tostig.' His voice, too, was tight with anger. 'He's arrived on the Isle of Wight with forty ships and is laying waste to the land. Our land.' He stood up, glancing round the room to see who was assembled there, then he turned back to Ældyth. 'Get dressed. The Council must be summoned. We need to decide what to do.' He turned back to Leofwine. 'In the meantime, get some food and clean clothes. I'll send word to the carles to prepare to leave. Can someone find Brynn for me?' Then, as he began to shrug off his nightclothes, he suddenly slammed his hand down on the robing chest. 'Treasonous bastard!' He shouted. 'The bloody, fucking, treasonous bastard!'

Part Five

Treason

'And then he, Tostig, went thence, and did harm everywhere by the sea-coast where he could land, as far as Sandwich. Then was it made known to King Harold, who was in London, that Tostig his brother was come to Sandwich. Then gathered he so great a ship-force, and also a land-force, as no king here in the land had before gathered.'

The Anglo-Saxon Chronicle

There was a tense silence in the Council chamber. Harold at the head of the table, Leofwine on one side of him and Gyrth, who had ridden all night to be there, on the other side. Archbishop Stigand was present and Ældyth, who looked shocked and anxious. At the bottom of the table the scribe was waiting expectantly, his quill hovering over the inkpot.

'What do we know for certain?' Edith asked. She was surprised how shaken her voice sounded.

'He has forty or fifty ships and has taken more from the Isle of Wight by force. Maybe sixty altogether. A small army of Flemings and Norman mercenaries.' It was Leofwine who spoke. 'He sent me a message telling me that if I joined him to topple Harold he would give me generous lands and an earldom!' Leofwine laughed derisively. 'He's probably offering every ealdorman in Wessex the same deal.'

Harold was considering. 'Sixty ships and their crew. That's only a small force.' He paused. 'Tostig can't do much unless he gains more men. My worry is that he's only the advance party for William's main army, testing our preparedness.'

In the silence after Harold spoke, Gyrth cleared his throat. 'There's only one way we can safeguard the kingdom. We have to burn and lay waste to the country all along the coast so that neither he nor William can rely on it for supplies. Without provisions they would have to leave.'

'No, Gyrth!' Harold said forcefully. 'Those are Godwins' manors, our lands, our people. I know every one of those farms, every village, every church.' He stopped for a moment and then went on, 'Are you forgetting the Northumbrian rebellion? How many villages were burned there in revenge for Tostig's actions? I'm resolved that no more people will die because of him if it can be helped.' He paused for breath. Edith could see the veins standing out on his forehead. 'I swore an oath in St Peter's church to protect my people, and I'll not do that by laying waste to their fields and burning their barns.'

Gyrth shrugged but refrained from saying anything. It was well known that he thought Harold too forbearing.

'So, what are you going to do?' Leowine asked.

'Call out the fyrde. I want every hale man assembled on the south coast.' He put up his hand as Gyrth opened his mouth to protest. 'I know the ealdormen and the sheriffs won't like it. Summer's a busy time on the land. And we're going to have to impose a levy to pay for the army. That won't be popular either, so you'll have to tell them there's never been so great a danger to the kingdom. I want all the ships you can find requisitioned and brought to Sandwich. William won't arrive with less than three hundred. The information I have is that it might be as many as five. We'll camp on the Isle of Wight and keep watch. Fortunately the winds are still unfavourable.' With a sudden loss of control he thumped his fist down on the table. 'God damn my brother!'

The archbishop stirred as though in discomfort, and then said, 'I can raise about a thousand men for you. Would you want them with you on the Isle?'

Edith was surprised for a moment, until she remembered that Stigand too was a war-lord, an old friend of her father's, a warrior of the church who campaigned with book and sword, a man who had fallen out with two popes.

'No,' Harold appeared to be thinking hard. 'I want Gyrth and Leofwine at different locations on the coast in case William chooses to land somewhere else – he's as sly as a fox. And Tostig will certainly make his way along it hoping to gain support. Your men, archbishop, will be best deployed in Kent.'

'Are you going to send for my brothers also?'

Edith was surprised to hear Ældyth's voice. Harold looked at her with his eyebrows raised, while his hands rearranged the papers in front of him disturbed by his outburst. 'I've sent messengers. Edwin should be here tomorrow, but I won't take him with me. We need to keep a guard in the north. We have enemies who may come from the east too. I want Edwin and Morcar to keep watch there.'

Then Harold looked across the table at Edith. It wasn't a pleasant look.

'Well, sister? Have you nothing to say in the matter?'

'I'm still struggling to believe it. Our mother's taken to her bed.'

'I hope,' Harold spoke evenly but his voice was hard, 'that you've realised the extent to which our brother will go to further his own ambitions. Are you on my side this time?' He emphasised the last two words.

'It's difficult to take sides when it's family.' Edith was looking down at her hands twisting themselves together in her lap.

'I must be able to count on your loyalty Edith. I'm remembering the Christmas of '64 and Uhtræd's son Gospatric.'

Edith felt as if Harold had struck her. Everyone in the room, except perhaps Ældyth, would remember Tostig's enemy, Gospatric, from Northumbria. And that it was she, to protect Tostig, who'd given the order for his arrest and execution.

'Sometimes you're too like our father for my liking,' Harold said.

'And you're too unkind!' She spat out the words. Suddenly it felt like a quarrel out of childhood. Edith tried to sound less emotional. 'Why should I, as a woman, be blamed for doing the things men do without ever being challenged? When you're in a position of power, as you well know,' she emphasised the phrase, holding his gaze, 'there are difficult decisions to be made.' She paused, knowing that he would be thinking of Gruffydd, and added, 'and then lived with.'

Harold's direct gaze flickered briefly. He grunted an acknowledgement, (or was it an apology?) and then turned his head and looked at Ældyth again.

Yes, Edith thought, *Gruffydd is on his mind and we're even on points.*

Harold was still looking at Ældyth. He said, 'Your little scop? Could he have heard anything, do you think?'

Ældyth shook her head. 'I doubt it very much. He spends his time in the company of Lady Margaret and sometimes also with my youngest brother, Arthur. They seem friends, of sorts.'

Harold nodded. 'I've told Arthur and my son Edmund to keep an eye on him.'

'I think you're making too much of it,' Edith said. 'He's a child and a slave, having to beg for his bed and board with his songs.'

'I agree.' It was Ældyth's quiet voice. 'There's something about him – a sweetness – that doesn't sit well with knavery. I'd swear he speaks the truth.'

Harold smiled, but the smile didn't reach his eyes. 'I hope you're both right, but it seems that these days we can't even trust our own kin.'

There was an uncomfortable silence before Stigand offered a prayer for the wisdom of the king and the safety of the kingdom. The Council was over.

~ ~ ~

Ældyth's first, irrational, emotion was relief, that it wasn't her own two brothers who had featured in her dreams. The two ravens were Harold and Tostig. But then her next thought was that one was probably going to kill the other. Her hand went straight to her belly where Harold's unborn child was already stirring. What would she do if Tostig Godwinson killed Harold? Where could she go? Who would protect her?

Outside the window it was full summer in the fields, the grass grown high, already the month of three daily milkings for the cattle. Soon it would be the first travelling month when roads were dry and the sea calm and a man could travel easily. And, she thought, catching her breath with fear, so could an army.

Edwin arrived in the early afternoon and went straight to Harold, remaining in conversation with him for over an hour before coming to her room. The temperature seemed to drop the moment he entered.

'Well, sister,' he began, settling himself down on the

largest chair beside the fireplace. He looked oddly pleased with himself. 'Nothing like a good falling out among the Godwinson brothers to advance our cause. I imagine Morcar's sword-arm is itching at the notion of coming within striking distance of Tostig. The Northumbrians certainly don't want him back!'

Ældyth put down her book and asked, 'How is it to our advantage?'

'A skirmish with Tostig, the unrest he could cause in Wessex would weaken Harold's authority and strengthen ours.'

'But you will remain loyal?' Ældyth felt the beginnings of anxiety.

'We'll protect our own interests, sister. I'm not dragging an army south to settle the Godwinsons' disputes.'

This wasn't the conversation Ældyth had imagined having with him. His use of the words 'ours' and 'our interests', claimed her as Mercian. But she had married a Godwin, surely her interests were now on the side of her husband, rather than her brothers?

'What do you have against the Godwins?'

'It was Earl Godwin who accused our father of treason and had him exiled.' Edwin was looking at Ældyth oddly. 'You've no reason to look kindly on them either, particularly Harold.'

'I think you wrong him. He's a good man. He really cares about England. If you're so hostile, why did you support his coronation?'

'Because he was the best man for the job, and he agreed to marry you.'

Ældyth controlled the spasm of anger she felt running through her. 'You're a ruthless man, Edwin, but, when you gave me to Harold for his queen, did it occur to you that, as queen, I now have power over you?'

'Much good that will do you, unless you can command three thousand carles!'

'I have something much more powerful. I have the king's ear and his trust.'

The mocking smile vanished from Edwin's face.

Ældyth pressed on. 'Be careful. A united England under a strong king is much more to your advantage than one fractured by fighting.' Then she added, 'And I'm no longer yours to wager with.'

~ ~ ~

'You're going to Sandwich?' Eadgifu was surprised.

'Yes.' Harold was already cloaked and booted for departure. 'We'll lie there for a while, until I have enough ships and then set up camp on the Isle of Wight. If William comes, Sandwich is the most likely landing place and I can surround him by land and sea.'

'You could be there for a long time.'

'That's the annoying thing. It could be days or weeks. Who knows what's in William's mind. My spies tell me he's waiting for a favourable wind.'

'I think I might come down to Bosham, bring the children.' Eadgifu waved away the protest she knew he was going to make. 'Yes, I know we'd be close to danger, but at least I would be near to you, and Edmund. You're taking Edmund this time as well as Godwin aren't you?'

'Yes. I thought it was time he saw how an army moved.'

'Perhaps I might even see something of you at Bosham?'

Harold grinned. 'It's possible. With an available ship and a favourable wind. But I worry about you being so near, if William should come.'

'Then we'll have to leave quickly. The infant isn't due until the early autumn, so there's time.' She sighed, then made up her mind about something. 'Are things all right between us Harold?' It was hard to keep her voice steady.

He didn't look at her. 'In what way?'

'You know what way. You haven't been the same since you came back from York. Less open, not so easy with me. It's the queen, isn't it? Ældyth.'

'Don't be ridiculous! I'm just pre-occupied. Things have been harder than I imagined, and I haven't always the energy for two . . .' he hesitated for a moment and then added, 'It's a damnable situation.'

'Are you in love with her?'

'Eadgifu!'

Not even 'Swan'. There was a warning note in his voice. 'I don't talk about you with her and I don't want to discuss her with you. Do you understand?'

'I suppose I do. Not the only middle-aged woman to be cast off for one that's younger.' The moment she'd said it she could have cut off her tongue. It sounded so bitter as it spilled out into the silence between them.

Harold looked fierce with anger. 'You aren't cast off, damn you! God, I can't talk about any of this now. We've Tostig and his men ravaging the south coast and an imminent invasion and you want to start a jealous spat about my wife!'

Then he seemed to realise what he'd just said and looked at Eadgifu, with a stricken expression on his face. His anger subsided.

'I'm sorry, Swan. But I have to go.' He looked drained and exhausted. 'Do what you think best.' And then he turned without embracing her and left, his red cloak swinging behind him as he went out of the door.

Eadgifu would have given anything to take the words back. Why, why, why, had she said those things when he was going off to battle and God only knew when she'd see him again. *I'm turning into a scold*, she told herself, *and it can only lead to misery.*

I was breakfasting in the hall – empty, since Harold's carles were preparing to leave – when the king's son Edmund came and stood beside me.

'Get your things,' he said. 'You're to come with us.'

Half in surprise, half in fright, I said, 'Where?'

'To the south coast. I can't tell you more. Those were the king's instructions.'

'But what about the queen ... Earl Edwin?'

'The king's given orders that you're to come with us. You can't argue.'

I picked up my lyre and then collected my meagre bundle from underneath the bench. I slung them both on my back.

'Take some bread,' Edmund said, 'It's a long journey.'

'You're coming too?'

He looked pleased. 'My father says I can, for the first time as a thegn.'

'And Arthur?'

Edmund gave me a strange look. 'He's to stay to guard the queen.'

I was given a stout pony, much the same as I had been given for the journey north, and once again I rode in the van with the servants and the carts loaded with foodstuffs, tents and baggage.

I've never been to the south before. It's lush, rich country with thick grass, herds of grazing cattle, lazy, meandering rivers and thickets of trees. I thought I saw a deer in one of them, the sunlight just catching its head as it startled from the rattle and clatter of an army on the move. There were more habitations here than in the north – wooden houses with roofs thatched with reed, or wooden shingles, thin trails of smoke lifting to the clear sky, and sturdy stone churches rearing their towers among clusters of buildings.

We camped the first night on a broad river meadow. The servants erected the tents of willow and hide, the king's tent dyed red, bigger than the others, with the royal standard bearing its golden dragon planted outside and, next to it, his own personal standard showing the image of an armed man wielding an axe. The cooks soon had a fire going and roasted a quantity of fowl and game. It was difficult to identify anything in the scorched portions of meat on the wooden platters, but there was plenty and baskets of bread to mop the juices, and there was ale to wash it down.

The next day we began to encounter small bands of carles, some with axes, some with spears, one or two with bows on their backs. They joined us and, band by band, our numbers grew.

'It's the fyrde,' I was told by one of the cooks riding next to me on a gaunt bone-shaker of a horse he told me had seen many campaigns and would see many more.

'You don't want looks in a war horse,' he told me. 'It's hardiness that's wanted.'

We reached the coast on the fourth day and by now we had begun to look like an army. There were men in front of me stretching to the horizon, and when I looked back, as many men behind.

'Over there's the king's own manor, Bosham,' the cook told me, waving his arm to the west, as we sat on a log beside the fire finishing our ale. 'It was his father's before him. Very grand. They say he built a palace fit for a king before his son was one, if you get my meaning.'

'Have you always been with the family?'

'I worked for his father Godwin until he died in '55. Fell down under the table at the old king's feast, just as he was raising a toast. He was taken up for dead – dumb and unable to move a limb. They put him in the king's bed at first, thinking he wouldn't last, but he lived three days before he had another seizure and died. There's some said it was a just punishment.'

'And Harold inherited?'

'All of it – Wessex, the earldom, the money. Not but what it used to be a kingdom in its own right. King of Wessex was a grand title once. There are stories I could tell you about that.'

He was full of stories; King Alfred hiding in the marshes at Athelney, of Viking raids, betrayals, abductions. I listened, entranced, already reworking them into tales fit for a king's hall.

~ ~ ~

Edith wasn't surprised to see Gytha the next morning. Her mother looked older, and still very troubled.

'I saw them go,' she said. 'But when I'll see them back, I don't know. Little Edmund too.'

'You're being pessimistic, mother.'

'You're a hard woman, Edith, but then perhaps you've never waved those you love off to battle without knowing whether you'll see them again.' There was a plaintive note in Gytha's voice and Edith knew what was coming. 'I've already lost one son, Swein, and my youngest Wulfnoth is a prisoner in Normandy. And now Tostig's risking his neck, stirring up trouble.'

If I'm a hard woman, how would you describe yourself? Edith thought. *I've never seen you cry over any of them. Stop trying to make me feel pity for you!* But what she said was, 'You can rest easy – Harold will be back. He's a good general.'

Gytha laughed grimly. 'It's true. Your brother can organise an army, but where women are concerned he's got no idea.'

'What do you mean?'

'He's having trouble with Ældyth and the Swan-neck. He came to see me before he went and said, 'Having two wives is harder than I thought'. What did he expect? It's plain he loves both of them and has no idea how to deal with it. One is the love of his life, the other a spring-time love for an ageing man. He's dazzled, cunt-struck.'

'Don't be vulgar mother.'

'When did you get to be so mealy-mouthed Edith? Among the nuns at Wilton? I'm telling the truth. It's what I see, just as I see what's in your head when you look at that monk.'

Edith felt her face flush scarlet.

'And you have to watch your brother Harold fucking women and getting them with child as easily as a ram in a flock of sheep. No wonder you're as sour as a crab-apple.'

'And is it my fault I missed out on all that marriage might have given me?' The words were wrung out of Edith against her will. She gripped the arms of her chair to try to regain control.

'Your father made you queen. That was worth something.'

The complacency of Gytha's voice broke something inside Edith. 'To whom? To him? I can tell you now the price was too high, and I was the one who paid it. You even changed my name!' She heard herself screaming. 'Get out! Get out! I can't bear to listen to you any longer.'

Edith was sobbing on her knees beside the bed when she heard someone come into the room. She presumed it was Mathilde until she heard a male voice say,

'Forgive me.' It was Goscelin. 'I've come at a bad time. I'll leave you in peace.'

'No! Please.'

Then his arm was around her, helping her to her feet. Her legs folded under her and he sat her down on the edge of the bed, sitting down beside her. His arm was still around her and Edith was sobbing into the wool of his habit.

'I don't want to be a queen. Just an ordinary woman, with an ordinary woman's desires. God help me!'

Afterwards, Edith never knew whether she had pulled him down onto the bed or whether he had laid her there, but she was holding him tightly in her arms, feeling the bulk of him pressed against her. Then they were kissing and he was protesting, but weakly, and soon it was too late. She pulled up her gown and then his habit and they were writhing together as she had sometimes allowed herself to imagine.

'Forgive me,' he murmured into her neck, as they lay together, gasping for breath. 'God forgive me.'

'I'm the one who should ask for forgiveness,' Edith said. 'For I was the one who led you into temptation.' She was surprised to find herself not even remotely penitent. 'But I feel thankful for God has given me, just once before I'm old and withered, the experience of human love.'

Goscelin raised his face from her shoulder and looked at her. There was compassion in his eyes. He caressed her cheek with his free hand. 'But I have broken my vow of chastity and the trust that was placed in me to be your scribe.'

Edith thought of her chaplain and confessor, Frobert, a swarthy Saxon foisted on her by Archbishop Stigand. How could she ever consult him for spiritual guidance now? This was a sin she could confess only to God. To confess to anyone else would mean immediate harm for Goscelin. He would never be allowed to stay at court. The thought of never seeing him again turned in her stomach like a knife.

~ ~ ~

It was known throughout the court that Countess Gytha had fallen out with her daughter. The Dowager queen was in a strange mood and Eadgifu avoided contact with her. The court was uncharacteristically silent since Harold had left and taken most of his carles with him. A few hundred remained, a mixture of Earl Edwin's and Harold's men, to guard the queen and the palace. A few hundred more were left to garrison London against an attack in case Tostig chose to sail up the Thames. Eadgifu found it strange to have only Magnus and little Gytha around her. Godwin and Edmund had gone with Harold and her older daughter, Gunhild, was still being schooled at Wilton in the family tradition.

There was high summer everywhere, lying across the fields and marshes like a heavy blanket. Eadgifu found the heat and inertia in the air intolerable; six months pregnant and restless, she felt desperate for a change. She wondered all the time where Harold was and what he was doing. The last report sent to the Dowager was that Tostig had taken fright and left Sandwich, chased by Harold's forces, and was now making his way along the coast and up towards East Anglia – her own manors. She'd sent word to her ealdormen to raise whatever forces they needed and give Earl Gyrth every assistance to repel Tostig before he did any damage.

Eadgifu had been awake all night thinking about it and wondering what she should do. Towards dawn she made up her mind. As soon as she was dressed and breakfasted she went to Gytha's room. Her mother-in-law was being read to in Danish by one of her waiting maids, who put the book down as soon as Eadgifu entered and slipped away.

'How are you?'

Gytha snorted. 'You should know better than to ask a woman of my age how I am!'

Eadgifu smiled. 'But I should like to know, all the same.'

'Weary of waiting for news. And you, Swan-neck?'

'The same. Otherwise in better health. Six months gone now and over the sickness.' She changed the subject. 'I'm here because I've made up my mind to go down to Bosham to be nearer to Harold while he's in the south. And it'll be better for the children. The marshes here will be swarming with mosquitoes in a few weeks. I wondered whether you'd like to come with us? It's your manor, after all.'

Gytha inclined her head as if she was thinking. All she said was, 'Bosham's lovely at this time of year,' in a wistful tone of voice.

'The sea air will be better for the children.'

Gytha sighed. 'It would certainly be good to remove myself from my daughter as well as the queen. If it wasn't for the company of Theo and Hilde it would be miserable here.'

'I agree. It's too quiet with everyone gone. There's a sorry lack of music and conversation. Even the archbishop's packed away his pallium and put on his chain mail. Will you come?'

Gytha smiled, showing the gaps in her teeth. 'I will. I've a great fondness for Bosham and I'm tired of Westminster.'

Eadgifu wondered privately why, if that was the case, she hadn't gone down to her own manor already. Perhaps she couldn't bear to be so far away from the centre of the news that involved her whole family.

'I'll instruct the men. We'll need a guard to go with us. And I'll write to Harold.' She lowered her head briefly to hide the expression in her eyes. 'I said rough words to him before we parted and I must make it up.'

A few days later their cavalcade left Westminster and crossed the bridge over the River Thames. Both Eadgifu and Gytha were travelling in litters drawn by horses, accompanied by chaplains, waiting maids and stewards. The whole troop was surrounded by about fifty carles bearing the scarlet livery of Wessex, all heavily armed.

The first night they spent near Wilton Abbey, at Gytha's manor there, taking a day's rest so that Eadgifu could visit her daughter Gunhild who, at thirteen, was apparently considering whether to stay on at the abbey after her schooling finished. When Gunhild walked into the small solar the abbess had allowed them to use, Eadgifu saw that her daughter had grown in the six months since she had last seen her and looked very womanly in her grey linen over-dress and white head-covering. Eadgifu, who had not been convent educated, observed Gunhild's quiet deportment and her graceful manners with envy, hardly recognising the tomboy she had once been. For some reason Eadgifu couldn't explain, her daughter's maturity alarmed her. When she commented on how much Gunhild had grown, and that perhaps it was time for her to come home to the court, the girl reacted with annoyance.

'I'm sure my father would want to marry me off,' Gunhild said. 'But I don't want to just yet. If I'm to have a husband, I'd like to choose my own.'

Eadgifu reassured her that nothing would be done with-out her consent. 'The abbess wrote in her last letter that you were thinking of staying here at Wilton to take your vows. Do you seriously consider a cloistered life?'

Gunhild looked amused. 'The abbess would like me to stay, but I don't think it would suit me, except as an alterna-tive to marriage.' She seemed almost relieved when the visit was over and Eadgifu felt saddened by the distance that had grown between them.

She said as much to Gytha as they prepared to travel on,

'You worry too much,' Gytha said, 'She's growing up into a woman, and just as spirited as you were – head-strong as you still are.'

'There's nothing wrong with knowing what you want,' Eadgifu said. She was packing her clothes back into the chest. 'And at the moment, it would be very helpful.' She sighed. 'I've got to make a life for myself now, you know. Harold has a kingdom and a queen to take all his attention. I have my lands and my children. Where do I go and what do I do?' She put down the robe she was holding. 'You know he wants me to stay permanently at Waltham, my manor at Nazeing?'

Gytha was silent, waiting for her to continue.

'It makes sense I suppose. Our manors meet each other there. They share a border. And the abbey is special to both of us, since we jointly endowed it.'

'Harold was healed there ,' Gytha said. 'After a fall from a horse.'

'I remember. It was just after we were married and we feared the worst. He lost the use of his legs, until he was taken to Waltham and prayed at the altar. He made a vow to God, he said, though he never told me what it was.'

'And will you go there?'

Eadgifu looked troubled. 'I don't know. Probably. I'll see what happens when the babe's born.'

~ ~ ~

"The King sends his greetings and hopes that you are in good health," it began, written in the regular script of the scribe. Ældyth thought she should be grateful that he made contact with her at all. The perfectly formed letters marched on, "Since Tostig has left the port of Sandwich and been chased along the coast by the ships and landforces of Earls Leofwine and Gyrth, the King has sent a message to the Ealdormen of East Anglia and also to your brothers in Mercia and Northumbria, to warn them of his incursions and the threats widely made to the security of the realm." She wondered whether this was a hint to write her own encouragements to her brothers. But it would scarcely be necessary. Edwin and Morcar were steadfast in defence of their own lands.

Ældyth searched the parchment for anything that might resemble a personal message. But at the bottom, only this: "The King would like to thank you for the loan of your scop who is providing good entertainment with both stories and songs and hopes that your court is not too silent without him." Not entirely silent, Ældyth thought, as Harold had left his own elderly verse-maker behind. But the music was not the same.

The court was very empty without Harold and his carles. Almost every able man, or bishop, had gone with him. And then yesterday the Swan-neck and her mother-in-law had also gone south to be near Harold, where Ældyth herself was unable to go and where she most wanted to be. Instead, she had to share the palace with the remnants of the court and the dowager queen who considered herself regent in Harold's absence. Between Aeldyth and the Swan-neck there might be some sympathy, but between herself and Edith, none. The dowager was a Saxon, a southerner, half Danish, brought up in the luxurious extravagances of Earl Godwin's household. Ældyth had been born a northerner, reared to hardship, daughter of a man outlawed for treachery, married by that father to a brutal man while still a child. Ældyth thinks fondly of her grandmother, Earl Leofric's trouble-some wife, Godiva, still living on her manors in Leicester. A formidable woman. Could she ever be like her?

Ældyth was still thinking nostalgically of the few times she had stayed with her grandmother, when Merwenne came quickly into the room. She seemed excited. 'Forgive me for intruding,' she said in the Mercian dialect. 'But I've stumbled upon something that, as queen, I think you should know about.'

~ ~ ~

The second time was better than the first; running her hands through the brown curly hair under his shift, feeling his nipples harden under her fingers, and then his manhood. Dear God, the pleasure of it, the aching, desperate pleasure of it.

'This isn't the first time I've given in to the sins of the flesh,' Goscelin said as they lay, exhausted, side by side on the bed. 'It's my greatest weakness.' He was quiet for a moment and then said, 'You know I'll have to confess this?'

'Can't you wait a little longer,' Edith said. 'They'll send you away.'

'I know. But it will have to be done. I made vows and I must try to keep them. I'm not alone in finding it hard. Some of the brothers lie with each other; others don't seem to feel the need for relief. I envy them.' He turned over to look at her. There was laughter in his eyes. 'You know we're automatically forgiven for what they call 'night emissions' providing they're involuntary and not the result of lewd thoughts?'

'It seems unnatural to deny the needs of the body.'

'If I agreed with you I'd be going against the laws of the church. But I find myself questioning them. I'm thankful to the Order for raising me out of poverty, but I'll never make a good monk.'

'So beautiful a writer of prose and poetry will always have a place in the world.'

Goscelin murmured some reply, but after a silence, Edith noticed that he'd gone to sleep with his head on her shoulder, his long lashes lying dark on his cheek, his breath warm on her skin.

After he had left, Edith stood in front of the mirror in her shift and ran her hands down her body. It was still slim, her breasts still full and firm. She thought she could see a difference in her face – a radiance that had not been there before.

Mathilde had come through the curtain and was laying out a new robe and overdress. She didn't speak.

'Do you judge me, Mathilde?'

'No, my Lady. How could I begrudge you a little happiness. But I think it very unwise.'

'Tell me why, as queen dowager, unmarried, I should be denied what other women take for granted?'

'Because, my Lady, as the dowager, as a Godwin, you may take whatever you want with little consequence, but he is not a plaything. You may cause harm to come to him.'

'He will confess and be forgiven.'

'And the archbishop will punish you both, him more than you.'

Edith allowed herself to be draped in an overdress of dark green with gold clasps at the shoulders. Then she knelt at the prie-dieu to pray for him and then, reluctantly, for herself.

~ ~ ~

Bosham was cool in summer, an impressive stone buildng, fit for an abbey. Harold had installed an indoor privy for their comfort after his father died. Two wooden halls stood outside the main building inside the outer fortifications to house the carles, and the servants were bedded in smaller buildings near the stables.

It was now the second travelling month and the days had lengthened. Eadgifu's life at Bosham assumed its usual routines. The children played in the orchard and the fields when they weren't at their lessons. They learned their catechisms from her chaplain, Anselm, and then Danish from their grandmother Gytha, and Magnus reluctantly conjugated his Latin verbs, marking the time until he could disappear to the falconry, while little Gytha set her first stitches with a lady of the household.

Eadgifu was grateful for the salt air off the sea, but not for the winds that blew constantly from the north and the north east, straight from Norway and its cool cousins. Her mother-in-law mostly stayed indoors, which Edith was thankful for, spending her time in the herb garden and the orchard. It was going to be a good year for apples and pears, the plums already ripening, the children's lips stained with blackcurrants and raspberries. There had been no news for weeks – the last that Tostig had landed in East Anglia on manors he must have known were hers and plundered them until Gyrth had arrived with his carles and chased him northwards, hugging the shore, sailing against the wind, presumably set for Northumbria to take back his earldom.

In the middle of the month Harold arrived unexpectedly with almost a hundred carles, banners flying, bringing Edmund with him and his scop. Eadgifu greeted them, bringing her son and his father their welcome cup as they dismounted. Harold grasped her in his arms for a brief hug, as though unsure of his welcome, but she pulled him to her and gave him her lips which he accepted gladly. She kissed Edmund and invited them into the house. Behind her she could hear the steward giving orders for horses and men.

As he accompanied her indoors, Harold said, 'Leofwine's on his way, he sent a message that he wanted to meet me.'

So, not a visit of pleasure. Eadgifu felt a small twinge of disappointment, but her life with Harold had always been like this, small joys snatched from an active life of duty. She felt sorry for Leofwine's wife, Hilde, who was attendant on the queen and hadn't seen her husband since he left court at the beginning of summer. For the rest of the afternoon she was occupied with her stewards making sure that there would be enough to eat for everyone, that beds were made up for them.

Leofwine arrived about an hour before dinner, tired and dust-stained. Both Eadgifu and Harold went out to welcome him.

'I've brought you some guests,' he said as soon as they had greeted each other. 'They're with my carles under close guard.'

Harold raised his eyebrows, but Leowine didn't immediately take the cue.

The steward poured Leofwine a flagon of ale which he downed almost in one. 'Travelling's dusty, thirsty work at this time of year,' he said, wiping his mouth on his sleeve. He went on, 'Two young Danes we found, half-starved in the woods on the edge of the Andredsweald. Some villagers told us about them. They'd escaped from Tostig's troop, or so they say.'

'Spies?'

'I doubt it. They don't speak English. They've got an interesting story to tell. I'll bring them in after we've dined and you can hear it.'

~ ~ ~

"My Lord, my brothers have probably already sent messages to you by other means, but I have received news from them that Earl Tostig has entered the Humber with a force of sixty ships and has ravaged the countryside around, but my brothers went there quickly with a good troop of carles and put him to flight. They have told me that many of the men he had constrained to come with him from the south coast and East Anglia have abandoned him and he left Lindesey with only twelve ships and some of the troop he was given by Count Baldwin. Morcar says he is of the opinion that he has gone to Scotland to take refuge with King Malcolm but doubts that we have seen the last of him.

I know you will be glad that he has been driven off. As for ourselves, I am well and Nest also, though we miss your presence. It must be tedious, camping so long in the field waiting on the Norman duke. I'm glad that my scop has entertained you so well – he is a great loss here too, for Wulfere, your old skald, has become so forgetful he can scarcely recite anything from beginning to end."

Ældyth was beginning to feel heavy with pregnancy. This was a big baby. She could feel him – she was sure it was a boy – kicking angrily inside her, particularly at night, so that she found it difficult to sleep. In those long dark hours she wondered when she would see her husband again. Perhaps not until after the invasion everyone seemed so sure would come. And if it didn't, he would be back when his army had to be disbanded. Her chaplain, Bishop Ælfric, had told her that the fyrde could only be kept for a certain amount of time before they would have to return to their farms and occupations.

In some ways, she was glad that the court was so quiet and she could rest during the day, but Ældyth was sad that it wasn't possible to go into the country to fresher air away from the marshes and the swarms of insects that bred there in summer.

Ældyth went back to her letter. She wondered whether she should tell Harold about the other problem that was occupying her mind, but it wasn't something that could be communicated in an open letter, which almost any one of Harold's scribes could read. Ældyth had no doubt that the dowager queen was in moral danger, but perhaps that was no business of hers. That's what she had told herself when Merwenne had come to her, big with gossip. For the moment, she'd done nothing. But Harold would want to know that there was a French priest in his sister's bed.

Would there be political consequences? Ældyth was loathe to ask her chaplain for advice, for that would publicly confirm the affair and that was distasteful. It should be dealt with privately within the family and Harold was the one to do it. However, in his absence, perhaps she should approach Edith herself? She was the queen after all, though Edith begrudged her that position.

Observing her sister-in-law over the past weeks, Ældyth had realised that Edith was a competent administrator, as good as Harold himself. In his absence she was essential for the smooth running of all the different systems of taxation, the oversight of the court, the bestowing of privileges and endowments. Fluent in Latin, French and Danish, Edith could talk to all the ambassadors and messengers and read all the communications that came into the court. Ældyth had often felt overlooked and inadequate in her presence. Sometimes she thought that she had made a mistake in allowing Edith to continue in her role, but Ældyth was aware that it was one she herself could never fill with such efficiency.

Ældyth took up another sheet of parchment and wrote a short letter before rolling it up, tying it with cord and securing it with the queen's seal. She wrote on the outside, along the length of it, 'For the King's eyes only' and then enclosed it within her letter.

~ ~ ~

My ears had caught the words 'two young Danes' in the conversations around the table and my heart fluttered at the thought of two of my countrymen being here. I tried to remember whether Tostig had had any other Danes at his court when I was there, but I couldn't think of any. Dinner seemed to take a long time. It was obviously a welcome reunion between Leofwine and his brother and they ate and drank a great deal and both Gytha and the Swan-neck were in lightened spirits. I played and sang a little and Leofwine tossed me a coin for a riddle he couldn't solve. Then, late in the evening, when the Swan-neck had already gone to bed, he gave an order to one of his carles and two men were brought into the hall.

They were about eighteen or nineteen, I estimated, the same age as Godwin, the king's son, dressed in linen tunics and britches with woollen cloaks over all. They looked unkempt, which was unsurprising, since they had been living in the woods.

As their faces came into view I realised that I knew them both. I felt hot and the room spun around my head. Without being able to stop myself I cried out 'Thorkild!' And in that moment I thought I would faint. Everyone turned to look at me.

Harold said straight away, 'You know these men?' He spoke in Danish.

I pointed a shaking hand to the taller of them. 'He's my brother. I thought he was dead.' Then my legs gave way and I sat down on a bench and put my head between my knees.

'Is that your name?' Harold's voice was hard.

'Yes. I am Thorkild Magnusson.' He held his head up and spoke proudly.

'And you?' Harold was pointing at the other.

'Wulfgar Sigurdsson. I was fostered at Earl Magnus' court.'

'You'd better tell us how you got here.'

It was Thorkild who answered. He was still looking at me with a puzzled expression on his face. I returned his gaze, pleading silently for him not to give me away. After a moment he looked back at the king and began to speak. 'On the day that Harold the Landwaster raided the town and laid waste to my father's hall and property, I was out hunting in the forests with friends. We saw smoke in the distance and rode back to find a scene of devastation – the Landwaster's ships were just pulling away from the shore and everyone dead or so sorely wounded there was no hope of recovery. One of them, still in possession of his wits, told us that they had taken all the young people to the ships as slaves.'

'So what did you do?'

'After much discussion, once we had honoured the dead, we travelled south to the court of Sweyn. My father and Sweyn had not always seen eye-to-eye, so our welcome was uncertain.'

I was surprised when Gytha spoke up. 'Sweyn is my nephew. I hope he treated you well.'

Thorkild gave a small bow. 'Very well my Lady. He took us in, gave us weapons and let us train with his carles. We served him for nearly two years. Then, Earl Tostig arrived from Flanders.'

Harold leaned forward and fixed his whole attention on Thorkild. 'What did he want?'

'He told Sweyn that he'd been dispossessed of his earldom and asked for his support to take it back. But Sweyn merely invited him to stay in Denmark and offered him an earldom there. He was very generous.'

'And what did Tostig say?'

'The earl refused immediately. Then he told Sweyn that perhaps the best way to get his own lands back was to promise Sweyn his support and that of his followers in England, if Sweyn would invade the country as his uncle Cnut had once done. He said that he could make Sweyn King of England.'

There was an intake of breath and a murmur around the room. Leowine swore. Harold asked 'So how did Sweyn respond to that?'

'He refused him in absolute terms, none too polite.

Sweyn has just restored a troubled kingdom to one more settled, if it were not for the raids from the Norwegian Vikings. Sweyn has no appetite to start another war. Earl Tostig was not best pleased and they parted on bad terms.'

'So what happened then?'

'The earl offered us – and any other warrior with an impatient sword-arm – new-forged weapons and mail and our share of the plunder if we went with him.' Thorkild lowered his head as if this was something he was ashamed of.

It was Leofwine who asked, 'And so you, ripe for adventure, agreed?'

Thorkild nodded, but he didn't look up.

'So why did you desert him?'

'I found I had no taste for the kind of raiding that Earl Tostig had in mind. Murdering innocent country-folk and burning their crops and their houses isn't to my taste, or Wulfgar's. We thought we were going to fight a proper war, not lay waste to people's homesteads – which makes us no better than the Landwaster. I didn't become a carle to kill children.'

'So you stayed behind?' It was Harold who spoke this time.

'It was easy enough to slip away into the forests. We knew we would be given up for dead.' Thorkild was quiet for a moment and then added, 'And, since we were captured, Earl Leofwine has told us another story.'

He moved to stand closer to Harold, looking him in the face. 'My lord, we would plead earnestly to be given our lives, by your mercy. We are young and both good swordsmen and would be happy to serve you.'

'That,' Harold said, with just a flicker of humour in his eyes, 'is scarcely a reliable offer. In the space of two or three years you've already served two masters – three if you count your father. And you've run away at the first taste of real warfare.'

Thorkild answered him boldly. 'I swear,' he said, 'that we would be faithful to a good lord. We served Sweyn well. Our mistake was to leave him. We seek only a place in the world, my father being dead.' Then unexpectedly he turned towards the corner where I was sitting. 'It seems that you already have one member of my family in your court.'

Everyone was looking at me again.

'Well Hari?' the king said.

'Is that what they call you?' Thorkild asked.

I nodded. 'I'm one of the court scops.'

'You always did sing well,' he said, and I knew then that he had recognised me.

After my brother had been taken back to the carle's quarters I sat for a while so shocked by what I had seen I hardly knew what to do. Harold and Leofwine were in deep conversation with each other. I saw them look in my direction occasionally, but no one spoke to me. I heard Leofwine say, 'Are they cowards do you think?' and Harold reply, 'No. Perhaps they'd never killed a man before. Do you remember how you felt when you were first blooded? They're not war-hardened yet.'

Then they went on to talk about how long they could keep the fyrde before supplies ran low and the crops spoiled in the fields for want of labour.

When I'd recovered myself a little, I got up and went out. The last of the light had faded from the sky, though it was still bright in the west. There was a fire lit and some of the carles were sitting around it keeping watch. They would be there all night. I went up to one of them, a man I knew called Egberth and asked him if he knew where the Danes were kept. He waved me over to one of the smaller huts in the compound.

Thorkild and Wulfgar were sitting outside on the ground. Someone had given them a dish of bread and meat, and some ale.

'Can we talk?' I said to Thorkild.

Wulfgar got up and moved away with a little bow.

'What's going on Hannë?' Thorkild said.

'I'm called Hari here. When the Landwaster arrived I borrowed some of your clothes and cut off my hair. I thought I had more chance as a boy. You know what they do to girls.'

He nodded. I thought how handsome he looked in the late evening summer light, his face tanned, his blond hair curling round his ears, the grey eyes like our mother's.

I told him everything that had happened since I was taken and enslaved. I cried when I told him I'd thought all my family dead. 'And now I'm at the royal court and scop to the queen, which is a good position.'

'I don't like to see you in this state, Hannë.'

'So what would you have me do? Since we no longer have a home and family we have to fend for ourselves. You have a sword; I have a lyre.'

'It's unseemly of you to dress as a boy and to sleep among men. Could you not take refuge in an abbey?'

I shook my head. 'It would be like being in prison. I've no vocation for religion. I like playing music and telling stories to entertain people.'

Thorkild's eyebrows contracted. He looked furious. 'It's not fitting Hannë. I'll talk to the king tomorrow.'

'You'll do no such thing.' I was surprised how angry I felt. I didn't want anyone telling me what to do. It spilled from my mouth in a torrent of words. 'I've survived very well without you these three years and I'll continue to do so. I was so glad to see you and to know that you're still alive, but if you betray me I'll never forgive you. And what can you do for me? You have no home to give me, no money to support me.' I paused for breath and put my hand on his arm. 'I beg you. Keep my secret!'

'It's the very devil not to be able to protect my own sister!'

'Who knows what may happen, Thorkild. Our fortunes

may change. There's a lot of land and privilege in Harold's gift. He's a good king.'

'If he lets us live.'

'I'm sure he will. He's half Danish himself. Our father was his mother's cousin.'

Thorkild grimaced.

'You can protect me best by not betraying my identity. I'm your little brother Hari.'

'It's a ridiculous name.'

That too made me angry. I hadn't expected to feel like this. 'Short for Harold – Viking or Saxon, take your pick.' I got up stiffly. 'Now, I must go to bed. I sleep in the hall near the fire, with the king's hounds for protection. Tomorrow you'll meet his wife, Lady Eadgifu, the one they call the Swan-neck. She speaks very little Danish, so you're going to have to learn the Saxon tongue. There, at least, I can help you.'

We had two days together. Thorkild told me everything that he'd done after the Landwaster's raid, skimming over some of it. There had been a girl, he said, a farmer's daughter. He was a man now. But there was a distance between us. We'd never been close – there was the four-year age difference, the fact that he was a young thegn among thegns, while I had been a girl, still in the schoolroom among the women. We were strangers.

I told him about the court in Norway and then my time in Tostig's Hall in Northumbria before being sent south.

'What did you think of Earl Tostig?' Thorkild asked.

'Like sunlight on a sword blade. Changeable. And there was always a ruthless edge to him.' I tried to remember what I could about my former lord. 'You could see Tostig's thoughts moving over his face like cloud shadow. He could turn to anger in a moment and then be utterly charming the next.' The joy of speaking my own language – not having to search for words to shape my meaning – was intoxicating.

'He thinks only of himself, as far as I can see.' Thorkild grunted. 'But what about his brother?'

'Harold? No, not like that. But he's deep. There are some who think he's too lenient, but that's not true. He's as ruthless as Tostig – he just has a different way of getting what he wants. A kind of quiet power.'

After I left them, the two Godwinson brothers had Thorkild and his friend under hard questioning all afternoon. That night in Hall, Thorkild and Wulfgar swore fealty to Harold, presenting their swords, bending the knee and kissing the ring. They were to go with him to the Isle and train with his carles.

The following day, Harold called me in to talk to me. 'This changes things,' he said, looking very serious. 'The queen has written to say she misses her scop and I feel obliged to send you back.' He paused and looked down at the ring of state on his hand. Then he went on, 'It isn't possible for your brother to be a free man in my service, while you are a slave, particularly as it seems we are kin. I'm writing to the queen to ask that you be freed. Lady Eadgifu will send you north in a day or so, with some messages I have for Westminster.'

I felt my stomach lurch with disappointment that I was to be parted from my brother so soon.

Harold was looking at me very carefully. 'Before I go, I want you to swear your oath to me, as your brother has just done, that you will be loyal, that you will fight for me if that day comes.'

'Willingly, Sir.' I meant it.

There was a moment's silence before the chaplain brought the holy book. I put my hand on it and said the words and then I knelt and kissed the big gold ring with its red garnet and the dragon curling round the band. It reminded me, for one shuddering second, of the gold dragon ring that coiled around the Landwaster's upper arm.

And then I was free.

Part Six

For the Sake of Ellisev

'The closer the army came, the greater it grew, and their glittering weapons sparkled like a field of broken ice.'

Snorri Sturluson, *Harald's Saga*

Ælyth remembered it afterwards as the summer of '*an-bi-dung*' – the endless weeks of watching and waiting; watching for invasions, waiting for the birth of a child, waiting for Harold's return. Everything felt held back – even her own position at court, nothing could be established until the kingdom was secure and she had presented Harold with a son. She was a queen in waiting.

At least she was no longer waiting for Harold's instructions on what should be done about the dowager queen, his sister and regent. He had written to her from Bosham, where he was visiting the Swan-neck, but in a manner that determined nothing. 'I can't see that anyone is being harmed by it,' he had written. 'She isn't cloistered, she has no husband, and no public position except by proxy. I understand your concerns. He will have to address his conscience with the Order and she, too, will have to seek forgiveness from the Church and her God. Edith is deeply Christian, so this will cause her some heart-searching. On the political side, I hope my sister is awake enough to the danger of giving away any information to one who might make use of it. Do what you think best. In any case, I can't be here many more weeks and will talk to her when I come back.'

Harold hadn't forbidden her to talk to the dowager privately, Ældyth thought. That was left to her own judgement. The letter ended with a personal greeting that seemed affectionate, and he had sent her scop back, so perhaps he did feel something for her after all.

The following morning Ældyth walked along the corridor, unaccompanied by her ladies, to visit the dowager. Edith was sitting at her desk, writing, while her maid Mathilde was sewing in a chair by the window. They bowed to each other and Edith indicated a chair for Ældyth to sit on. Edith was subtly changed, Ældyth thought, though she couldn't quite identify what it was that was different. There was a certain ease in her manner, a lessening of that critical tightening of her face that had always been there, pinching it into creases.

'Can I have words with you alone?' Ældyth asked.

Edith looked across at Mathilde who collected her materials and left the room. 'What is it? I know you've had a letter from my brother.'

Ældyth nodded. 'I wanted to ask you how your Life of Edward was progressing. The king's interested to know.'

Edith turned away, but Ældyth could see the red blush spreading to the side of her neck where it wasn't covered by her veil.

She pressed on, sure now that Edith knew what she was referring to. 'I want to tell you that it's known. All of it. The gossip is rife in the court. Not what you would want, I think.'

The dowager turned back to face her. Edith's cheeks were

still flushed. 'Gossip! Why should I care about that? It's no business of yours, in any case.'

'But it is my business. As queen, it's my responsibility to be answerable for the moral state of the women of the court, as you once were for yours.'

Ældyth thought that Edith was going to explode into anger, but the dowager gripped her hands tightly in her lap and pressed her lips together. Eventually she raised her head and looked straight at Ældyth.

'That's a deep cut, is it not? The "women of the court"! Is that what I'm reduced to?' She took a deep, gasping breath. 'What are you going to do?'

'Nothing. That's for you to decide. It's between you and your conscience. But I thought you should know what's being said.'

'How dare you!'

'It's troubled me a great deal. I know you're unhappy and I suspect that Goscelin gives you much needed comfort. But it can only end badly. When the archbishop returns . . .'

'Aren't I entitled to a little happiness? After a miserable marriage and now facing a miserable widowhood? Don't you think I know what's involved? You must leave me to make my own decisions.'

Ældyth could read the unspoken accusations in her eyes, *you, with your husband and your unborn child,* and indeed, what could she know of Edith's suffering. Ældyth got up. Edith remained seated. 'That's what I intend to do,'Ældyth said. 'And I'm sure you'll make the right choice.' Then she left, feeling no satisfaction for what she had done. And, when she knelt in confession later that evening to tell her chaplain that she had reproached another woman for her actions, she wondered whether there had been an element of self-righteousness, or perhaps even of asserting herself. Had her motives been completely pure? What had she said? *'Responsibility for the moral state of the women of the court'.* The sanctimonious words made her shudder now. It had been uncharitable, she confessed to an impassive Ælfric. She had cast a stone at someone who didn't deserve it. He gave her absolution, but she did not feel forgiven.

~ ~ ~

I had a strange dream. I was on a ship, at sea in a great storm. The sail was ragged and the men were rowing hard to keep the prow into the wind. At the top of the mast was a large bird, as big as a raven, and I remember thinking, 'How can a bird perch there in so strong a gale?' One of the rowers was shouting, warning that he could see land, perilous rocks that could cast us away if we were washed up on them. I can't remember any fear. Then Merithien was there, standing beside the mast, untouched by the wind, her hair and clothes still, as if in a dead calm. She was smiling at me. 'Don't be afraid, my little shape-shifter,' she said. 'You will see rougher seas than this.' She pointed to the bird at the top of the mast. 'You have a protector now.' And then she vanished and there was only the howling gale and the terrible sound of the sea growling against the rocks.

When I woke up, I could feel something wet and sticky between my legs. My stomach ached and I knew straight away what it was. The thing I dreaded – my women's courses had begun. My first thought was thankfulness that I hadn't bled within the military encampment; my second that this would have been a joyous time if I was still at home. I re-member celebrating the coming of my sister's womanhood, when my mother had put the veil over her head; there was a feast and preparations had begun to find a suitable marriage for her. I suppose I should be glad to escape that.

Panic rose inside me. How was I going to deal with this, to conceal it from those around me? In truth, it wasn't possible. As I lay there, in despair, I thought about who could help me. One of the serving women? No, for they couldn't be trusted not to reveal my identity to everyone. Such a juicy piece of gossip would be impossible to resist.

I got up and went to the latrine to clean myself as well as I could. It was unpleasant and not very successful. I tied the piece of linen between my legs with the ragged napkin inside and wondered what I should do when it needed changing. There was my old tunic; I could tear it into strips, but that wouldn't last forever. Who could I ask what the women of the court did when they had their courses? Every one of them must have the same problem. I thought about confiding in the Lady Margaret, but she would, I knew, immediately insist that I put on women's clothes and lead a more conventional life. She would be scandalised to know that I was not a boy.

I've been in the habit of slipping in and out of the palace through the kitchens at the back so I know the servants' areas very well. Outside, in wooden structures built against the wall, open at the sides, are the wash houses. The women who work there, I've been told, are slaves, Welsh or Frankish, some from Ireland or the far north. When I went in, there was a brief pause as they looked up. Two of the women were stirring an enormous vat over a brazier with long poles. They looked at me curiously. Another was beating some linen on a wooden board. She looked no older than myself and so I went to her first.

'Do you speak English?'

She made a strange gesture with her hand over her mouth.

One of the other women called over, 'You'll get nothing out of her. She's as deaf and dumb as a doorpost.'

There was a moment of disappointment and I could feel the panic rising again. Who should I talk to? Then, I wondered if perhaps the gods had deliberately guided me to one who couldn't tell tales.

I made some gestures, with my back to the other women, trying to describe what it was I needed. I mouthed 'moon-courses' once or twice, as she watched me and saw the moment she understood. She opened her mouth to laugh and I saw that where her tongue should have been was an empty space. Someone had cut it out. When she saw my expression she opened her mouth wider and laughed again, a strange guttural sound deep in her throat.

I spread my hands in a gesture of helplessness and horror.

She left what she was doing and put one hand, the skin reddened and raw around her fingernails, on my arm. She pulled me along with her into the corridor just outside the laundry and gestured to a door on the left near the latrines. Then she left me, putting one hand up to her lips again in the same gesture that she'd made before.

I opened the door and found myself in a small laundry cupboard. On the shelves were towels and linen under-garments, neatly stacked. A wooden bucket on the floor had three or four bloodied cloths in it. On the shelf above there was a pile of red linen napkins. I could see, from the quality of the linen, that this wasn't a servants' room. This was for the ladies of the court. A washbowl and pitcher of water stood in the corner. I thanked all the gods who looked over me. But at the same time I knew that my life had become more complicated and my situation more precarious.

~ ~ ~

After Ældyth had left, Edith walked up and down her room seething with anger. How dared she! How dared she! But when some of that energy had evaporated she felt nauseous with shame that her secret, her precious secret, had been tarnished by gossip. There was also anxiety and sadness.

It was almost three weeks since she had seen Goscelin,

and Edith was afraid that he had left the palace for good. Last week he had sent a note to say that he had a room in the abbey scriptorium and was working on the Life without danger of interruption. He would, he said, give it to her to read when he had finished the first part. She knew he was avoiding her, using the abbey's thick stone walls as protection.

Edith was racked with guilt. Only a few days earlier, her courses had begun – a few days late; long days of fear and hope as well as the horror of what she had done. But when she saw the blood she had felt such devastation and grief that she had burst into tears. Now she felt empty and desolate. To have slipped from grace, after a lifetime of service to God and king as well as loyalty to family – a lifetime of duty dishonoured by one act of passion – was a great fall.

~ ~ ~

Late summer was in rich abundance, hay and corn high in the fields, but as yet no men to harvest it. The fields were being worked by women and children. The horses had gone too, so they were pulling the carts themselves. Despite the season, there was no letup in the cool, easterly breeze that rippled through the grass, threshing the trees in front of it. At night the wind gusted across the roof, sighing in the chimney. Eadgifu was tired of it. Several weeks now since Harold had left to go back to the Isle. His men were still keeping watch on the headland, ready to light the beacon at the first sight of William's fleet. But there was nothing but the usual merchant vessels, coastal traders, hugging land, still unable to brave the open water. The sea was choppy and grey, raked by the wind, the sharp waves like steel teeth.

Eadgifu had been restless all day and had walked down to the headland gazing over to where the Isle was simply a shadow on the horizon. Then she had picked windfalls in the orchard for the cooks to conserve before they were too worm-eaten. Her back ached from all that bending and straightening. As she lay in bed, sleep eluded her. The moon was sending a shaft of light across the bed from the lancet window in the wall and an owl was shrieking murderously as it hunted in the long grass.

As she lay awake, she realised that she needed to pee urgently, as she did every night now at least once, and made her way down to the privy, blessing Harold's forethought in building it indoors. As she sat on the wooden seat she was suddenly overtaken by a wave of pain and felt the hot gush of fluid pouring out of her. She put her hand between her legs and was shocked to feel the fuzz of hair on the crown of a small head. In a panic she slipped down onto the stone floor, shouting out for help. All was lost in pain for a while until she realised that one of the maids was holding her hand, Gytha was standing beside her, and another maid was crouched at her feet holding a baby. Its body was red and blue and it was crying with a long, thin, wailing sound.

'It's a boy,' Gytha said, with great satisfaction. 'Harold has another son.'

'His name is Ulf.' Eadgifu's voice was shaking with the shock of it. 'He's not due for another three weeks.' She took the small bundle the maid handed to her, bloody and half blind, blinking at the candlelight like a new-born kitten, and still attached to her by the cord.

Gytha was giving orders. Someone came with a leather thong and a seax knife. Then she held the cord and began to say prayers in her own language, to what gods Eadgifu didn't like to speculate. The cord was severed. Eadgifu tightened her grip on the child and put her mouth against his matted hair, clotted with birth fluid. '*Ulf,*' she thought, '*my little Ulf.*'

Then Gytha sat her up against the wall and began to knead her stomach to release the after-birth. She pulled down Eadgifu's night shift at the shoulder and placed Ulf to her breast. 'Bring her some mead,' she shouted.

'I'd rather have wine,' Eadgifu protested.

'Mead will give you strength,' Gytha said, 'and bring in your milk.'

One of her maids put a glass to her lips. It was mead, thick and much too sweet. The babe had a strong suck, despite the fact that he was small – such an early baby. The pain of his sucking went through her and she could feel her stomach contract. That was the truth of children; pain and love.

~ ~ ~

'Do you remember your mother?' Arthur asked quietly. We were lying in the long grass on the edge of the marsh watching a heron fishing.

'I do. But it's not a pleasant memory. She was put to the sword by one of the Landwaster's men. I try not to think of it.'

'Sorry.'

'And yours?'

'Not really. She was an ealdorman's daughter, I think. When I was five or six, Ælfgar's men came for me. I was taken to his hall to be brought up with his other sons.'

'And Ældyth, the queen?'

'No. She was brought up by her own mother. I don't think Ælfgar spent much time with any of his wives.' He was silent for a moment and then said, 'Do you miss your home?'

'Yes.'

I must have answered curtly because he said, 'Forgive me. I'm just interested in your family and the place where you belong.' He glanced sideways at me. 'You're such a mystery, Hari.'

The heron had got hold of an eel which it was waving in the air as it struggled to get a good grip.

'Maybe one day I'll tell you,' I murmured. It would be a relief to tell someone, particularly Arthur. I was still bleeding, though only a little, and very conscious of my new womanhood.

Arthur was laughing and pointing towards the water. 'Look! The heron! It's trying to swallow it whole!'

It was strange to be back at court. On the second day, Ældyth had called me to her room and given me a small roll of parchment. 'That's your freedom, Hari,' she said. 'You're no longer a slave.' She looked anxious as I took hold of it. 'I hope you'll feel that the court is still your home and that we can count on your music and stories?'

I bowed. 'The houses of Mercia and Wessex have been kind to me. I'm happy to stay. But I have a brother now, in the service of the king and I may have to go with him at some future time.'

'The king's told me, so I understand. You must be very pleased.'

'Yes, my Lady. And I'm grateful to the king for his kindness to my brother.'

The queen gave me a purse of silver, which she said was for my service to her and then I was dismissed. To be a wandering scop, not belonging to anyone, feels precarious, though old Wulfere, the king's scop, has told me that it can be lucrative. It was a hard living, he said, but every town and village would give me bed and board and money in return for music and stories. 'It's a young man's life though,' he went on, revealing his toothless gums in a broad grin. 'Not for the likes of me.'

Nor, I thought, newly blooded into womanhood, for the likes of me.

Later I went down to the market in town with the purse that the queen had given me. I bought a new cloak in green wool, big enough to wrap around me and keep the weather out, as well as to conceal what was underneath. Then I paused beside a silversmith's stall. When I was at home, I'd worn jewellery often and I missed it. The new cloak demanded a shoulder clasp. There was one, in silver, engraved with the shape of a raven with a small, dark stone where the eye of the bird should be. The price the vendor demanded made me catch my breath. It cost me more than I was willing to pay, making the purse considerably lighter, but I wanted something of my own, something beautiful that would remind me who I was. The man looked at the coins I'd given him and then looked across at me curiously. 'These are Harold's. Haven't seen any of these yet. Where'd you get them?' There was suspicion in his voice.

'I live at the court and earn my living there.' I indicated the lyre on my back and the man seemed satisfied. He nodded and handed me the brooch. For the first time in many months I felt just a little more like Hannë Magnusdottir.

~ ~ ~

Goscelin came a few days later, accompanied by another brother from the abbey. He looked very solemn, but there was great kindness in his eyes, a warmth that made Edith ache inside. He presented her with a thick wad of parchment. 'This is the first part of the *Vita Edwardi Regis*,' he said. 'The part that addresses the lineage of the Godwin family and your life before marriage to the king. Can you read it and tell me if there's anything I've written that's incorrect?'

Edith took a long breath and accepted the manuscript. It was heavy, the parchment new and stiff, covered by his firm, familiar, handwriting. His hands had moved over these pages, she thought, as her fingers gripped it. His touch was everywhere. She forced herself to behave formally, inclining her head and saying, 'Thank you. I will read it carefully.'

'As to the second part,' Edith thought she saw compassion in Goscelin's eyes. 'I intend to begin that immediately and I will be returning to Wilton. There are many people I have to talk to, so I may have to travel in order to collect the facts of his life – from the beginning, you understand. You have already told me what you know.'

All Edith understood was that he was telling her that he didn't need to talk to her any more and would be going away. Her tongue felt wooden and there was nothing she could say.

The brother who accompanied Goscelin was standing just inside the door. Goscelin made a bow and said quietly in French, 'I've made my confession my Lady, but I named no one. I wasn't asked.'

It was all Edith could do to stand straight and make her face blank. She nodded.

Goscelin said, 'I wish you God's mercy, for He has been good enough to give it to me.' And then he went out of the room.

~ ~ ~

Harold was on horseback, his gyrfalcon on his wrist, hounds running at his horse's legs. As Eadgifu watched from the window, he lifted his arm in a graceful gesture and the hawk went free, soaring up into the blue air, the jesses dangling beneath until it went out of sight, a mere dot in the sky.

Eadgifu felt glad. Harold had looked so angry and frustrated when he arrived two days ago, swearing that he had had to let the fyrde go back to their houses, their farms, their families. William still hadn't come and now the coast was undefended except by his own carles. Out in the fields he looked so carefree, like the hawk he had just released.

Gytha was beside her, watching the men ride towards the woods, their cloaks billowing behind them in the wind; Gyrth, Leofwine, Harold, with Godwin and Edmund behind them riding with the archbishop and the falconers.

'My boys,' Gytha said.

'And mine, though I don't include the archbishop in that.'

'He rides well for a cleric.' Her tone was grudging.

Eadgifu was walking the room with Ulf on her shoulder. He had fallen asleep, but she thought more out of exhaustion than satisfaction. Her breasts ached and her nipples were raw. No amount of lanolin or oil of marigold could soothe them. She cried every time she tried to feed him.

'Maybe it's because he was such an early baby,' Eadgifu said, returning to the conversation she had been having with Gytha before they had seen the hunting party riding out. 'Maybe my body just wasn't ready. Or maybe I'm just too old. It seems terrible not to be able to feed my own child!'

'Don't blame yourself.' Gytha put a hand on her shoulder. 'Sometimes we just can't. Get a wet nurse.'

Eadgifu sighed. 'My maid was telling me today of a girl in the village who has a three-month child without a father. A good, clean girl.'

Ulf was stirring, his mouth seeking against the skin of her neck. Her heart sank. Her milkless breasts hurt so much she couldn't bear the thought of trying to feed him again. Her eyes went back to the window, to Harold. The men were only small figures in the distance now.

'It does me good to see them playing together like boys again,' Gytha said. 'After so much worry and care.'

But, Eadgifu thought, the care was still there. She had heard the late-night conversations between them as she sat up nursing Ulf after Gytha had gone to bed. Heard them running through different possible events – making plans, altering them, saying 'What if . . .' again and again. It was Leofwine who had the best imagination when it came to trickery, but Harold who always had the solution. It was good to be a family again, to see Harold playing with the little ones, holding Ulf up to his shoulder while he talked, to give her a rest. Tomorrow the archbishop was going to bless the babe in the church, to baptise him as Harold wished. Leofwine and Godwin were going to stand as his sponsors. Eadgifu hoped that he wouldn't cry through the whole service.

She handed Ulf to Gytha. 'I must talk to my maid. To carry on is madness – I'm starving the child.'

At night Harold slept in her bed as he had always done, until the old king died. His familiar bulk on the other side of the bed gave her comfort, and the animal smell of his skin was intoxicating. The first night after his return he had caught her up in his arms eagerly, the weeks of celibacy in the camp taking hold of him. Still sore and bleeding after the birth, she had given him comfort in other ways, their bodies so familiar together that there was no need for words. Harold had always been a generous lover, and it was good to give something back. She couldn't help thinking that the Welsh mare, heavily pregnant, wouldn't be in a position to give him anything when he went up to London. If, as Gytha had said, their relationship was based on lust, a wife who was eight months gone would cool it.

Why did it hurt so much, Eadgifu asked herself, even though she knew he still cared for her? There was no answer.

Lying together in the early morning light, Harold said, 'I'm very loath to go. But I must. There's urgent business waiting for me in London.'

Eadgifu rested her head on his chest, listening to his heart thumping against her cheek. 'Can't it wait a little longer?'

She felt him laugh. 'No. We've agreed on a plan between us and I've got to organise the men. Besides, I've been absent for months and there are pressing things for me to take care of. I can't leave it all to my sister.'

Eadgifu lifted her head and looked down at him, his hair tousled, crumbs of sleep in his eyes, stubble on his jaw, lines she hadn't seen before scoring his brow and cheeks. 'I'm glad you stayed so long this time. I'm just greedy for your company.' She paused for a fraction of a second and then said, as lightly as she could, 'Shall I come back to court?'

A shadow passed over his face. His eyes were like slate. 'Why don't you come up to Hildburgh with Gytha, or go to Waltham which is nearer to London. It's better for the children in the country, but I want you out of reach of the Normans, and Bosham is one of the places they might land.'

Eadgifu was circling one of his nipples with her finger. 'What's William like?'

Harold caught her finger in his grip and kissed it. 'A cruel man. In those months I was with him in Normandy I saw him treat people like vermin, even his own family. I watched him kick his wife downstairs for saying something not to his liking. The mark of his spur was in her breast. He cuffed her often too, and his stewards. He wasn't above humiliating anyone he didn't like.'

Eadgifu shuddered. 'I pray he doesn't come.'

'He'll come,' Harold said. 'I know the man. He'll come. He has scores to settle with me.'

The church at Bosham was old, as sturdy as their manor. Cnut the Great had once worshipped here, and it had afterwards been endowed and improved by King Edward. Cnut's small daughter, who had drowned at sea, was buried in the crypt. Eadgifu often thought of that small body, encased in stone – every mother's horror to lose a child. She herself had lost one, at birth, and knew the cost. Bosham was now part of Harold's gift, as king, but, like the manor, it was also part of his childhood and Eadgifu knew he loved it. The stonework was pale stone with a squat tower and soaring oak beams to hold up the roof. So much beauty, Eadgifu thought, with such an atmosphere of calm.

They were all there, Gytha, Gyrth and Leofwine, Godwin and Edmund, Magnus and little Gytha. Harold carried the infant Ulf, soundly, blissfully asleep after the village girl had shared her breasts with him. It had filled Eadgifu with guilt to watch him sucking at them, his little fist pawing the girl's soft flesh. Eadgifu felt that she had failed in the most profound part of being a mother. But at least he would thrive and the girl would also be properly fed. She was far too thin, though her own babe was as plump as one could wish for. One of Harold's carles was the father, Eadgifu gathered, unwilling to honour his part in it. She had already asked the girl to come with them when they went up to Waltham.

Archbishop Stigand was standing at the font, reading the prayers in Latin, which the men understood perfectly and could respond to, but which meant very little to Eadgifu. The basic words she knew, enough to deal with her sheriffs and bailiffs, but not this complex liturgical language.

Harold put Ulf into Leofwine's arms and he and Godwin stepped forward to offer Ulf to the archbishop and make their promises. Ulf offered no protest as his head was dipped in the holy water, only curling and uncurling his fists and sighing. Like a small bear, Eadgifu thought, having eaten enough for its winter sleep. It made her feel very strange to see her eldest son with her youngest – almost twenty years between them.

At Bosham the cooks had prepared a feast of the game caught at yesterday's hunt, ducks and a hare, as well as one of the pigs that had been slaughtered the day Harold had arrived. And then it was time for them to go; dogs barking, the horses stamping and whickering, the carles shouting, harness jingling, the smell of horses and harness grease. Eadgifu and Gytha brought out the stirrup cups for the men – hot wine mulled with spices. Harold and his company and two hundred carles rode out of the gates, bound for the north; Gyrth and Leofwine were bound east for their own manors, accompanied by their own carles.

The silence they left behind was terrible. Eadgifu watched the horses and fluttering banners vanish into a dust cloud. *The king rides*, she thought. And Harold was gone. That moment was burnt into her memory.

~ ~ ~

The court was clattering with noise and the bustle of people, as the carles returned from the south with their retinues of servants. They were sun and wind-bronzed, from camping all summer on the Isle. I recognised quite a few of them, and among them was my brother and his friend Wulfgar. Thorkild has gained in confidence since Harold accepted his service, and he's grown, his arms more muscular and his chest broader with strenuous sword practice. He's much more like my father now, though he has my mother's eyes. But I've noticed that he avoids using my name.

That first night in hall I sang some Danish songs, which pleased the dowager, but were really meant to remind Thorkild of home. It's painful to sing those songs, but if I don't then they'll be forgotten and then home will be just a faint memory, unreal as a dream. I've talked to Lady Margaret about this, but she's of the opinion that the past is best put behind us, since we can never go back. She wants to travel on into the future unburdened by it. I only want to forget some of the things that have happened, but I know that I must remember the rest. The difficulty is that I can't separate the two.

I didn't get an opportunity to talk to Thorkild for two or three days. He was spending his time with Edmund and Godwin Haroldson after the king's return, and sometimes also with Arthur. Edgar the Ætheling was often with them, though several years younger, equal in rank, if not in age – a quiet, shy boy. Thorkild had learned to speak a little Saxon during his time on the Isle, and Harold's sons spoke Danish, so they all managed to talk to each other after a fashion.

Thorkild sought me out in one of the solars, waiting to play for the queen when she rested in the afternoon.

'You promised to teach me the Saxon language.'

I shrugged. 'It's not so different to ours. Some of the words are the same, haven't you noticed?'

He grinned and opened his hands in a helpless gesture. 'Probably, but I'm no good at speaking it!'

'The only way is to speak it, all the time.' I switched into Saxon. 'What have you been doing this morning?'

'Oh,' he paused to think for a moment. 'I understood *hwhaet*, and *merigen-tid* – that's the same as *morgen* isn't it?'

'It is. You'll see it's really easy.'

Since then, we've spent an hour or so every day speaking a kind of muddled Saxon-Danish. It would be very pleasant if he didn't keep pressing me about my situation.

'Who knows?'

'Only one of the laundry maids and she's dumb.'

'Even so, you can't keep it secret forever.'

I knew that, but my hope was that perhaps I could keep it secret until I found some permanent place of safety. There was only the vaguest idea in my head of what that would look like, but I knew it was there somewhere in my future.

'And what about Arthur Ælfgarson? You spend a lot of time with him.' Thorkild's eyes were hard.

'We're friends. That's all.'

'There's lewd gossip among the carles about the two of you. I can't bear my sister to be spoken of like that, when I know it can't be true. If you were known to be a girl. . .'

I shook my head. 'I know what's being said. It hurts Arthur more than me.'

'I would wish you in the queen's court among the women.'

His words made me cross. 'Until you're in a position to offer me a home, you must leave me to lead my life as I wish.' I sounded harsher than I intended. 'While you're only a wandering thegn, there's nothing you can do.'

The strength of my feelings surprised me and at night I sometimes lay awake trying to make sense of them. I'd longed to have some member of my family returned to me, had despaired of what was to become of me, alone in the world and unprotected. But now that had happened, I didn't feel as I'd expected to. Thorkild was a stranger to me, even though he was my kin, and the choices he gave me were alien to my nature. I no longer wanted the life that had been laid out for me as an earl's daughter. Marriage was unlikely now, since Thorkild had no money to pay a dowry, and his own position was precarious, which left only the cloister and that was not what I wanted. To be enclosed and spend your life praying to a god you only half believed in and not have the freedom to go where you wanted, to sing and compose stories and poems was hateful. I thought I might suffocate between the four walls of a nun's cell.

He agreed not to say anything but wouldn't promise. He said that I was too young to know what was best for me. I was so angry I could barely be civil.

~ ~ ~

Edith spent the day after Harold's return closeted with him to discuss all the affairs she had managed while he was away – their personal holdings as well as matters of state. After a few hours, Harold was showing signs of boredom, shuffling his feet and glancing out of the window, where the early autumn sunlight was slanting down on the stone floor.

'You haven't said anything about that other matter,' Harold said suddenly. 'I presume it's dealt with?'

'What other matter?' Edith was very conscious of the scribe sitting with pen poised at the end of the table – Ældyth saying, *It's known everywhere*.

'The Life of King Edward.'

Edith felt her stomach contract. 'I didn't need to. It's all taken care of.'

'Good. I thought I could trust you to end it.'

'You didn't ask the queen to talk to me?'

'No. Did she?'

Edith said nothing, but she went cold with anger. Ældyth had wanted to humiliate her. Those words, *'the moral state of the women of the court'*. She sat up straight in her chair. 'Can we discuss the latest news from Normandy?'

'If we must.'

'There's a rumour that Pope Alexander has sent the duke a papal banner. Apparently he believes the tale of the broken oath. Do you think it's true?'

Harold groaned. 'Spare me! I think I've done all I can bear to do in one day.' He stood up and stretched. 'The light's still good. There's time for a couple of hours hunting on the marshes before nightfall.' His expression changed to one of pleasurable expectation as he spoke, and the corners of his mouth lifted.

Edith was annoyed. 'So, you'll leave all this for me to deal with?' She waved a hand over the rolls of parchment scattered over the table.

Harold smiled down at her. 'Why don't you leave it for my scribes. You don't have to take everything on your shoulders Edith. Perhaps you should share some of it with the queen?'

He didn't wait for her reply. Edith watched him go, clenching her fists in anger. Administration was his least favourite activity. She tried not to feel resentful.

~ ~ ~

The hall was crowded with returned carles and chaplains and the whole of Harold's retinue, but not the younger Godwinson brothers or the Mercian earls who had gone back to their own manors. Ældyth sat next to Edith, without saying anything more than pleasantries. The atmosphere between the two was cool. She knew that Edith had not forgiven her. Harold had said nothing on the subject. Ældyth looked across at him – his face and arms were weathered from months outdoors and he was leaner. Camp fare was not so substantial as the food in the palace. Ældyth thought he also looked preoccupied.

Just as the platters were being cleared and the stewards were bringing more wine a messenger came into the lower hall, his spurs ringing on the paved floor. He was travel-strained and weary, she could see, as he spoke to one of the stewards who brought him quickly forward towards Harold's table. It was an important message from the north, he said.

'It's from Morcar,' Harold said as he opened it. Ældyth saw his face change. He closed his eyes and breathed hard for a moment, as if to calm himself. 'Tostig's back,' he said curtly, 'with a Viking army. Harald of Norway and two hundred ships.'

Ældyth heard her sister-in-law gasp.

'Now will you believe?' Harold said, looking at Edith.

She put her face in her hands.

'Are my brothers ready?' Ældyth asked. 'It will take a while to raise an army to face numbers like that.'

'Morcar's called out his men and he says Edwin's on his way with another three thousand. Harald's landed on the northeast coast and burned several towns. Morcar fears that the Vikings may be heading for York. It's Tostig's old stronghold after all.'

'My brothers will stop him, surely,' Ældyth said. 'They won't want to lose their lands.'

Harold ran his hand over his moustaches, smoothing them down around his mouth – a sign of anxiety, Ældyth thought.

'I hope so. But neither of them are experienced generals in major battles. The Norwegian's cunning and powerful – probably the most successful warrior alive. I don't think he's ever lost a fight. He's prudent enough to walk away from anything he thinks he can't win. Tostig's obviously persuaded him that England's worth fighting for.'

'Who else is with him? Does Morcar say?' Edith said quietly.

'The earls of Orkney and Shetland, as well as a troop from Flanders. I thought Count Baldwin was our friend, but it seems not.'

'Perhaps his daughter fancies herself as Queen of England,' Edith said. There was acid in her voice.

'And she's also kin of the Norman duke.' Harold sounded curt. 'It's easy to see what advantage William gets from this invasion.' He got up. 'It's all deeply troubling. I must go and see the archbishop and consult my thegns.' He looked down at Ældyth. 'I need to be ready if your brothers can't hold him'.

~ ~ ~

The court is loud with gossip. Apparently, Harald and Tostig have landed on the east coast and are harrying the land north of the River Humber. Mercian land. Edwin is going to York and Morcar is coming down from the north to drive them back. They are collecting as many men under arms as they can, since Harald's force is so large. Edwin has had reports of two hundred ships full of warriors and has sent word for his brother and the other Mercian carles to join him as well as the fyrde.

Arthur told me about it while we were playing chess. He said, 'Come north Hari. Come and see what a real battle is like. Besides, I expect we'll need something to cheer us up in the evenings.'

'This is your first time?'

Arthur nodded. 'A few skirmishes on the Welsh borders, but nothing that needed any strategy. I want to see how the shield wall holds against a real enemy. Now that the king's back with his carles, I can be spared to join Edwin. I'm tired of kicking my heels at court like a milkling.'

'Harald of Norway isn't an enemy to be wished on anyone.' I moved a pawn Arthur was threatening but my mind wasn't on the game anymore. 'I've seen him fight. They call him the Hadrada – the ruthless one. He spares no one. At home we called him the Landwaster, because that's what he does best.'

'My brothers will soon put him to flight,' Arthur said confidently.

I was less certain than him but didn't say so. I went back to his first request. 'Besides, aren't you forgetting I'm the queen's scop?'

'You're free now, Hari.'

Reluctantly, I said, 'It's true, but here I have a roof over my head and food in my stomach and somewhere to sleep and must be grateful. I'm not free to go where I please without risking that.'

Arthur looked serious. 'Everyone says you're a Danish Ætheling, Thorkild Magnusson's brother. Is that true?'

I nodded, wondering if Thorkild had said anything to him.

Then he said, slowly and deliberately, 'I'm guessing your name isn't Hari.'

I looked at him without answering. Perhaps my brother had said something.

'What is your name. Can't you tell me? We're supposed to be friends.'

I couldn't help but remember the time when he had pushed me away from him; the times he had told me 'we can't be friends'. What would he do now if I told him my real name? I couldn't be sure he wouldn't expose me.

'If I gave it to you, I'd be in even more trouble than I am already,' I said quietly. 'I must find my own way out of the tangle I'm in. Trust me.' I met his eyes. 'But to go north would suit me. I'd be nearer to my own people again.' I wondered if Ingrid would welcome me back, whether I'd find Merithien on the quayside with her cherrywood stick.

Arthur picked up one of his knights, peering at the board. 'You must be nearly sixteen now, Hari, if not already.'

I nodded, not sure where this was leading.

Arthur set down the knight, threatening another of my pawns. I could see doubt and speculation moving over his face. 'But you still have no hair on your chin. You aren't like your brother, are you.'

He was probing again, looking at me in a way that set my heart thumping inside my chest, my cheeks pink, a swarm of bees inside my head. He was giving me the chance to explain, but I still couldn't say the words. The risk was too great. So instead, I said, 'I'll come, if you can arrange it.'

It was a long, weary journey before we met Edwin's main forces just south of York. He told us that Tostig, together with the Hadrada's men were camped along the river at a place called Fulford, intending to move on to York the following day. We dismounted at a distance and moved quietly up through woodland, on the other side of a small hill that Edwin said would give us an advantage, and pitched camp in the growing dark. We lit no fires to give us away, eating only bread and cold meat. And then we went to bed, exhausted.

I found that I was sharing a small tent with Arthur and two other young carles who were fast – and noisily – asleep. I was so used to sleeping among the carles in the hall I thought nothing of it. Arthur was lying beside me in the dark and I could hear him breathing. I knew he was awake. 'Are you afraid?' I asked softly.

'Not afraid exactly. Not of the fighting anyway. But perhaps the thought that I might die. It hadn't occurred to me until tonight. There's such a lot of my life I haven't lived.'

I turned towards him and put my head on his shoulder. It was a simple gesture of comfort. He laid his cheek against my hair and I could feel his breath on my brow. He was breathing fast.

I felt his fingers on my arm, then his hand on my breast, felt the pause of recognition and knew I was discovered. I touched his face in the dark, the smooth skin of his throat. He said nothing as his lips pressed mine and then moved across my cheek and down towards my breasts. I made no sound as he lifted my tunic, pulled down my britches and began to explore the soft skin of my stomach, the downy cleft between my legs. Now he could not be in any doubt as to my sex. And then he was on top of me and I had to bite his shoulder so's not to cry out. It was quickly over and he lay, panting, his head on my shoulder.

'It's Hannë,' I whispered. 'My name's Hannë.'

'You're beautiful,' he murmured into my ear. Then, after a moment, 'I'll take care of you, I promise.'

I think I wept, but I don't remember anything else.

Afterwards I don't know how long I slept. I was woken by the noise. Arthur and the carles were gone, had slipped quietly away without disturbing me. In the distance I could hear the clash of wood on wood, the clang of metal, the shouts of men, and knew what it was. I pulled on my britches, crawled out of the tent and stood up. At the end of the field, beyond the tents, was a small mound and some trees where Edwin and his troops had left their horses. I put some bread in my pouch, climbed up to the top where I could see what was happening and lay flat peering over the edge.

The river was broad and there were ships drawn up on the banks, a forest of masts and curved prows as far as I could see. Below me, in the curve of the river, on the flood plain, I could see the Landwaster's men glittering in their mail and polished helmets, and Harald himself, a tall figure standing beside the standard bearer carrying his banner – the Landwaster, a flying raven, black on white. I had a terrible feeling in my stomach, like hunger, only worse. Further along, where the river turned back on itself, Tostig's men were clustered around him, and his banner, the white stag on a green ground. The two armies were locked, shield to shield, the wall of wood flowing like the river, backwards and forwards, the thud of shield on shield. Men were fighting with swords and axes and behind them the archers were firing across the massed ranks. Where a man fell, another moved forward to replace him in the shield wall. Why, I kept thinking, did men regard this as honourable? A noble calling, to kill and be killed? It made no sense.

I could see Edwin's silver eagle fluttering above his position. It seemed to me that he had less men behind him than the Landwaster and as I watched I could see that they were being pushed back by the sheer weight of the Vikings who were screaming like berserkers, swinging their axes above their heads as they charged. There was a sudden movement on the right, where Morcar's men were fighting and the Landwaster's carles had somehow pushed round between Morcar and the river bank and were bearing down on the main army, threatening to surround them. Morcar, the younger and less experienced brother, was outmaneuvered. The shield wall broke and it was slaughter. I saw the moment Edwin knew he was going to lose, saw him give the signal and then he and Morcar and as many of their carles as still stood on their feet turned and made for the horses, running up the mound towards where I sat. I watched them disappear into the trees and heard them ride off leaving the field to Harald and his men. The marshland to the left was choked by the bodies of fleeing men and their pursuers.

There were many horses still tethered where we had left them. Mine was there and, next to it, was Arthur's beautiful, black destrier.

I didn't think of my own danger but, after they had all left and I had waited long enough, I walked down towards the battlefield. The fallen men were all being picked over for anything of value. Alive or dead they were stripped of their helmets, mail shirts, belts and weapons, even their rings and shoulder clasps. Somewhere I would find Arthur, I knew – wounded perhaps, and I could beg for his life, rather than leave his body to the carrion birds already circling. Was he a prisoner? Had he thrown himself into the river to swim to safety as I had seen some men do? Had he gone with Edwin on another horse?

I was still searching for Arthur among the dead, when one of Harald's men saw me. 'Hey, you!' he cried as I tried to run, but he grabbed me by the arm and I was marched off to the Norsemen's camp. Harald the Landwaster was cleaning his sword. No mean feat, given the blood that he had shed that day. But he looked up as they marched me past and bade the carles stop. 'I know you,' he said. 'You're the little scop I seized in Denmark. Tostig's little princeling!' He laughed. 'So, scop, what praise song will you compose now?'

I had to swallow the vomit that rose in my throat. No longer a girl, a woman, stinking of semen and virgin blood, those I loved most put to the sword, it was a wraith that smiled and spoke through her teeth. 'What words can celebrate the greatest warrior that ever lived?' and Harald put down his sword and said, 'Oh I can suggest a few.' I had forgotten his reputation for scaldic verses in the tradition

of the Boast. He thought for a moment and then began to
declaim.

> *'Even among the blizzards of steel,*
> *the king would never crouch faint-hearted*
> *in the shelter of his shield, but heave his sword*
> *aloft, Scourge of the Saxons, for the honour*
> *of Ellisev, to cleave the skulls of Saxon warriors.'*

'So, can you put that to music do you think?' he said, laughing as he put a blood-stained hand under my chin and tilted
my face up. 'You are intelligent and resourceful, my little
Danish changeling. You will survive.'

And I saw that he knew, had probably known all along.

Part Seven

Barriers of Ash and Steel

Against the barriers of ash and steel
he pitched his heart, the sinews of his sword-
arm wielding the Scourge of the Saxons.
When he was offered truce, he asked
what they would give him. 'Seven feet
of earth,' was the reply. 'No more –
no less.' A warrior's destiny, to be
buried where he fell, staining a part
of foreign soil with his blood, his bones
under the victor's feet, the final conquest.

Hadrada [KJ]

Ældyth was writing to her mother-in-law, Gytha, at Bosham, knowing that her letter would also be read by the Swan-neck. After she had made the necessary greetings and pleasantries, she began what was a difficult letter to write, and what she knew was going to be a difficult letter to read.

'I have grave news, which Harold has asked me to give to you, as he has left in haste. My brothers, the Earls Edwin and Morcar, have been defeated by the Norwegian King and Earl Tostig at Fulford, near York. They lost a great many of their men and have been forced to agree a truce with the Vikings. My youngest brother, Arthur, is among the fallen.'

She paused to keep herself from weeping. Tears were useless. When the news had arrived yesterday, Harold had had to be restrained. He had kicked the legs of the oak table in hall shouting 'Fuck them! Fuck them all!', so that the platters and glasses clattered on the table and the dogs had jumped up from the hearth, barking. Then he had hurried, almost running, from the hall calling for the archbishop, his most senior thegns, his scribes and messengers. The chaos of that scene could not be put in a letter.

'Harold left London within hours of the news and is going north with the utmost haste taking all his carles and recruiting the fyrde as he travels. He talks of reaching York in three days and has sent forward to have horses ready for him at every point along the road.'

He was facing a huge force, he had told her during their brief farewell, perhaps as many as eight thousand men even after the battle with Edwin and Morcar. Seasoned troops, Harold had said gravely, not untried recruits, all battle-hardened mercenaries from the Norwegian's many campaigns. Harold was putting his faith in the shield wall and the strength of his archers – better than those of his opponent, he claimed. There was also the element of surprise, if he could travel fast.

Without Harold, Ældyth felt vulnerable. There was now only Gyrth and Leofwine between her and the Norman threat. But the wind was still in the east and she prayed it stayed there until winter set in.

'Harold has asked me to send his greetings,' she ended. 'And tell you not to worry about the outcome. He is confident of winning ...'

But he was not, Aeldyth knew from the deepening worry

lines on his face. Harald of Norway was a serious opponent who had already slaughtered half of Edwin's army.

'. . . and he wanted me to assure you that he will deal fairly with Earl Tostig, with all the forbearance and respect due to a brother.'

That, too, was weighing on him. Ældyth hoped that she had been tactful enough, to spare Gytha too much anxiety; she had already lost her youngest daughter to the wasting sickness last year and Ældyth knew that she would fear for her sons' lives. What mother would not? Ældyth completed the letter with more reassurances and pleasantries, sealed it and turned to give it to one of her ladies. It was Hilde who came forward, Earl Leofwine's wife.

'I was thinking, Countess, that I might give both you and Countess Theo leave to go to your own manors for a while. You've seen little of your husbands for some months and they're likely to be in the south for longer now that the king's gone north again. Would you like that?'

Hilde smiled. 'We would indeed be pleased to go. There are affairs relating to our own lands that need to be dealt with and we both have children at home.'

'Will you tell Theo? My three other ladies will be quite enough.'

Hilde hesitated. 'And if the babe should come while we're away?'

'Lady Edith is here, and Lady Margaret and I am very well looked after by my Welsh ladies. And there's the arch-bishop in attendance. He's not going north.'

Hilde nodded, though there was still a worry line above her eyebrows. Had she been primed to oversee the birth to make sure no cuckoos were smuggled into the nest? Whenever the Godwins were around she felt watched. But perhaps she had imagined it. Seemingly satisfied, Hilde bowed out of the room with the letter.

Æeldyth's dream still hung over her. She had been more than relieved to know that both Edwin and Morcar had survived the battle, but it was all still in the balance. Edwin had written to her, bearing the news of Arthur's death, while the blood was still drying on his sword. 'Tell Harold,' he wrote in a hasty scrawl, 'We have lost too many men to give him any support and cannot jeopardise our own people by breaking the oaths we have sworn to the Norwegians, in case Harold, too, is defeated. The Norwegian king and Tostig have a formidable army – the biggest ever seen in England since the Great Viking Army of Cnut in our grandfather's time. But rest easy, sister, we will keep you safe, whatever the outcome.'

That Harold doubted the outcome, she knew. He told her that he believed that the Norse king was part of a trap to draw him north, 'keeping me in Northumbria, while the Norman duke, informed by my brother, presses me from the south.' Harold spoke matter-of-factly, as if this was something he had always known might happen. 'We have to crush Harald before he even gets a hold and make sure he never comes back.'

'And Tostig?'

Harold said nothing for a while and then, 'It's damnable. I loved him. We were allies under Edward. But something changed and I've racked my brains to know what. For the past few years he's been my enemy.'

'You were allies when he helped you kill my husband.' She spoke gently, putting into words something that had always been between them, feeling that it was time to lay it to rest.

'Gruffydd was harrying our borders, threatening peace, killing our own people – your own Mercian people. We did what we had to do.' He was looking at the floor while he spoke, but now he looked up at her. 'Did you love him?'

Æeldyth shook her head. 'But you grow fond of the people you share a bed and have children with.'

'That's true.'

Ældyth hoped that he might say more. Was he fond of her? But he changed the subject.

'So, I intend to leave this afternoon and go north as quickly as we can travel. We'll have to change horses along the road and there'll be precious little rest, but I reckon we can do the journey in three days and gather enough forces from the fyrde to face the Norwegian down.'

Ældyth could only see the risks. 'Prepare yourself,' he had said at the beginning of their conversation, and she knew what he meant. They all might be killed if the Norwegian Viking's reputation was true; her brothers, even Harold himself. She couldn't bear to think of that possibility, but the question niggled at the back of her mind. What might happen if they lost?

He got up to go and she stood up to say goodbye. He embraced her, though it was difficult to do that over her swelling stomach. Harold put his hand on it. 'Take care of my heir,' he said. 'I'm leaving Godwin and some of the best of my carles here to keep you safe. And Gyrth and Leofwine are guarding the south. If all goes well I should be back in two or three weeks, more or less.'

'I'll pray for you.' Ældyth made herself smile.

He kissed her on the cheek and turned to go, his pace increasing as he swung out of the room, calling to his carles as he went.

Ældyth put away Edwin's letter and closed her writing box. If Harold had calculated right, he would be a third of the way to York by now, riding as if all the inhabitants of hell were behind him. Ældyth closed her eyes and put her hands together on the table and prayed to God to keep him safe.

~ ~ ~

I was told that this time I was a hostage rather than a prisoner, and more hostages were expected to arrive from the city in the next few days as well as the tribute money agreed with Earl Edwin. I was taken back to the camp where they had drawn up the boats. The sunlight glinted on their gilded prows, belying their dreadful purpose. Fires had been lit in the field and the men were roasting sheep captured from the nearby farms they had raided. I was told, ordered, to entertain them with stories and songs which I had never felt less inclined to do. Arthur was in my mind and an ache in my chest and head as though grief was an illness that afflicted my body like fever.

But there were many Danish tales I could tell, and one in particular that Ellisev had liked, and that had been well received at Harold Godwinson's court. I called it *Út-Lagr,* the outlaw, and it was a lament about an unhappily married woman who lives on an island and is in love with a man who has been outlawed to another island, surrounded by fenland, protected by fierce warriors. She's expecting his child, but knows that if he comes to take her, he will be killed by her family and if she goes to him, his people will kill her and the child she's carrying. She sits weeping, watching the rain fall, sick with longing for her lover, but she knows what the end will be. *'It is easy to sever what has never been joined.'* The violent men that surrounded them both, would make sure of it.

It seemed that the Viking army liked the tale, because I was thrown a good collection of coins afterwards. It never ceases to amaze me that men who live by the sword should be so susceptible to romance, but I imagine that many of their lives and loves are like the couple in the story.

They kept me closely observed. When Earl Edwin came for talks with the Landwaster they made sure that I remained hidden at the landing place. There were three other hostages, taken at the battle, or just after. A farmer, too old to fight, had resisted the men who came to take his sheep, but, rather than kill him, they had seized him, along with his two sons. It seemed that Tostig at least, wanted to enforce cooperation with the people of his old earldom by threat rather than burn their dwellings and lay waste to their land. Listening to the men's conversations, it was clear that Tostig and the Landwaster had done a deal; Tostig was to have his earldom back and occupy the throne as regent for Harald. There had been a precedent, it seemed, when the Landwaster's cousin Cnut had ruled England, Norway and Denmark, appointing his relatives as regents.

The weather was beautiful, hot and still, and the carles had taken off their helmets. chain mail and leather jerkins and were sitting in the river meadows in their tunics. After several days of idling the Landwaster told them they were to go to the fields outside York to receive the hostages and the tributes, which would be brought out to them, escorted by Edwin as a pledge for his oaths. Then the earl would be allowed to go in peace. A large body of carles were assigned to guard the ships, already filled with the loot from the battlefield, and too precious to risk a raid from the rear. Harald and Tostig were in a merry mood and both left their chain mail behind at the ships with their men when they went to the river bridge to meet Edwin, wearing only their tunics and helmets.

I followed them along the edge of the river, unchallenged, unremarked, for who notices a boy child armed only with a lyre? After we had sat for an hour or so, the hour of the meeting already gone, there was a dust cloud in the distance on the road coming from York.

'That will be them,' I heard Tostig say. 'They've taken their time.'

Then, out of the dust came – not dray carts and a ragged band of hostages behind Earl Edwin's banner – but the cold glitter of sunlight on helmets, the jingle of chain mail carrying on the breeze, and there, on the other side of the river, an army was approaching.

The Landwaster swore in Norwegian and called to one of his men to go back to the boats for his mail coat, the one he called 'Emma', and summon the rest of the men. But the army was on them before the messenger had even left the field, and before any of Harald's men could recover their own armour and put it on.

Under cover of the confusion I slipped into the willows growing over the river near the bridge. There were tall reeds I could hide amongst. I wrapped myself in my green cloak and watched as eleven hearth-carles rode up to the bridge on their destriers, all in chain mail with steel helmets, but wearing red tabards bearing a golden dragon – the King of England's colours. One of their number rode out in front, stopped at the approach to the bridge, and asked to speak to the King of Norway and Earl Tostig. His voice sounded strangely familiar. When they came a little way towards the other side of the bridge, the carle said that he had a message from the King of England for Earl Tostig.

'And what would that be?' Tostig called over the water, in a jeering kind of voice.

'The king promises to restore all the earl's honours and lands and grant pardon for his treason, if he will lay down his arms and go in peace.'

Tostig made a rude sign. 'Tell the king he can go fuck himself,' he said, turning his back as he did so.

Then Harald stepped forward, leaning on the pommel of his sword as he surveyed the men on the other side of the river. 'And does the King of England have a message for me?' he asked.

'He does,' the mounted warrior replied.

'What will he give me to lay down my arms and go in peace?'

'Seven feet of English earth,' was the terse reply. And the carle turned his horse and the group galloped back to the main army.

Harald walked to where Tostig was standing. 'The thegn spoke very fairly to you. Weren't you tempted?'

'Thegn?' Tostig spat. 'That was my brother!'

Harald's eyes turned to steel. 'You should have said so. We could have killed them all and there would have been no need to fight.'

Then I saw the Saxons begin to group themselves for battle, shield to shield. King Harold's red armed-man standard was furthest away from me on the other side of the river; Tostig's white stag in front of me. I slid down the bank into the reeds where I cowered under my green cloak as the fighting began. The shouting, the clash of steel on wood, the smell of blood – the reek of it was like an abbatoir. It was all too familiar. I shut my eyes and my ears and curled up as tightly as I could, but I was back in my father's hall, behind the tapestry – the stench, the screams, the crunch of bone . . . and any moment I would be discovered and feel the bite of steel in my own body. Death seemed inevitable, I was so close to the fighting.

And then it seemed quieter, as if there was less fury. I heard voices on the river bank above me. King Harold, his voice harder and colder than I had ever heard it. If he was here, then perhaps I was safe. I crawled cautiously to the lip of the bank where the willows grew and peered over, still in their shade. Harold was standing, a bold figure in his chain mail and leather jerkin, with his carles crowded behind him under the banner. I recognised the captain of his carles, Brynn, standing beside him, his sword raised as if to protect the king.

Opposite, with his own men, was Earl Tostig, his blond hair shifting in the wind. He was not wearing a helmet and there was blood among the fair strands as if he had brushed his hair back from his eyes with a blood-stained hand. Both men were panting with the effort of battle.

Harold's carles began to move in front of him for protection, but he gestured them away. I heard him say, 'Why, Tostig, why?'

'I've come for what's mine by right!'

'I'd have given you an earldom gladly if you'd asked. You've no right to the kingdom.'

Tostig laughed, resting on his pommel, his sword point down on the ground. He looked weary. 'The king promised me. For services rendered.'

'Edward promised the throne to everyone. And you know as well as I that it wasn't his to promise. The Witan makes the choice. You weren't there when they decided.'

Tostig was smiling oddly. 'Smooth-tongued Harold, always with the reasonable answer. I have as much right to the throne of England as you do. Why shouldn't I have it?'

'Is it worth the slaughter of so many good men?'

'Only one man needs to die.'

Tostig grasped his sword hilt and began to swing it, but Harold was quicker. His weapon flashed in the air, and seemed to twist as it turned to descend, slicing into Tostig's shoulder and down into his ribs, splattering blood on those nearest to him. There was a sigh of air escaping from Tostig's chest as he crumpled to the ground. Then, as Harold raised his sword again, it was Brynn who stepped forward and plunged his own sword into Tostig's heart. I saw the spurt of blood and felt the shock of it as if it had been my own.

Harold was on his knees beside his brother, his hand on Tostig's head. He was murmuring to himself and I saw him make the sign of the cross over him. To kill a brother is not only to commit the ultimate sin in Christianity, but also to offend all the Fates.

Brynn was wiping Tostig's blood from his sword. 'You

did what was necessary. And, anyway, it was my blow that put an end to his life.'

Harold stood up and clapped him on the shoulder. 'It's over now. You're a good man, Brynn. God go with you.'

It was Brynn who discovered me and strode across to grasp me by the hair, pulling me from my hiding place. I felt no fear, only numbness. He looked me up and down.

'What're you doing here? You're only a lad, barely older than my own.' He paused. 'I know you though.' His eyes went to the leather bag on my back. 'You're the little scop who plays in the hall. What the fucking hell are you doing here?'

I opened my mouth, but no words came. In front of me was a scene of carnage. Tostig's carles were sitting on the ground around his body, weary and defeated. Some of Harold's men were beginning to drag the corpses into piles, stripping their armour, their helmets and swords and setting them aside.

'This is no place for a child.' Brynn said.

'Is Harald of Norway dead?' I hardly recognised the voice that escaped from my mouth.

'He is.' Brynn jerked his head to the left of him. 'He took an arrow in his throat.'

I slipped out of Brynn's grasp and over the blood-stained grass to where a group of Norse warriors were sitting. As I drew nearer, I recognised one of them as Harald's son, the others as Tostig's boys – the young thegns he had been so proud of when I played for the Viking in his hall. In front of them, Harald's body lay, awkwardly stretched out on the ground. He had taken several serious wounds to his arms and legs before he died. There was an arrow at the angle of his jaw and the soil around him was soaked with his blood. His people would believe him a hero. I looked at my father's killer, no longer the great warrior, just an ageing man, his flesh falling away in death, his face lined and scored by battle. He was pale from loss of blood. I should have felt triumph, should have gloated over his fallen body, but I didn't. I felt completely empty.

Brynn was shouting at the boys as I turned to cross the bridge to walk back towards the city.

'The king's given orders that you're to be taken to the ships and may go back to your own country, on the condition that you swear an oath never to invade our country again.'

One of the boys was weeping. The other said, 'How could we do that since you've killed the best of our warriors? We came with two hundred ships and there are scarce enough of us left for twenty.'

'Can I take my father's body back to my mother?' The weeping boy asked. It was Harald's son Olav.

'No.' Brynn's voice was hard. 'The king has ordered that he be left here with his men.' He turned and walked away, calling to a group of men who had arrived with a cart. 'You! You're to take Earl Tostig's body to the Minster.'

The funeral pyres burned all night and the air was tainted with the stench of burning flesh. The following morning, they buried Tostig in the crypt with all the honours due to the king's brother, rather than a traitor whose actions had killed thousands of good men – his own and his brother's. I could see Harold's face, as Tostig's coffin was carried past towards the altar, and it was impassive, not a single emotion flickered across it, not a muscle twitched. But afterwards, as I sat near the fire in the hall, in the shadows out of sight, I heard the men talking.

'It's bad luck to kill a brother.'

'He deserved it. But the king doesn't seem to care'.

'Oh, he does.' It was Brynn's voice. 'He would have done

anything to avoid it, but Tostig deliberately sought him out on the battlefield, told his own carles to stand back and leave the king to him. And I saw the king's grief as he dealt him the blow. That's why I stepped in, to deal the final stroke while Tostig still lived.'

'He killed his brother though. Tostig wouldn't have survived the sword-strike Harold gave him. It was butchery.'

'Whatever you think, you must never speak of it. The last stroke was mine.' Brynn sounded grim and final.

'What I want to know,' one of the men said, 'is why York surrendered so easily to the Vikings so soon after they'd sworn allegiance to Harold at Easter?'

Another man answered him. 'It's my opinion there's still men here that supported Tostig. Not all Northumbrians rebelled.'

Brynn sighed. 'The north's a wild land that won't be easily subdued. Morcar will have a hard road ahead of him.'

The men went off to fetch their bed rolls, but Brynn sat for a much longer time, gazing into the fire. Then he got up to go, slowly, as if his body ached from the effort. He looked into the shadows, directly at me.

'Time you were asleep too, stripling.'

I stood up. He was still looking at me.

'What I want to know is, what's a youngster like you doing in all this? Your place is at the court.'

'I was with Earl Edwin's brother, Arthur, at Fulford when the Norsemen won the battle and killed my friend. I was taken prisoner.'

'Poor sod,' Brynn said. His voice was kind, but weary. He ruffled my hair with his hand. 'God bless you.'

I had thought my heart already broken, but it broke again at his kind words. Curled up in my cloak in a corner of the hearth, my mind re-lived every moment of the past days, the people I had most loved put to the sword. I didn't even know if Thorkild was alive. Had he taken part in the battle?

My lyre was pressing hard against my shoulder as I tried
to get comfortable. But how could I ever play music again?
What was it that Merithien had said? *'You have a destiny.'*
Her voice floated across my waking nightmare. *'You have
seen terrible things and people you love have died a hard death.
There will be more bloodshed before you are a grown woman, but
you have the strength and the grace to survive.'* Did I? At that
moment it seemed impossible. But, since I was alive, I had
no choice but to try.

~ ~ ~

Ældyth's letter was unsettling and neither Eadgifu nor
Gytha had yet decided what to do about it. Eadgifu had
agreed, when Harold was here, to go to Waltham, since he
didn't want her in London. She could see his reasoning;
the queen's presence upset her – to see Ældyth and Harold
together was torture. So, it was better for all of them to be
apart. But Waltham wasn't far from the palace in London,
close enough to Harold for him to visit, and she knew he
would. Waltham Abbey was sacred to him – it was a place
of miracles.

Both Eadgifu and Gytha were reluctant to leave Bosham.
Autumn was such a beautiful time. They had been harvesting
the apples from the orchard, storing them in barrels, and the
men were out in the fields bringing in the harvest. Eadgifu
felt thankful for such abundance. And she was free to take
pleasure in it – getting a wet nurse for Ulf had been a great
relief. He was a happy, sunny baby now that his stomach
was full.

As she walked in the orchard, Eadgifu was aware that
something had changed, but at first she didn't know what it
was. It was only when she went out of the gate and turned
towards the sea that she realised; the wind had changed. It

216

was no longer a cool breeze blowing from the east, but a warm, purposeful wind coming directly from France.

When she came in she went straight to Gytha's room. 'I think we need to leave here soon,' she said, surprised by the urgency in her voice. She told Gytha about the wind's new direction and what it might mean. 'It makes me feel uneasy. I'd feel safer if we were further north, nearer to Harold.'

'If you think so,' Gytha said, nodding her head.

Eadgifu was surprised that she was so compliant, but she had been very subdued since the news of Tostig's death. Whatever the reason, Gytha raised no objections to their removal. Eadgifu wondered if she, too, was feeling uneasy. 'It will be a long, difficult journey for the children. Harold wants me at Waltham, not London.'

Gytha smiled as if she knew why. 'So we must spend some nights on the way there – make it easy for ourselves. I should like to see Hildburgh again.'

There was a great deal to do to close up Bosham for the winter, leaving it in the charge of the stewards, housekeepers, falconers and stable men and a few carles to guard it. There were instructions to leave behind and arrangements to make for pay and provisions. And there were two babies to prepare for travel. The girl, whose name was Ann, was loath to leave her family, but ultimately persuaded with a gift of money.

Eadgifu thought long and hard about the money. Harold's treasury at Bosham was full of gold and silver, not something to risk if there was an invasion. Suppose William landed here first? The carles dug a pit under the cellars and one chest of coins and some goblets and jewellery were hidden there, the paving slabs replaced as if they had never been disturbed. The rest was shared between Gytha's litter and the cart containing Eadgifu's belongings and the children.

It took three days, travelling slowly, to reach Hildburgh, Gytha's Kentish manor. It was not fortified, as Bosham was, just a wooden hall with two stories and a thatched roof, with smaller wooden buildings surrounding it for the children, the servants and the carles. Hildburgh was one of Gytha's favourite places, built on a low rise above a loop of the river, with the church and its small monastery down on the plain below. It had been one of Godwin's first strongholds, a manor he had inherited in the time of Athelstan, before he gave his allegiance to Cnut, before his marriage to Gytha.

It felt safe, with a pastoral calm, cows and sheep in the fields surrounding it, crows returning to their roosts in the trees in early evening, and the smoke rising gently to the sky from the hall. 'Simple beginnings,' Gytha said, as she drank her mead and addressed a spit-roasted chicken. 'But he was always ambitious. Not a Saxon hall, but a king's palace – that's what he wanted. And that's what he got in the end.' She was full of reminiscence. Tostig's name was never mentioned.

In bed, in one of the ground floor rooms, Eadgifu watched the light from the moon move across the quilt, then across the floor as she lay awake. The moon must be almost full. She missed Harold and the uneasy feeling she'd had, since Ælldyth's letter had come, refused to go away. But soon they would be in Waltham, her own manor, and Harold would surely come.

~ ~ ~

'Self-punishment,' Archbishop Stigand said, 'is not advisable. Punishment must be left to God who, alone, knows how to apportion blame. What you must do is to make amends.'

'You mean money, don't you.' Edith, still grieving Tostig's death and filled with anger, said caustically. 'You want me to endow an abbey and then it will be all right.'

Stigand looked offended. 'I didn't say that. But, if my Lady felt inclined to do so – it would be, after all, for the glory of God.'

It seemed to Edith that the church had its own system of weregild for sins. If you paid enough you could even get away with murder. She thought of her brother Swein, who had died while walking barefoot to Jerusalem to expunge the murder of his cousin. No doubt the Pope would have advised him to endow an abbey on his return. And what, she wondered, would they ask of Harold for the death of his brother?

'I'll give it some thought,' Edith said.

'And prayer, my Lady,' Stigand lowered his head in a semblance of humility.

He irritated Edith. She could always smell the odour of hypocrisy when he was near her. He lived like a prince, was openly guilty of pluralism, holding the Sees of both Canterbury and Winchester against the laws of the church, and yet he always seemed to want more. But, since he was a worldly cleric, Edith had deemed it wise to confess her sins to him. Now, she must endure his response, which was a kind of spiritual blackmail as well as a personal humiliation.

Mathilde had entered the room and signalled that she wanted speech with her.

'What is it?'

Mathilde was trembling. 'A messenger, my Lady. He needs to speak to you urgently.'

'Send him in,' Edith said. It was a welcome diversion.

The messenger was a young man, in Harold's livery, looking as close to exhaustion as anyone she'd ever seen. He was out of breath and coughed when he spoke. 'The Norman duke has arrived,' he said. 'Many, many ships – more than five hundred. He's landed at Pevensey and is camped in the old Roman fort there. The king needs to know.'

Edith's stomach clenched in panic as she listened. That

William should come when Harold was at the other end of England! But then, she acknowledged with a bleak honesty, perhaps that was intentional, perhaps Tostig had been in league with him all along.

'I must try to raise my men and make preparations. Most of them have gone home already,' Stigand said, rising to his feet. 'Will you excuse me, my Lady?'

Edith dismissed him, her mind already leaping ahead. She shouted for scribes. Gyrth and Leofwine needed to be told. Harold would want a full meeting of the Council when he got back. She decided to write to him herself. He would need to be reassured that his mother and the Swan-neck were at Hildburgh and not Bosham. They too would need to know what had happened. Heaven only knew when Harold would return from the north. She took a moment to pause and calm herself. There were people Edith needed to consult and she needed to clear her thoughts.

She turned to Mathilde. 'Can you make sure the queen is informed?' Mathilde bowed and went silently out of the room.

Now Edith would have to make sure that London was secured, in case William marched north immediately. With Harold away, what did he have to lose?

~ ~ ~

I found it hard to realise that it was only five months since we had left York. So much has happened in that time. After the battle I was allowed to stay in the abbey with the thegns and the king's party. The carles were in a tented encampment outside the city walls and the wounded, of which there were many, were in the abbey infirmary being tended by the holy brothers. Arthur was not among them. Nor was my brother. The steward in charge of the young thegns told me that Thorkild had been left behind in London at the request of the king as part of the queen's guard. I wondered privately whether it was because Harold didn't trust Thorkild and Wulfgar to fight against Tostig.

The first thing I did, when I was given leave, was to walk down into the old quarter to find Ingrid. The houses there were smaller than I remembered and poorer. It was as if I'd become a different person in the intervening months. Ingrid was sitting on the threshold of her house, gutting fish into a bowl and then putting the flesh to soak in salt water. I'd seen her do it a thousand times. I watched her for a moment until she felt my eye on her and then she looked up.

'Hannë!' She put down the bowl and sprang up. She came towards me as if she would embrace me, but she stopped at the last moment and looked at her hands, silvered with fish scales and smeared with herring blood. She laughed. 'Hannë! You look so prosperous. I wouldn't have known you in the street. Did you come with the king's army?'

I'd brought some mead from the market, and we sat and drank it in the doorway while she carried on cleaning the fish and I told her what had been happening to me since we had last seen each other.

'Your fortunes have changed, I think,' she said with a smile, looking across at me.

I nodded. 'I was freed by the queen little more than a sennight ago, after my older brother was discovered alive. He's now one of the king's thegns. Harold has been very good to us both.'

'Well, he's a half-dane, so he should be. Not a traitor like his brother.'

'You know Earl Tostig's dead?'

'With the Landwaster. Yes. That was a good day's work. There will be no tears shed for him here. We've been so afraid. Ansgar said we'd have to leave rather than live under his rule.' She looked at me very closely. 'Are you happy Hannë?'

I couldn't meet her gaze. 'A boy I cared about died in the battle.'

Ingrid slid across the wooden step, wiped her hands on her apron and put her arm around me, murmuring words my mother used to say to us when we were children – nursery words to comfort a child who is hurt. I cried a little and allowed her to comfort me.

'You're still living as Hari, I see.'

'It's easier.'

We talked about the children, Ansgar's work in the tannery, and then I stood up to go.

'Will you not stay and eat with us? They'll be back soon.'

I shook my head. My heart was too full of tears. 'I'm expected back to the king's hall. But I'll come again before we leave.'

'Wait,' she said, and went inside. She returned with the silver cup in her hands. 'You must take this back. I was so cross when I found it after you'd left. How could you leave something so valuable, when you yourself had need of it?'

'I left it for you and your family. I'm well provided for. You might need it in the future. It's for you.'

She put her arms around me again and kissed me and I walked away up the hill, back to the abbey, though I didn't go straight there. I climbed up the ramparts to my old viewing point and looked out over the meadows where the river curved like a silver fish in the autumn light. When I was with Ingrid and her family I felt at home, among my own people. Was it time to go back? To see what was left? King Sweyn had been an enemy of my father when a throne was at stake, but he'd been kind to Thorkild. Then there were other lands I'd never been to, over the shining sea, waiting to be discovered – the 'foreign lands' that Merithien had foretold. And who was the queen I was to serve 'in great prosperity'?

Both Edwin and Morcar were at dinner in hall that night, with the Archbishop of York. The conversation, what I could hear of it, was terse and business-like. I sat among the black-robed brothers at the lower tables and I knew I'd be expected to play later on. I was running over in my head what might be suitable, when a messenger came in to deliver a letter for Harold. There was a sudden lull in the conversation. It was curious for a messenger to arrive so late. He strode forward, brushing aside the steward. It was from the Lady Edith, he said, to be delivered into the king's hands.

Harold opened it, unconcerned, but then, as he read, he became very still. He gave the letter to Earl Edwin beside him and then put his head in his hands. When he lifted it up again, I don't think I've ever seen a man look so weary.

'I can't help you,' Edwin said. His voice sounded sullen. 'My army's in tatters. I've barely enough men left to guard my own borders.'

Harold's expression changed to one of resolution. He looked like a man who has seen his own doom and knows he must go to meet it.

'I need to talk to Brynn,' he said, and got up and left the hall.

Part Eight

Nightmare and Lament

A Geat woman too   sang out in grief;
with hair bound up,   she unburdened herself
of her worst fears,   a wild litany
of nightmare and lament: her nation invaded,
enemies on the rampage,   bodies in piles,
slavery and abasement.

Beowulf, l. 3150, trans Seamus Heaney

Harold was reading out to the Council the letter he had received from the Norman duke in answer to his request that the duke agree to leave the kingdom and make treaty with him. '*Fitting greetings, O king, from the duke, whom you are forcing unjustly to do wrong. And this is so, because as many bear witness, King Edward with the assent of his people and the advice of his nobles, promised and decreed that William should be his heir.*' Harold put it down on the table. 'And so it goes on with the same old lies. But he won't budge. There's no prospect of any meeting with him, or of an agreement.' He gave a weary sigh. 'I'd hoped to resolve it otherwise, but we'll have to fight.'

The Council meeting was tense and angry. There was an atmosphere Ældyth had never felt before. Gyrth and Leofwine were there with Harold, Archbishop Stigand and two or three bishops, one of whom said a prayer. Harold's captain of the carles was sitting next to the scribe at the end of the table, close to Ealdorman Bryhtnoth and the high reeves of Sussex and Kent who sat with Edith on the other side.

'How many men can we raise?' Harold asked, his voice flat. 'William will have at least six thousand and he's had time to dig himself in.'

One of the bishops said, 'He's already built a fort at Hastings, but he seems in no hurry to move further inland.'

Harold nodded, busy with his own thoughts.

Gyrth shifted restlessly in his chair. 'It's unwise to move quickly, Harold. You're exhausted and so are your carles, having just fought a long battle and been marched up and down the country at speed.'

'The best strategy is to take him by surprise – he thinks we're still in the north.'

'The best strategy is to rest for a few days and wait for reinforcements to arrive. The whole of the fyrde hasn't come in yet. Maybe as many as two or three thousand.'

Leofwine agreed. 'He won't move much away from the coast. Gyrth and I can keep him penned in until you're ready. Our carles are still fresh and we can gather about three thousand between us.'

Harold looked undecided, running his hand over his moustaches, staring down at a parchment on the table where he had written notes and drawn a quick diagram. 'We're all agreed on Senlac Hill?'

There was a murmur of agreement.

'We'd have the advantage of the trees as cover, and the slope. William's method is to fight on horseback, but he'd be continually trying to ride uphill which will tire the horses.

And he can't get round us because of the marshland on the flank.'

'It's the best plan,' Leofwine said.

'But it'll be useless if William reaches the hill before we do.' Harold was reasoning aloud. 'We have' – Harold stressed the word – 'we have to go quickly and gain the element of surprise.'

'I still think it's madness,' Gyrth said abruptly. 'You're too tired to think clearly. Taking weary troops into battle against a fresh Norman army! They're not a fyrde. They're all mercenaries and William's own elite carles, seasoned fighters and they've been sunning themselves on the south coast for more than two weeks.' His voice rose as he spoke. 'Listen to me, Harold. For God's sake, listen to reason.'

Harold looked at his brother and Ældyth thought there was just a flicker of amusement, tempered with affection, as his eyes met Gyrth's. 'It's a gamble, I grant you that. But it's a gamble I think I can win.'

Leofwine interrupted. 'In a day or so, Edwin and Morcar may reach us with whatever they can muster of their forces. Earl Waltheof has promised us his carles too. Another three thousand men would make all certain.'

Harold's eyes flicked to Ældyth and then round the room. 'I don't have any confidence that the Mercian earls will come, after their mauling by the Vikings and our brother.' He sighed. Ældyth noticed that he was turning the ring of state round and round on his finger. He pursed his mouth up for a moment as though tasting something bitter. 'We'll go,' he said suddenly. 'Get everything ready, we leave tomorrow morning.'

Gyrth looked as if he was going to argue again, but Harold just got up and turned away. He left the room without saying anything to anyone.

Leofwine sighed and turned to Gyrth. 'He's getting older, and he still thinks he's immortal.'

Gyrth's expression was grim. 'But he'll drag us with him, and we aren't.'

The next morning, early, Harold came to Ældyth's room before she was dressed, still with her hair down around her shoulders.

'I've come to take my leave,' he said. 'Don't worry about me, it will be all right. I went to Waltham on my way back to London and spent an hour praying there. I've trusted my soul to God.'

Ældyth didn't know what to say. Her tongue felt numb, but she managed to form the words, 'I will pray for you and for your success.'

'Thank you. I've left sufficient carles to ensure your safety and Edith's.' He turned away towards the door. Then, just as she thought he was gone, he suddenly turned back towards her and said, 'I hope I have treated you well, Ældyth.'

'Very well, my lord.'

He looked at her intently for a few moments and then strode forward to take her into his arms for a long, passion-ate, ruthless, kiss. Then he almost threw her away from him, turned and walked out of the door without looking back.

As soon as she could compose herself, after he was gone, Ældyth called for her writing box and began an angry letter to Edwin. She sensed that he was dragging his feet and wanted him, and Morcar, to recognise the urgency of the situation. Ældyth was past caring whether she offended them. 'I've kept my part of the bargain by marrying Harold,' she wrote, 'and you undertook to support him on your part. But I've yet to see it. If William of Normandy wins, we lose the kingdom. Doesn't that matter to you? This is no longer an argument between the Godwins – it's a matter of survival.' But Ældyth no longer had any faith that they would come. She knew her brothers better now than she had formerly. She had thought herself a peace-weaver, but Edwin and Morcar had used her as a gaming piece in a game of their own making. It was one they were, evidently, still playing.

~ ~ ~

I've been left behind. Barely more than a week back in London, after a gruelling march from the north, Harold summoned his weary carles and departed. Thorkild was proud to go with them as one of Godwin's thegns. He came to say goodbye but stood looking at me for a moment with a kind of embarrassment before he spoke, as if he was uncomfortable in my company. Then he said, 'I hate leaving you here like this, among slaves and servants.'

I smiled at him, in sympathy with his awkwardness. 'You don't know me very well, do you?' I said. 'Nor I, you. We've both changed since the Landwaster arrived in Nordjylland three years ago'

'One day I'll be able to take care of you, Hannë.'

'Has it occurred to you that I don't need taking care of?'

He looked angry. 'It's unseemly for you to be among common carles. You're too innocent to take care of yourself.'

I stared at him and almost laughed at his lack of understanding. 'Innocent? When I was twelve I watched my parents and my sisters butchered in their own hall. I lived for three years as a slave evading licentious men. I was at Fulford when the Landwaster slaughtered the Mercian army and I saw the bodies lying so deep in the marshes you could walk over them dry-shod. At Stamford Bridge I watched the Viking army scythed like grass before Harold Godwinson's swordsmen. But I lived through it all and survived.' Now I was the one who was angry. 'And you would still call me innocent? I would think myself a blood-maiden!' I didn't add, 'and no longer a virgin'.

Thorkild was white-faced. 'But is this the life you want for yourself? When I come back from this battle – and I will come back – we'll talk more.'

I just shook my head. 'Fight well, Thorkild. May the gods be with you.'

He smiled uncertainly and put his hand up to the silver hammer of Thor he wore on a leather thong under his tunic. 'I've made my peace with the fates.'

I reached up and kissed him. He was going to be tall when he finished growing. Thorkild the Tall.

We said nothing as he turned to leave. Goodbye was too final a word for either of us to say.

After he'd gone, I walked across the fields towards the marshes. I sat on a fallen tree trunk and got out my lyre to tune it in the late autumn sunshine. The marshes were unusually silent, but I knew that later, as the light faded, the sky would darken with clouds of birds, swirling and blending, scarving themselves through the dusk in a last dance before they reached their roosts. Overhead, an arrowhead of geese went honking south, just as they had in my homeland, fleeing the approaching winter cold, and I wanted, desperately, to follow them. The need to fly was an ache in my bones. The urge was difficult to resist. Was this how birds knew it was time to move from one place to another? Something was telling me that it was time to make a new story. Stories are a kind of magic that can transform one thing into another, the ache of wanderlust and the search for a homeland can become a voyage of words, even the creation of a paradise, in the firelight of a king's hall. The gods have seen fit to give the gift to me and I must honour them. But where am I to go and how am I to get there?

~ ~ ~

Edith restrained herself until the men had gone and everything felt empty and forlorn. The palace corridors echoed with the absence of feet. It was then, trembling with unfamiliar emotions, that she took the first part of the *Vita Edwardi Regis* from its wrappings and began to read. She hadn't known what to expect, had left it to Goscelin to shape their family narrative in polished prose and verse. At first sight, his handwriting was uneven for a monastery-trained scribe – a bold, irregular italic hand, yet still shaping elegant Latin phrases which unfolded across the page in a tracery of black ink.

With a shock, she realised that he had begun with an invocation to a muse who seemed suspiciously like herself. *'Wake Muse, with all your maids attended, rise from your sleep.'* This muse was apparently a *'mistress of truth, to falsehood stranger.'* Holding her breath, Edith read his praise-song to his patroness, herself. *'A woman whose mind is schooled in all the arts, impatient of worldly things.'* He went on to describe their first meeting in prose. *'On first acquaintance it was her education that surprised, matched by her modesty and the beauty of her body.'* Had he thought her beautiful?

Such hyperbole was perhaps to be expected, but as she went on, there was more – little secret messages that seemed to be embedded in the text, personal phrases aimed directly at herself. One in particular appeared to refer to his present state, separated from her and from love. *'When pens lie idle, the mind decays and my own self laments its ruined state.'* She remembered the way he had placed the manuscript in her hands, his whispered words.

Edith tried to prevent her tears from falling onto the parchment and blotting the ink. She read it over again and again, particularly this one sentence, *'and while she lives, so then do I, and that's enough.'*

When Mathilde came to put her to bed, she found Edith in tears, but as happy as she had ever been in her life. Goscelin loved her; Edith was sure of that.

~ ~ ~

I've been feeling lost without Arthur. I can't help thinking, particularly at night when all is silent and there are no distractions, what might have happened if he had come back from Fulford. And then, worse, what had become of him on the battlefield – images of his mangled body bleeding through the terrible dreams that make a torment of my sleep. I keep seeing his dark, straight hair and the pale, soft skin of his face with just the beginnings of a moustache above his lip. I have prayed to the wælcyrge to take Arthur to the resting place of valiant warriors. But then, as he was a Christian, I suppose I should pray that the angels will take him to heaven. When I say it to myself like that, they seem almost the same thing, but in translation.

Was it love that I felt for him? Those strange feelings I couldn't understand? There's no one to ask. In the middle of some of the worst nights I begin to long for my mother – something I've never allowed myself to do in the past because it's too sad and I can't bear it. I'm missing Thorkild too and worrying about him. He's never been in a major battle before and I know what he faces. Am I to lose my only remaining family member?

I'm not the only one to worry about the outcome of the battle.

'Have you thought,' Lady Margaret asked this morning as we sat in the solar waiting for the queen. 'Have you thought what would happen if things go awry?'

I nodded. 'But perhaps that's because I've lived in a place where everything did go wrong. I've never trusted anything since. One moment we were a happy family, the sun came up in the morning, and the tides went in and out in an orderly way, and then the Landwaster arrived, killed almost everyone, burned the town to the ground and took me away within the space of a few hours. I think, after that, nothing will seem safe any more.'

I've been spending more time with Lady Margaret since I came back from York. The revelation of my relationship with Thorkild has altered my standing in the court. I'm no longer a slave, but a young person of good family, distantly related to the king. I've talked to her about it. She is the granddaughter of a king, and I too have a king for a grandfather, so we are more equal. Only a little more though, for Margaret is the official guest of the king, lady in waiting to the queen, and I am but an itinerant scop, of no consequence whatever.

'What will you do if William wins?' Margaret asked suddenly.

Her Saxon has improved but she still speaks with a strange, often abrupt, formality.

I answered vaguely, for the truth is I have no idea. 'Go back to Denmark or Norway perhaps? Somewhere different. A new life. What about you?'

'I have family in Hungaria, and in Kievan Rus. But there is my mother and sister in the Abbey at Winchester, and my brother Edgar is here, the last of Æthelred's line. Would William kill him? Or send him back into exile? I think perhaps my duty is to stay with him. My mother will definitely stay.'

Margaret seemed to think that her brother would be the heir to the throne, but I wondered whether the Witan might choose one of Harold's brothers, Gyrth or Leofwine, or even his eldest son Godwin, rather than Edgar – an even younger boy – still little more than a child. It was worrying that there was no one who was an obvious successor to Harold. I even wondered whether the Mercian earls might have their eyes on the throne.

I sighed. 'We must just hope that Harold is the one to win. I saw him fight at Stamford Bridge and he's a clever and courageous warrior.'

Margaret agreed. But our spirits didn't lift. The brothers in the Abbey are apparently praying all day and night for victory. Everywhere in the palace there's an atmosphere of gloom tinged with fear. Autumn is wearing in towards winter with shorter, darker days and all our thoughts and hopes are on King Harold's army going to battle against the Norman invaders. I prayed to Thor last night, for my brother Thorkild. May he live.

~ ~ ~

It was evening, already dark. Gytha and Eadgifu were sitting beside the fire sewing. There was a hammering on the door and Eadgifu's steward opened it to find Brynn with Godwin, Edmund and a few carles. One look at their faces when they came into the hall told Eadgifu everything. Godwin sat down on a bench and put his head down on the table. His arm was bleeding.

'I'm afraid the king's dead, my Lady,' Brynn said. A tear ran down the side of his weathered cheek. 'He ordered me away when he saw that all was lost. "Take Godwin and Edmund and go," he said to me. He wouldn't hear any different.'

'I didn't want to go,' Godwin said, raising his head. 'It was a cowardly thing to do. I should have stayed with my father.'

'Aye and died with him,' Brynn said, raising his voice. 'What good would that do, and you the eldest son of his line. Who else could he trust to leave his kingdom to? How could you fight if you were dead?'

'What happened?' Eadgifu asked, hardly able to control her voice. She was amazed to find that it was anger, not grief, that was running through her. Not even anger. Pure uncontrollable rage.

'Harold should have won. He got the best position – he beat William to the top of Senlac Hill, looking down on the Normans, with the trees behind him and the marshes at the bottom. But somehow, William had got wind of Harold's plan and he was waiting there for him, had been there below the hill all night so the king lost the advantage of surprise.' Brynn paused. 'I'd like to know who it was who betrayed him. There are still Normans at the court who see Harold as a usurper. Someone told William of his plans.'

'Harold was a good general,' Eadgifu said, 'But if he was betrayed. . .' Her heart almost tore apart when she heard herself speaking in the past tense.

Brynn carried on, his voice bleak. 'But then the Normans fought from their horses – William had three cut down under him – and the shield wall isn't made for that kind of attack. They could fight from above, on their destriers, cutting men down behind their shields.'

Edmund spoke from where he was sitting on the hearth close to the fire. 'If we'd only been able to hold on for another hour, the light would have faded and the battle would have been abandoned.'

Brynn nodded. 'But perhaps it was always a hopeless case. If it hadn't been for the marsh land, there would have been a massacre much earlier. The Normans had more archers than we had, and better. They had crossbows and our shields and mail weren't any defence against those. And our men were tired, having already fought another battle and ridden the length of the country.' Brynn paused.

'And what news of my other sons?' Gytha interrupted, her voice hard in the silence.

Brynn wiped his eyes on the back of his hand. 'Both dead, my Lady. Gyrth was brought down by William himself; Leofwine by the hand of Eustace of Boulogne.'

Gytha's face was stiff and expressionless, as if she had been turned to stone. Her voice was almost a whisper. 'Blood for blood. Eustace never forgave my husband for the insult he gave him. Godwin refused to punish our people for the insolence they showed Eustace when he behaved so badly at Dover. Now he has vengeance.'

'So, how did . . .' For a moment, Eadgifu found it impossible to say the words, her lips suddenly cracked and dried. She ran her tongue over them. 'How did Harold die?'

'The Normans appeared to draw back as though in retreat and the fyrde at the front believed their trickery and pushed forward at speed, leaving a gap where William could break through, splitting our forces and surrounding us. Then he came up the hill on his horse with the best of his men, Eustace of Boulogne, William FitzOsborn and Hugh de Ponthieu, and they fought their way to Harold hand to hand, cutting his carles down one by one. That's when Harold ordered me to go, otherwise I would never have left his side. I found Godwin and Edmund and we went for the horses. As we mounted to ride away, I saw his banner fall.'

Eadgifu could hear the fire crackling in the silence. Then Gytha said, 'We must find their bodies and bring them home for burial.'

Eadgifu nodded. She looked at Brynn. 'Can you take us?'

She glanced across the table, to where Godwin sat with his head buried in his arms, his shoulders shaking. Edmund's face was colourless in the fire light, his eyes glazed.

Eadgifu went on, 'My own carles can take the boys to London tomorrow morning. They'll be safe enough until then. But you are the only one who knows where Harold fell.' Eadgifu got up. There were arrangements to be made, carts for the bodies . . . bodies! Oh, dear Christ . . . horses for herself, a litter for Gytha, some carles to come with her, which ones to go with Godwin. No time to think about what this meant. She must get Harold back for a burial befitting a king, before the carrion pickers got to him. And then there was Ulf and the other two children, they would be safer in

London too, so they must go with Godwin. None of it felt real. It was a vision of disaster – beyond the worst of all her fears. Harold, Gyrth, Leofwine, all gone. Her legs shook. But there were things to be done – she mustn't fail. What if he wasn't dead, a prisoner perhaps, wounded perhaps? After all, Brynn hadn't seen him killed.

~ ~ ~

'Is it certain?' Ældyth said. She stood very still with one hand on the back of a chair.

'Yes, my Lady.' Bishop Ælfric looked pale and the hand that held his staff shook. 'The messenger arrived early and spoke to the Lady Edith. And now, other men are beginning to arrive, those that fled the field after the king fell. They all tell the same tale.'

'Did Lady Edith not think fit to tell me as soon as the messenger arrived?' Ældyth felt the shock of anger pouring through her body. Her heart raced and she could feel its pulse even in the fingertips that gripped the chair. 'Did she not think I should be told that my husband was dead as soon as the reports came in?'

The bishop flinched. 'Perhaps,' he sounded hesitant. 'Perhaps she thought that such terrible news should be given more gently to one in such a delicate condition. Perhaps . . .' His stammering excuses tailed away into silence.

Ældyth began to move restlessly around the room. In her mind the words 'Dear God, Dear God, please, please,' swirled without meaning. She felt, rather than heard, Merwenne and Angharad come into the room. Merwenne had her by the arm. 'Sit down, you must sit down,' she was saying in Welsh. 'You must be kind to yourself.'

Angharad was talking to Bishop Ælfric, ushering him out of the room. 'My Lady must rest. She must have quiet.'

The bishop murmured something about a prayer, but Angharad interrupted him and shortly afterwards he was gone.

'It's not prayer she needs,' Merwenne said brusquely, 'nor a prating priest.'

'Harold's dead.' It wasn't until she said the words that Ældyth realised it was true.

'And his brothers with him,' Angharad said.

'His sons?'

'We have no word of them yet.'

The babe in Ældyth's belly moved, pressing up under her ribs. This child at least was still alive. For a moment Ældyth felt unable to think what she should do. What did this mean?

'Fetch me my best robe,' she said suddenly. 'I'm going to see the Lady Edith.'

The dowager was walking up and down in her room. There were three scribes seated there and she was dictating to all of them at the same time – jerky phrases, tossed out of her mouth impatiently. She glanced at Ældyth when she entered the room, but gave her no acknowledgment, making her wait like a servant. Ældyth had to clench her fists to contain the anger that she felt.

'Could you not,' she said, as evenly as she could, 'spare the time, or the merest shred of compassion, to tell me of the death of my husband until now? I'm his wife, his queen, did it not seem important for me to know?'

There was a startled silence as Edith turned to face her. Edith's eyes glittered with tears and her face was white, although her expression was fierce. 'You're no longer the queen, Ældyth. You are, like me, a dowager.' There was no bitterness in her voice. 'But you're expecting Harold's child and must be protected. Once I've sent off the messengers to make sure that every earl and thegn in the country knows what's happened, we must get you to a place of safety.'

All anger drained out of Ældyth at the sight of Edith's

stricken face. 'What can I do? There must be something?'

Edith shook her head. 'When everyone arrives, there'll be a Council meeting. We need to decide what can be done. I've sent for your brothers.'

Ældyth's dream, and the Seer's interpretation of it, nagged at her memory as she walked back to her room. One brother would kill the other, the woman had said, and he would be cursed for it as in the story of Cain and Abel. Ældyth remembered that the Seer had also given her a warning. What had she said? *"You are not safe, even in your own garden."* Ældyth did not feel safe. Was there anyone she could trust? She was certain that, as Harold's widow and the mother of his child, she had never been in as much danger as she was now.

~ ~ ~

It was a strange cavalcade that set out for Senlac. Eadgifu and her chaplain with Brynn, four holy brothers from the little monastery at Hildburgh, six carles, all on horseback, the carts following behind with Gytha's litter. Eadgifu knew that this journey would always stay with her. The dark road lit by the torches held by the carles that accompanied them; the way the flickering light made the trees appear grotesque – their contorted branches looming out into the light, and retreating into shadow, like creatures in a nightmare, clawing at them from the dark forest. Then, as they neared the battlefield, the bodies began to appear; some lying beside the road where they had fallen as they escaped, some propped up against the trees. All dead or at the point of death. And on the wind, a suffocating smell, the odour of carrion, the stench of death.

The numbers increased as they approached Senlac and soon, they were too thick on the road to continue. It was necessary to leave the carts and the horses and go forward on foot. About half a mile further on, a Norman foot-soldier came out of the shadows and held up his arm. He was swaying as he stood and Eadgifu wondered if he was in drink. Brynn spoke to him, having learnt much Norman-French when he was at the duke's court with Harold.

'He won't let us go any further,' Brynn said. 'The duke has given orders that no one is to be removed from the battlefield without his permission.'

'Barbarians,' Gytha muttered. 'Swine! I'm sure if the price is high enough his permission would be granted.' She moved forward and stood in front of the Norman. 'I'm an old woman. All I want are my sons' bodies to give them a Christian burial rather than leave them to be picked over by the crows.'

It was difficult to know if the Norman understood any of it, but Brynn did a rapid translation. Two of the Benedictines had moved up to stand behind Gytha who was close under the guard's face now. 'Would you not take pity on an old woman? I will make sure you are properly rewarded for such a charitable deed, and God would be gracious to you for your compassion.' The monks nodded. One of them said something in Norman-French.

Eadgifu saw obedience to his lord, religious duty and personal greed fighting in his eyes as they passed from Gytha to the monks and back. There was a smell of beer on the breeze. But who wouldn't be drunk in this scene of horror. She saw Gytha take a purse out of her satchel and pass it, almost invisibly, to the Norman. He opened the top of it slightly and Eadgifu saw the glint of gold in the light from the torches. Then he said, in very poor English, 'Out of pity for you madame, out of pity.' His voice was slurred and he walked away unsteadily, sniggering to himself.

Brynn had told her that it was on the crown of Senlac Hill that Harold and his brothers had been cut down, so that was where they searched, two of her carles holding torches. It was a field of mangled corpses, Norman and Saxon piled on each other, some not yet dead, moaning faintly, some calling out – all beyond help. Eadgifu could hear Gytha stumbling and swearing at the carle who was helping her.

Eadgifu's feet in her leather boots were bloody – it was impossible not to walk on things that had once been men, their bodies mashed to pulp by Norman swords and their horses' hooves. But then, just as she had begun to think it was impossible to make sense of so much slaughter, Brynn called to her. There was a pile of bodies, two of them in tunics much torn and bloodied, but still recognisably in Harold's colours.

'That's Odric,' Brynn said. 'He was one of Harold's hearth-carles under me.'

From the pile of bodies, she saw a foot and a lower leg sliding its way out from under the fallen and thought she recognised the sickle-shaped scar on the calf that Harold had acquired on one of his Welsh campaigns. The carles pulled away the bodies on top of him. What was revealed resembled a piece of butchered meat, but she knew that it was Harold. One of his legs was missing, hacked off mid-thigh, and his head was gone. His body was pierced through the stomach and the chest by Norman lances. The bastards had made very sure. His chain mail had been stolen, and every piece of gold or silver had been taken; his sword belt, the clasps of his cloak and the ring of state – no doubt in William's hand by now.

'How can you be certain?' one of the carles asked.

Eadgifu lifted up the linen hem at the top of his missing leg and there was the blue tattoo of a swan. Above it, where his manhood should have been, was a bloodied mess. Not content with killing him, they had castrated him. She had a sudden memory that went through her like a sword blade, of herself threatening, when he married the Welsh queen, that she would cut off his balls with a knife. Dear God, how could she have said that? For a moment she thought she would vomit.

Gytha was standing gazing silently down. She looked ten years older, her face gaunt and ghost-like in the flickering light.

The carles found Gyrth and Leofwine nearby, lying with Hakon, Sweyn's son by the Abbess of Leominster. His mother would have to be told, Eadgifu thought. Hakon was her only child. And Theo and Hilde would have to be given the news. So much loss. Eadgifu could hardly bear it. The carles brought the men's bodies to lie with Harold, but Gytha's face was still like stone, her eyes without tears. This was a grief beyond mourning. *I have lost the love of my life,* Eadgifu thought, *but she has lost three more of her sons and a grandson tonight.*

The carles, assisted by the monks, carried Harold and his brothers to the carts. They had been unable to find Harold's head or his missing leg in the carnage. Brynn had been talking to the Norman, coaxing him to talk about the death of the king and he'd been told that one of the duke's thegns, possibly Eustace, had waved his head in the air and flung it away. 'We've no hope of finding it in the dark, my Lady.'

Brynn thought that perhaps it was a good thing – if William found it he might take another body for Harold's. 'The duke expressly forbade anyone to remove the bodies of the Godwins. It seems he has a fate reserved for them that only he can carry out.'

'He'll discover that we've taken them and search for us,' Eadgifu said fearfully.

'How is he going to know who is who in this carnage, when they've been stripped of all their possessions?' It was Gytha who spoke. 'Naked, one Saxon is very like another.'

There were other figures, cloaked, carrying torches, picking their way among the dead on the hill. Eadgifu thought of the Norman, laughing as he took the purse and felt angry enough to kill. Was that how men felt? Or did they deal death coldly, as something necessary, a task they had been trained for?

~ ~ ~

Thorkild is back at last, to my great relief. But he has changed. It's as though his eyes are a different colour, darker, without that glint of optimism they'd had before. He looked exhausted, but there was a grim determination about him.

'What happened?' I asked. 'If you can bear to talk about it.'

He hesitated, but once he began, he could hardly stop even for breath. 'We knew it was lost when we saw the Norman charging up the hill towards the king. Some carles and members of the fyrde were already beginning to slip away towards the trees where the horses were tethered. Wulfgar had been wounded by an arrow and I was tending to him when I saw the duke break through the ring of carles around the king. I put Wulfgar over my shoulder and made for the horses. He lost a lot of blood, but the healers are taking care of him and they say that he'll recover.' He shook his head as if trying to shake off the memories it contained. 'I thought Harold was a fine man, a good king, but the men were saying that his sword was cursed the moment he killed his brother.'

'What will you do now?' I asked – the same question that was being asked up and down the corridors.

'I've thrown in my lot with Godwin. He and Edmund talk of leaving London and going west, perhaps as far as Ireland to try and raise an army to take back the throne.' He looked down at his feet for a moment and then asked, 'And you? What will you do?'

I knew what it must have cost him to ask that – to admit that he could offer me no shelter or assistance. 'The Lady Margaret and I've been talking. She thinks of going back to the east, and I can be part of her retinue if I wish. But our lives are in the hands of the gods, or the three women who weave our fates.'

We were both silent and then I said, 'I once talked to a knowing woman, who told me something of that fate.' I smiled, remembering Merithien. 'It sounded like a life worth having.'

After he'd gone, I took up my lyre again. I've begun to compose a praise-song for Harold Godwinson. He was an honourable man who died honourably by the sword according to the warrior code. In my country he would be known as *gōd-kæning* – not just a good king, but everything those words implied; generous to his thegns, a welcoming host, defender of his people, courageous in battle and fair in judgement. I'm trying to put that into verse and calling it the Armed Man, after his banner of gold and red, embroidered by the Swan-neck and carried by him into every battle.

> I sing the song of the Armed-Man
> Harold, war-worthy warrior who slew
> the mighty Viking on the land he laid waste.
> I sing the song of the battle of Senlac
> King and defender, husband, father, friend,
> that was a good king, wise in council
> brave in battle, protector of the poor
> slain by the Norman horde on Senlac Hill
> I sing of the brave carles and thegns who fell
> to the Norman swords beside their king
> his sword-arm strong to the end.

It needs much more work, but when I've finished, I will give it to the queen.

Ældyth had not been outside the palace, but she had heard the reports. The streets of London were apparently crowded with carles. Some had fled the battle, many of them wounded; others were the fyrde called out by Harold, arriving after he had left. Men were sleeping in the streets. Inside the palace, all was chaos. Everyone was wondering when the Norman duke would arrive. There were rumours that he was imminent. Some of the carles and the servants simply vanished overnight, others declared their intention to stay. Edwin and Morcar arrived two days after the news of Harold's death. Both seemed stunned by it.

'He was a good general,' Morcar said. 'And he defeated a far greater army at Stamford Bridge. If it wasn't for that bugger Tostig, Harold would have been in London, with an army fresh and ready to fight the duke and win. It was all Tostig's fault.'

'Twice traitor – once for attacking his own country and twice for throwing in his lot with the Viking.' Edwin was frowning. 'But now we must get you out of danger. If William comes, he'll give you no quarter, since you are the queen and with child by Harold.'

'How can I travel now?' Ældyth felt angry. 'You can see my condition. The babe is due any day. I've no intention of giving birth in a ditch like some peasant woman.'

'You'll travel in a litter, as quietly as we can arrange. There's no time to argue. Morcar will take you and Nest to Chester.'

'I'd rather go to my own manor at Binley. It's closer and I'd be near our grandmother.'

'I'm sure you'd prefer it, but only Chester is fortified to withstand the kind of assault the Norman is likely to mount. And it's near enough to Wales and the seaports to get you out of Mercia if things don't go our way.' Edwin saw her stormy face and said, in a placatory tone, 'Later, when we can see the lie of the land, and you've had the babe, perhaps it will be safe to go to Binley.'

With Harold dead, Ældyth reflected, she was at the mercy of her brothers once more. She thought of her own manor, surrounded by trees, in soft, rolling countryside, close to her grandmother the Lady Godiva, and her heart longed for it. But she could see the sense of her brother's words. Whatever her own desires, she owed it to Harold to keep his child safe.

The Mercian earls didn't stay long. Edwin said that he must talk to as many people as possible about the vacant throne. 'We've asked for a full meeting of the Council tomorrow. Then, Morcar will escort you and your maids, accompanied by a midwife, to Chester.'

Ældyth lowered her head meekly to hide the fact that her eyes were blazing with rebellion.

~ ~ ~

It was a long, weary journey from Bosham to London and on the last stretch it began to rain. Eadgifu rode every mile of the road with the memory of that interment, under cover of darkness in the utmost secrecy. How the Hildburgh monks had wrapped Harold's body in a purple cloak, coffined it and then, by candlelight, said the mass for the dead over him. How Gytha had stood in the background, dry-eyed but ashen-faced as the monks prepared the bodies of her sons. A hasty pit had been dug under the floor in front of the altar and Harold was lowered into it with the accompaniment of prayers and psalms. How much more fitting, Eadgifu thought, would it have been to put him into one of his own longships and rowed him out to sea from Bosham harbour. Harold, like his father Godwin, had always been a good sailor, a lover of the sea, perhaps a throwback to his Danish ancestors. But at least he was close to the sea, within hearing distance when the wind was blowing hard.

'He'll be safe here,' Brynn said as he stood guard over the grave as the paving stones were replaced to leave no trace of disturbance. 'William will find another body to bury as his, to mock over, as I've no doubt he will.'

And, Eadgifu thought, even if he is found, who would expect a king to be buried so humbly, without gold or silver, in a plain wooden coffin.

That had been part of the argument on Senlac Hill, that Bosham, on a Godwin manor, the furthest distance from the battlefield, was the least obvious place to hide Harold's body. No one would look for him here, particularly if William believed his mangled corpse was still lying on the field. And Harold had company, in Cnut's little daughter, her stone coffin lying next to him.

His brothers had been laid under the chancel arch in graves that had been prepared originally for their father Godwin and his wife Gytha, but never used, since Godwin had been buried in Winchester and Gytha was still alive. A space had been found for Hakon beside Gyrth and Leofwine – Godwin's sons and grandson, fittingly buried in their birthplace at Bosham. Beside their tombs, Eadgifu and Gytha had held each other tightly.

Now, on her way to London, to reunite with her children, Eadgifu carried Harold's heart in a casket, to place it – like a holy relic – in the church at Waltham. Since it had been almost wrenched out of his body by a Norman lance, pale and bloodless, it hadn't been a difficult decision to remove it and take it to a place he loved so much – a place he had endowed because it was, for him, a place of healing. Eadgifu thought sadly of his broken body, his head on the battlefield, his body at Bosham, and his heart at Waltham. But the holy brothers had told her that he would be resurrected, whole and unblemished, on the day of judgement and that his soul would already be in heaven, so it didn't matter where his body was now.

As she rode, Eadgifu began to think what she might do after she reached London. She'd originally thought to go to their Waltham manor at Nazeing, but now that didn't seem practical. William would find them there very quickly. She must get Harold's children to safety against the future. Her mother-in-law Gytha too. Only three of Gytha's children were now alive, Edith the Dowager, Abbess Gunhilda across the channel at St Omer, and Wulfnoth, a captive in Normandy. She had lost six of her nine children, five of them in the past year. That kind of loss was beyond Eadgifu's knowledge or her ability to imagine. But it was also, she knew, common. 'How many kings and princes,' she thought, 'live out their days and die in their beds as old King Edward did?' Who would care for Gytha now in the absence of her sons? Edith, Eadgifu knew, would scarcely put herself out for her mother – the rancour between them ran too deep. Eadgifu made up her mind to take care of her, in the absence of her sons, though it would not be easy. Gytha was too independent, too outspoken.

It was late when they arrived at the palace, which was unusually quiet. Eadgifu let her maids help her to take off her damp cloak and riding boots and prepare her for bed. She enquired after the children and drank a cup of wine, then went straight to Gytha's room.

Gytha was still awake, sitting up in bed, her hair in one long braid on her shoulder, reading a prayer book. That surprised Eadgifu, for Gytha had never been conventionally religious. She watched Gytha's face and saw her eyes were so heavy with sadness that her cheeks sagged under their weight. It was Gytha who spoke first.

'You did well,' her voice shook slightly as she spoke. 'No one else could have done what you did.'

'It was carnage. I hadn't realised. So many good men cut down, and for what? A piece of earth and a title.'

'Men kill each other for less.' Gytha said.

'Are you all right?' Eadgifu asked, wondering how she could bear her losses.

Gytha didn't reply, but looked very directly at her daughter-in-law and said, 'Are you, Swan-neck?'

'No, but I have my children and that must be my comfort.' Instantly she regretted saying it. She had her children, but she had just buried Gytha's. There was an awkward silence and then Eadgifu said, 'It's late. Time to go and try to sleep, though I doubt there'll be much of it.'

'Goodnight, Swan-neck.'

'Goodnight, Gytha.'

Part Nine

The Pelican in the Wilderness

Psalm 102

No one sat at the head of the table in Council. Harold's chair was empty. It was a sparse assembly. Archbishop Stigand, Edwin, Morcar, Ælðyth looking pale, but resolute, Godwin and Edmund joining for the first time and three bishops from London, Essex and Kent. It was Edwin who took it upon himself to begin talking, his right, he explained, as the most senior earl present. That was the truth, but no one expressed approval.

'Shall we begin with a prayer?' Edwin said, glancing

briefly round the table and then nodding to the archbishop.

Stigand prayed lustily for Harold's soul, giving thanks for his life and acknowledging his service and that he had given his life for his people. A man who liked the sound of his own voice, Edith thought, as he began to pray for guidance, that each member of the Council should be blessed with a blinding revelation of the will of God.

Then Edwin laid out, in stark terms, the situation they were in. 'We are leaderless, without a king, unless we're craven enough to offer up the crown to William the invader, giving up what is ours meekly to a bastard of a Norman duke.'

'What are the choices?' the archbishop asked.

Quite a few eyes around the table moved to look at Godwin. Then moved on. 'You're not proposing yourself, I hope,' Edith said, looking straight across the table at Edwin.

'I'm not. It pains me to admit it, but I don't think I could command enough support.'

'Particularly as it was your tardiness to the battlefield that cost us the day,' Godwin said abruptly. 'If you had come when my father asked you. . .'

'And if he had been less impatient and waited a day or so longer for us!'

'Please,' Stigand held up his hand. 'This is no place for recriminations. We must decide who has the best right to be put forward to the Witan. In my mind, there's only one. The last heir to Æthelred, Edgar, grandson to King Edmund Ironside'

There was silence. Then Godwin spoke up again. 'But he's only a child. Fourteen, and young for his age. No match for William. The duke's strong and murderous in battle. He gives no quarter.'

'But Edgar has the blood of Æthelred in his veins. True Saxon blood.' Stigand was insistent, as if, Edith thought, blood was all that mattered.

Again, silence.

Edith studied Godwin's face. He was stubborn and had the same quality as Harold – not arrogance exactly, but that assurance of command, the air of someone who knows they are entitled to rule.

Edwin sighed. He tapped the table with his ring finger, thinking aloud. 'It's a true bloodline right enough. The people might be persuaded to support him. At least his claim is legitimate. Edward brought him from Hungaria to be the Ætheling. Why would he do that if not to make him his heir?' He paused for a moment and then went on, 'William's justification for the invasion is that Harold was a usurper. He can hardly argue that against Edgar.'

He made it sound such a reasonable argument, but, Edith thought, looking at Edgar's thin face, his hooded eyes, a shy child of fourteen would be easily manipulated by a cunning senior earl hungry for power.

'What about Godwin Haroldson?' It was Ældyth who spoke. 'He's of age, trained in diplomacy and warcraft by his father. The eldest son of the king. Why shouldn't he succeed?'

'Because he's not even an earl.' Morcar sounded exasperated. 'And who's going to support another Godwin after this disaster?'

'I'm older than you were when you were made Earl of Northumbria,' Godwin said. 'I fought against William with my father on Senlac Hill and, since he's dead, I should be Earl of Wessex as his heir. And, if you're arguing that because I'm not an earl, then Edgar isn't either. He has no land and no carles to fight for him. Don't you think I should have my chance?'

It was Stigand who intervened again. 'I think it's time to take a decision. Who is in favour of Edgar the Ætheling?'

Hands were raised.

'And Godwin Haroldson?'

No one put up their hand, not even Ældyth.

'So, it's decided,' Edwin said, nodding to the scribe at the bottom of the table. 'We'll present Edgar to the Witan and then, if they agree, declare him king. That will give William pause for thought.'

Godwin got up and left, followed quickly by Edmund, not even staying to sign the record the scribe was drawing up.

Edith noticed that Ældyth remained seated as the men left, and she too hung back until they'd all left the room.

'Your brother is taking you to Chester, I gather,' she said.

Ældyth nodded. 'I don't want to go. Partly because I've no desire to return to my brother's house,' she gave a wry smile, 'and partly because I've developed a dislike of being ordered about.' She stood up. 'Since I was a child, I've been trained in obedience and traded like a prize brood mare first by my father and then by my brothers. Now I have the opportunity to decide for myself what I'll do.'

'And what will you do?'

'I have estates near Coventry at Binley Woods. It's remote and feels like a good place to rear my children in obscurity. I hope to live simply. Perhaps marry by my own choice one day. And if the Normans arrive that far north then I can go into Wales or west into Ireland to the king that sheltered Harold.'

Edith nodded. 'I'll make sure that you're well provided for. I'm determined not to leave Harold's treasury for his successor. It's Godwin money and the Godwins look after their own.' Edith smiled as she remembered that it had been one of Harold's, half teasing, sayings – almost a family joke.

'And what will you do, Lady Edith?'

'Oh, I'll stay until the end. Whatever that is.'

'Even if William crushes Edwin's pathetic revolt?'

'Is that what you think it is?'

Ældyth made a shrugging gesture and nodded. Then she said, 'I admire your courage and resolution.'

'What have I got to lose?' Edith said. 'He can't take from me what I've already lost, and as Edward's widow, I have the right to be treated fairly. I hope that he'll let me keep my lands and live out my life in peace. I've no child to threaten the security of William's throne.'

She came across the room impulsively and put her arms on Ældyth's shoulders and kissed her on the cheek. 'Fare well, Ældyth. You were queen for such a short time, but I admire your dignity. We haven't made it easy for you, either Eadgifu or myself.'

Ældyth smiled and gripped Edith's arms. 'It hasn't been easy for any of us.'

After she had left, Edith sat down at the empty table. She felt odd, as if a knot had uncurled inside her, leaving her in danger of unravelling. It wasn't a feeling she had ever had before.

~ ~ ~

One of the first things Eadgifu did was to go to see Ældyth before she left. The queen was lying on her bed, pale and exhausted.

'You must take care of yourself,' Eadgifu said. 'I gather that Morcar's escorting you to Chester.'

Ældyth sat up. 'I hope to get there before my child's born.'

'Do you know what you're going to call the babe?'

'If it's a boy, Harold, after his father.'

Eadgifu smiled. 'It will be. The Godwinsons are very good at breeding boys. But if it's a girl?'

'Perhaps Gytha, after my formidable mother-in-law.'

'We could all do with some of her spirit. I wonder every day how she can cope with so much grief. Strange that such a short time ago all was so calm and we went on every day as usual as if all our tomorrows would be the same.' She paused for a moment to control her voice. 'Now it's wreckage.'

'Did you bury him?' Ældyth asked.

'I did. Where no one will find him, in an obscure grave, with his brothers.'

Ældyth nodded and Eadgifu could see tears flooding into her eyes.

'You loved him too, didn't you? I was so jealous.'

'And I of you. It seems foolish now.'

Eadgifu went over to the bed and kissed Ældyth on the cheek. 'Fare well. And God bless the child you carry. I'm going to my family lands in East Anglia, and then, if the Norman approaches, to Denmark to Gytha's nephew King Sweyn. Godwin wants to fight, but he's young and inexperienced. Edith told me what he said in Council. I fear for him, but I can't stop him. If he fails, he'll probably go to Ireland, or to Denmark.'

'I wish him well,' Ældyth said. 'He's a fine young man, growing more like his father every day.' She paused and then added. 'I'll write to you at the Danish court, if I can, and let you know what happens.'

The two women embraced and Eadgifu went back to her room to supervise the packing of the boxes. There was a great deal to organise. She had sent to her shipbuilder in Norfolk to order the building of six ships to take her into Denmark, but also as a gift for King Sweyn, together with a substantial quantity of gold and silver from Harold's treasury. There would be more from her own at Nazeing. She was also taking horses, carles and armour. Sweyn could not refuse her sanctuary after such generous gifts. As she made the plans and gave orders for the chests of valuables and vestments, Eadgifu knew that she would never come back. Reluctantly she admitted to herself that Gytha would probably not come with her. But Gytha would look after Godwin and Edmund and provide for them, whether they won their battle or not. Eadgifu thought not, but her mother-in-law was a force to be reckoned with. Gytha had been so angry when she heard that Edgar had been chosen at the Council before Harold's sons. She was adamant that Godwin must have his chances, mounting a rebellion from the west with troops from Ireland. *'I thought to look after her,'* Eadgifu said to herself. *'But she doesn't need anyone else.'*

~ ~ ~

I took my praise-song to the queen and played it to her and her assembled ladies the evening before she left. They all cried and I could hardly sing the words for my own tears. Somehow the tears I shed were not just for the king, but for Arthur, my parents, my sisters, and everyone I'd ever loved who had died by the sword. It's the first time I've cried publicly since I was taken from my home. Then the queen went to one of her chests, waiting for men to move them to the carts, took something out of it and handed it to me.

'I'm worried about you, Hari,' she said. 'You have no one to take care of you now and who knows what might happen. Take this to keep you safe on your journeys.' She handed me a purse. 'And if you ever need a place to lay your head, you are always welcome at my manor of Binley or my brother's palace at Chester.'

I bowed very low, too overcome to speak. When I opened it later, she had given me gold coins, enough to take me across the world and back. I need not want for anything. I tucked it inside my tunic to keep it safe.

The next day Edgar the Ætheling was declared king by the Witan. He was taken out into the streets of London and proclaimed by the archbishop and the earls. Edgar looked very young and frail standing between the three war-lords and I thought that he himself could hardly believe it. I noticed that whenever he spoke he looked to Earl Edwin first for his encouragement – perhaps even permission. There was great enthusiasm among the crowds in the street. But inside the palace it's different. Some in the hall are calling him a puppet king, controlled by the Mercians. We've been told that there'll be no coronation until he has the support of the people outside London.

Lady Margaret should be glad, for she's now the sister of the king, but she says that all she feels is fear. She doesn't believe that William will allow him to reign, even protected by her brothers. Edwin and Morcar are innocents, she says, if they think that they can withstand the might of the Norman conqueror's army, when they were beaten so easily by Tostig and the Vikings. Margaret has sent for her mother, Agatha, from Winchester. If Edgar is to be king then he must have his family around him. Margaret's shrewd where politics are concerned. She's well educated and can read Latin and French. I'm going to stay with her for the moment, I've decided. It's very pleasant to have intelligent female company, and I'll be interested to meet her mother, Lady Agatha, who is, Margaret tells me, a close relative of Ellisev, the Landwaster's wife, both being the daughters of Kievan Rus.

~ ~ ~

Eadgifu knew that the time had come. If she didn't leave now, she might not be able to leave at all. William had advanced towards London, coming not directly up the river with ships, as they expected, or laying seige to the bridge over the Thames, but had crossed the river upstream and was now threatening the city from the west. He had burnt and laid waste to great swathes of the countryside, harrying every village and every town. She had tried for two days to persuade Gytha to come with her to Waltham and then to Norfolk where they could take ship for Denmark. But Gytha was adamant.

'I'll go to Exeter, to my manor there. It's out of the main way, so the Norman duke won't bother me for a while.' She turned to address Godwin. 'Well? Are you all words, or are you going to put them into action?'

'If I can get an army, I'll show the bloody Mercians what a Godwin can do.' His hands were tightly fisted on the table in front of him.

'I'd prefer you safe,' Eadgifu said. 'Hasn't there been enough slaughter?'

Godwin looked at her. 'Do you really want me to lie down like a milkling and let the bastard duke take our land?' His voice changed, became more conciliatory. 'Mother, I have to do what I've been brought up to do; defend our land and our family. Edmund and I are going to Ireland, to the King of Leinster to ask for troops to recover as much of it as we can. We'll go north and then west with grandmother and take ship from Bristol. My father's got vessels there. There's got to be some resistance. I'm hoping that when we come back with a force, all the people of Wessex will rise up and fight for a Godwin. They're not going to do that for a foreign prince and a couple of Mercians.'

'Who's going with you?'

'Thorkild Magnusson, Wulfgar Sigurdson, Brynn and all that's left of our hearth-carles. While I'm in Ireland, some of them will stay with our grandmother in Exeter. It's well fortified.'

'It is,' Gytha said. 'Your grandmother, for one, will not give in easily.'

The boys left hurriedly and Gytha and Eadgifu were alone with the little ones. The Swan-neck didn't share

Gytha's certainty. Eadgifu felt as though there was no fight left in her body or mind, only fear.

'This is the end of our hopes,' she wept. 'What will become of my fine boys?'

'They'll do well,' Gytha said. 'They have strong sword arms and a ship full of their father's gold to ease their passage. The King of Leinster will be glad to welcome such thegns.'

'Harold thought to leave a line of Saxon kings behind him. That's all over now.'

'You despair too soon.' Gytha sounded cross. She was running her hand through her granddaughter's blonde hair as she lay, half-asleep, on her lap. 'Who knows the future? Only the gods. Perhaps it won't run through the male line at all.'

Eadgifu looked at her.

'Take this one,' Gytha said, indicating her small name-sake curled up with her thumb in her mouth. 'She comes from a line of strong women descended from the royal lines of two kingdoms. Little Gytha will go to Denmark with you and who can tell who she will marry and who her children will become.'

Eadgifu felt a degree of comfort. Ulf was tugging at her dress. He already looked remarkably like his father and his grandfather – fair haired, blue-eyed, sturdy. She must salvage as much of their estates as she could, before the Norman bastard ravaged them, to create a future for Magnus, Ulf and their sister.

She sighed. 'I must go, before it's too late. Waltham first and then to my father's manor in Norfolk. From there, as soon as the ships are ready, we'll sail for Denmark and seek refuge with your nephew.'

'Don't leave it too long. If Godwin and Edmund can resist William's advance, then I'll let you know that it's safe to come back.'

'And if they can't?'

'Then I'll join you at the court of Sweyn in Denmark. Though I've got no real wish to go back.' She sighed. 'Perhaps William will let me live out my days at Exeter.'

'If you're supporting Godwin and Edmund's rebellion I doubt he will. You'll be hounded into exile with your grandsons. I fear my boys will become like all the other dispossessed æthelings, young men like Thorkild Magnusson, wandering the world as mercenaries, lordless and landless, lending their sword-arms to whichever lord will hire them.'

'Have you told Gunhild?'

'Yes. She's decided to remain at Wilton for the present. She'll be safe there, under Edith's protection.'

There was nothing more to be said or done. Eadgifu sat a few moments longer, listening to the wood spitting on the hearth, the ash falling down into the grate. Now there was only the journey. Her jeweller had made a beautiful gold casket decorated with garnets to contain Harold's heart. She would bury it in a secure place at Waltham where it could remain hidden. Brynn had been right. William was boasting, mocking, that he had buried Harold's body in an unsanctified grave where he would be left to rot for his supposed crimes. She wondered which poor dead warrior had been selected for that ritual. Eadgifu was satisfied with what she had done. Harold's body was at Bosham, his birthplace and life-long home, but his heart would be at Waltham, where his heart had surely always been.

~ ~ ~

Edith came into Gytha's room. Her mother's maids were packing her belongings into chests, but they bowed and withdrew as Edith entered. Neither Edith nor Gytha said the words, but it was in the air, that they might not see each other again.

'I'm sorry Mother,' Edith said, but it was with a struggle. 'I gave you hard words, but you were right.' It was one of the most difficult things she'd ever had to say. 'I've made my confession to Archbishop Stigand and been forgiven. Goscelin has been sent back to Wilton and will continue his Life of Edward. He's written the first part, the history of our family, in such beautiful prose and poetry. You will be pleased with it, I think.'

Gytha came forward and, in an uncharacteristic gesture, put her arm around her daughter. 'You are very like your father. Godwin was loathe to admit it when he was proved wrong. I can only remember one occasion. It will be of no comfort to you now, but your father acknowledged, before he died, that he had made a mistake. Edward was not the man he had thought he would be, either as king or husband.'

Edith heard her words but couldn't think of any fitting reply. She nodded. 'Where will you go now?'

'We will be in Exeter, at Queen Emma's old manor. Send me word when you've seen the duke. Remember, he's not been crowned king yet!'

'He has Harold's ring.'

'But not yet the kingdom.' Gytha squeezed her daughter's shoulders. 'There's always hope.'

Edith felt her mother's grip and thought that perhaps this calamity had done her mother a deal of good, rousing her from the boredom of old age to become the strong, practical woman she had always been. *As thin and strong as a leather whip!* Was it Harold who had once said that, or Tostig? But it was true of Gytha – and of her tongue.

Gytha turned away to continue her packing. If she felt grief she wasn't expressing it. Edith felt, all over again, that lack of affection. Did Gytha not care for any of them? She tried to think whether she had ever seen her mother shed a tear but couldn't remember a single occasion.

It's too late for tears now, Edith thought.

~ ~ ~

The Mercians with their little puppet king have gone to meet the Norman Duke and swear allegiance to him. It seems no one is willing to go on fighting. They are all war-weary. Lady Margaret said that everyone was busy defending their own lands and making arrangements with the duke to protect their interests. She doubts he'll honour any of his agreements, not yet sworn. There's panic in the court now. I asked Margaret, 'Who was the goddess you prayed to?' Living in a Christian country, perhaps it was wise to pray to their gods. That was always my mother's way, to serve both the old gods and the new, for one never knew which one would be useful.

'Goddess?' Margaret looked puzzled. 'We don't have goddesses. Perhaps you mean saint?'

'At the summer feast?'

'Oh, Saint Walpurga.'

So, I prayed for protection and safety. But, since Harold died, nothing feels safe. There's no place of safety. The security of the court, the feeling of permanence in this palace guarded by solid walls, has been an illusion. I've come to realise that the only safety is in yourself and your own ability to survive. I'm not a man. I don't have a sword, so I must use my wits and the protection of the gods who watch over me. No one knows their own fate or what their doom will be. We have only our dreams and enough courage for the next day. Thorkild has gone one way and I will go another. But at least we know that we have kin in the world and who knows whether our paths will cross again.

I've been forced to tell Margaret the truth about myself, though it was hard. I feared that she would be shocked and try to force me to put off my boy's clothes and live the conventional life of a court woman. I'd even worried that she'd expect me to become one of her maids. But she didn't.

'I knew that there was something different about you, from the very first. But I did not know what it was. There was, between us, a friendship that could never have existed between girl and boy. I talked to you as I would to my sister. Now that you have told me, it seems clear. Can you tell me your name?'

'Hannë Magnusdottir, granddaughter of Danish kings through both my mother and my father, though that no longer matters, since they are all dead and our lands laid waste. I'm just another exile.'

'Like me,' Margaret said quietly. 'Born in exile, brought to a land that was foreign to me, and now exiled again. Where can I go, since I have no homeland to go to? I am an exile wherever I go.'

'But at least you have your mother with you, and you can go to her homeland.' For myself, having been a slave, I've found that belonging is a slippery thing, but I didn't know how to explain that to Margaret. I simply said, 'You could always stay in England you know. William has offered you and your brother safety here.'

Margaret laughed. 'Safety? If I stay, William will force me to marry some Norman knight. I am a descendant of Æthelred, and his blood would be used to legitimise William in some way or other. I had rather die.'

'Can I come with you? I've no wish to serve the duke either.' There's another reason too. I'm fond of Margaret and she is too innocent to know how to keep herself safe. She has never had to sleep with her hand on the shaft of a seax knife, but if I'm with her, perhaps I can be of help.

'Yes, Hari, I would like your company. Though perhaps I should call you Hannë now?'

'Hari will do.' Life is too risky at present to cast off my disguise.

We are going to Sweden first, where her mother has relatives, and are journeying north to the wild lands of Northumberland to take ship from there, since the north is still free from Norman troops. Some of Harold's old carles, still in the palace with nowhere else to go, are coming with us. But we must leave fast, as the duke advances nearer every day, ravaging the land and filling everyone with fear. When the wind blows in the right direction, you can smell the smoke of burning fields and houses. And, mingled with it, the odour of scorching flesh.

~ ~ ~

Nest had been an easy birth; this one was not. Ælfgyth's pains began in the early afternoon and went on all night. She walked the floors of Edwin's palace, had Merwenne and Angharad massage her back, but it was still agony. Waves of it, dragging her stomach down as if a giant had hold of her; making her thighs tremble as the pain rippled down towards her knees. Angharad gave her the bone birthing-stick to put between her teeth, the same one that her mother had used. Ælfgyth bit down until she thought her teeth would crack.

At noon the next day the midwife put her hand inside her, which was more agony, to pierce her waters, flooding the straw she was laid on under a thin linen sheet. And that was when the pain really began. Ælfgyth felt at one moment as if she was going to split apart, then she was floating on the ceiling looking down at her body spread across the bed, at the mercy of this child fighting not to be born.

It was a boy they told her. There was complete silence for a moment and Ælfgyth – through the haze of exhaustion and pain – wondered whether he was dead. But then the silence was shattered by the angry squalling of Harold Haroldson. Once the afterbirth had been delivered, the midwife gave her a tea containing syrup of poppy and, after she had drunk the bitter liquid, she slipped into blissful unconsciousness.

It felt strange to be back at Chester. Nest was miserable without the Godwin children to play with, and Ældyth too missed the company of the other women. Her scop too. There was no music here now. But most of all she missed Harold; the comfort of his nearness, just knowing he was there had made her feel secure.

'I didn't realise till now,' she said to Merwenne, 'the extent of my loss.' When Gruffydd had been killed, she had been sad, but this was grief, raw and violent, ambushing her when she least expected it. She could barely look at Harold's son, for the memory of that loss. Angharad had found a nurse for Harold and Ældyth felt guilty, but she had torn badly during the birth, and it took weeks to heal, while her breasts remained stubbornly empty. She wondered whether it was grief. She had heard, once, that tragic events dried up a mother's milk like a curse.

The news from London was grave. Her brothers' attempt to put an English king on the throne hadn't succeeded, perhaps because Edgar wasn't seen as English, or perhaps it was just that no one wanted to fight for Edwin. Without significant opposition the Normans were moving further and further north, destroying villages and towns wherever they went. In the end there had been a collapse of hope in London and support for the child king had evaporated completely in the face of the savagery that William was meting out. Once Edgar and his supporters had capitulated, the conqueror had taken Edwin, Morcar and Edgar to Normandy. Edwin had written to her to say that they were guests of the duke at his court and being royally treated. Ældyth laughed at his naivety. Why couldn't he see that they were hostages?

But Ældyth's future plans did not include her brothers. She had made a difficult decision for her own protection and that of her children. Ældyth had a daughter by one king and a son by another, and she was determined that they would grow up in peace, far from the risk and terror of the court. In her prophetic dream she had seen her tears fall to the ground and become white flowers, and sunlight had illuminated the upper branches of that dark tree rooted in blood. The Seer had said that it meant that something good would come out of darkness and bloodshed and that gave her hope. Ældyth, once Queen of all Wales and Queen of the English, was about to fall into obscurity, to become Ældyth of the Mercians, land holder of a small manor, mother, an ordinary woman of no account.

~ ~ ~

Edith waited in the great hall for William to arrive. She had dressed with great care in a blue overdress with gold shoulder clasps and was wearing the gold circlet that proclaimed her royal status on her head. Behind her, in the shadows, stood Mathilde. Edith could hear the clatter and jangle of William's retinue coming up the steps and along the corridor. Then, suddenly, he was there, stomping towards her with short, aggressive steps – a thin, swarthy man of no great height, but an air of absolute power. She could feel his presence like a dark miasma. She almost put her hand up to defend herself against it. When he spoke it was in a gruff, rasping voice that made the Norman-French he spoke almost unintelligible. Her skin crawled at his nearness as he approached.

'Welcome Duke William,' she forced herself to say.

He stared at her for a moment, rudely, and then said, 'Lady Edith. I hadn't expected you to be here.'

'I stayed to bid you welcome, and to ask a favour.' Edith bowed her head and asked, as humbly as she could, to be allowed to go to a monastery for the remainder of her days accompanied by her maid. 'I have to finish the life of your sainted cousin Edward, my late husband. I beg that you will let me do that.'

William gave a guttural laugh. Not a man of manners, Edith thought.

'You may. And, once you've given me the keys to the treasury, I'll give you leave to go.'

Edith indicated to Robert the Staller to come forward and put the keys in William's hand. He would find the treasury rather bare. That thought gave her great satisfaction. He was speaking again, in that loud, gruff voice.

'I think, once I've looked over them, that you may be allowed to keep your lands for your lifetime, providing they are to be gifted to myself afterwards. I'm not a vindictive man, you may even find me magnanimous, and Edward was, of course, my cousin.'

Your distant cousin – and he didn't like you very much. Edith almost said it aloud. She seethed inside but bowed her head in a semblance of meekness. This man, this mean little man, she thought, is to sit on Harold's throne, sleep in Harold's bed and we are all to swear obedience to him. A man who has no birth-right, or right of honour to be there. Nothing except brute force and a grasping spirit. He should be called William Streona – William the Grasper – rather than conqueror. There was nothing brave or valiant about this man – little in body and in spirit. Not a man you could ever trust.

Then Edith was dismissed, without courtesy, to supervise the packing of her belongings and the removal to Wilton. But now, at last, she would have no need to complain that there wasn't enough time for her needlework. And she would be near to Goscelin. That thought was both comfort and agony. In his introduction to the Life he had called himself a 'Pelican of the Wilderness'. She had wondered, as she read it, what he meant and had looked for some deep spiritual meaning. The Pelican was the symbol of self-sacrifice, wounding her breast to feed her young with her blood. So, did Goscelin mean that he was sacrificing himself for his faith? And then Edith remembered the psalm. 'I am like a Pelican in the Wilderness, an Owl in the Desert. . . for I have eaten Ashes instead of Bread and drunk my own Tears.' She thought, now, that he was talking about suffering. He, too, knew the wilderness of the soul and what it meant to sacrifice oneself for something.

Despite the pain, Edith regretted nothing. She felt herself changed by her love for him. And without the constraints of the court, the obligations that went with being a Godwin, she was free to devote herself to the same God. A God who was demanding and uncompromising but must be obeyed. That, Edith had vowed last night, in private prayer, would be her future. She must be the owl in the desert, the owl among the ruins in Goscelin's psalm, enduring loneliness and desolation as her daily existence, accepting the annihilation of her family. It was a hard fate, but there was security in its constraints and a sense of purpose that her life had lacked since Edward died. *God's will be done*, she said to herself as she directed the men to take the last of her boxes. Mathilde held the door curtain back for her and Edith walked purposefully through it.

~ ~ ~

We boarded the ship at midnight to catch the early tide. Margaret knelt to pray on the quayside before we boarded and insisted that a holy brother prayed and blessed the ship. For myself I silently entreated Meili the Mile-stepper, who keeps all travellers safe, as well as Njörthr, the god of sailors, to watch over us and give us safe passage. One can't have too much protection.

Margaret is mourning the death of her mother. Lady Agatha had not travelled well. In London, before we left, distressed by her son's enforced departure for Normandy, she'd become quite hysterical, fearing that the duke would kill Edgar. 'All the more reason for us to leave,' Margaret had argued. 'If we wait to see what happens, it will be too late. We must put ourselves in the hands of God.' I only knew what Margaret had told me, since she and her mother talked to each other in the language of Hungaria. So, we had left London quickly and Agatha had sickened with every mile. She was breathless and pale, barely able to walk when her maids lifted her out of the litter. By the time we reached Monkchester she was bed-bound and three days ago she had woken, confused and agitated, tried to get out of bed and had fallen senseless on the floor. Her maid had called Margaret, but it was too late; her soul was flying out of her body even as Margaret came through the door. One of the brothers gave her the last rites and we buried her in the church, under the chancel arch as befitted her rank. Margaret left money to pay for a carved memorial. I think she cried a great deal, for her eyes were red and sore in the morning, but afterwards she was stoical, holding herself together with dignity. We are now in the same state, Margaret and I, as orphans, though Margaret still has a sister cloistered in the south and we both have a brother, though I fear we aren't likely to see our siblings again.

Only a few of the carles have come with us, to manage the ship. Most wished to stay and fight. One of them said contemptuously, 'The north will not give in as easily as the southerners did.' But who will lead them now that both Edwin and Morcar are in Normandy, I can't think. They are leaderless.

The men rowed the ship up the River Tyne towards the sea. Just the smell of it, that salty, metallic smell, made me ache at the memory of my home. They raised the sail and soon the boat was lurching and pitching on the swells in the river mouth as we were launched into the open sea, still dark, the white froth of the waves glimpsed here and there in the light from the lamp on the masthead. There was also wind, blowing fresh from the west, an off-shore wind to fill the sail and blow us towards our destination.

The men made a bed for Margaret in the stern of the ship with pillows, near the steersman. I curled up with my cloak in the prow. It was cold, but I could hear the rushing of the water under the bow, the suck and gurgle of the waves under the keel, and I felt the thrill of the journey in front of me.

In Monkchester, as we prepared ourselves, Margaret had asked, 'What will you do when we arrive? Now you can be the lady, noble-born, that you once were.'

I thought about it before answering her. The truth is that I've got used to being dressed as a boy – the clothes are comfortable and easy to wear. And I like being a scop. I am the 'song-singer, word-bringer' that Merithien had named me. It's my destiny, felt in my bones, and, with no family to provide for me, it's a good living. 'I'll go on as I am,' I told Margaret, hoisting my bundle on one shoulder and my lyre on the other.

I clutched the wooden side of the ship, gazing out over the dark sea where the dawn was just beginning to show a pink edge, only the width of a fingernail, between water and sky. Above me, just visible in the faint light, a seabird was flying above the mast, soaring and swooping on the wind. What was it Merithien had said? *Your spirit will fly like a raven and when that moment comes, you will know your fate.* It wasn't a raven, but my spirit was flying like that bird. Somewhere over the horizon was a new land waiting for me, and I felt a great surge of happiness. I had a whole world, a whole life, in front of me.

Anglo Saxon and Norse Terms

Ætheling - Prince or nobleman

scōp - A court musician and poet, literally a 'shaper' of words and music. Sometimes called a 'skald' or 'bard'. Pronounced 'skop' or 'shoap'.

Witan - 'wise men', short for witenagemot, a council of the most important nobles and bishops who acted as advisers to the king and were also responsible for choosing the next king.

Hus-carles - Skilled, professional warriors.

Heorð-weroð - Hearth warriors' or 'hearth-carles'– the king or nobleman's closest carles.

Fyrde - A volunteer reserve, with only rudimentary training and armed with spears and axes rather than swords.

Weregild - Compensation paid for the loss or wounding of a man, a woman, or loss of land.

In More Danico - In the Danish fashion.

Ragnhild the Mighty - She was married to the 9th century

Norse king, Harald Fairhair, when she had her famous dream, according to 12th century Icelandic historian Snorri Sturluson. Ragnhild was the mother of Eric Bloodaxe. Born, 870 AD. Died, 897 aged 27.

The Long-haired Wyrme - Halley's comet arrived in April 1066.

Staller - The chief steward of the court. Other senior stewards of the king.

Haar - Sea fog. The term is still in use in Northumberland today.

Gang days - The days of going out to celebrate the coming of summer. From the verb *Gangan*, to go.

Merigen-tid - Morning time, morning.

Wælcyrge - Valkyrie

Streona - grasper

Characters

<u>**The House of Æthelred the Unraede**</u>

Edmund Ironside, son of Æthelred by his first wife, Ælf-gifu of York – half-brother to Edward the Confessor. See Elizabethan drama *Edmund Ironside*.

Edgar the Ætheling, grandson of Edmund Ironside. Born in exile in Hungary (Hungaria) in 1052. Brought to England again by his great-uncle Edward the Confessor. Elected king, aged about 14, by the Witan after the death of Harold Godwinson in 1066. King for 33 days.

Lady Margaret, Edgar's sister. Their mother was Agatha of Kievan Rus.

Queen Emma – sister to the Duke of Normandy, Æthelred's second wife. Mother of his sons Edward the Confessor and Alfred.

King Edward II 1042-66, the Confessor, son of Æthelred the Unraede by his second wife Queen Emma.

Alfred, younger son of Æthelred by Queen Emma. Believed to have been murdered by Earl Godwin on the orders of either Harold Harefoot, Harthacnut (his half-brothers) or Queen Emma.

<u>The House of Cnut the Great</u>

Sweyn Forkbeard, King of England 1013-1014, [Son of Harald Bluetooth].

Cnut the Great, King of England, Denmark and Norway 1016-1035. Son of the legendary Sweyn Forkbeard.

Queen Emma, Cnut's 2nd wife mother of his son Harthacnut. (See below)

Harold Harefoot, Harold I, 1037-1040, son of Cnut by Ælfgifu of Northampton – half-brother to Edward the Confessor, buried in Westminster.

Harthacnut, King of England 1040-1042, son of Cnut the Great and Queen Emma. Died age 24 during a seizure. Unpopular. His body was disinterred after burial and thrown into a fen near the River Thames. A fisherman rescued the body and it was reburied in the Danish cemetery in London.

Harald the Landwaster (Harald Hadrada) a relative, through Sweyn Forkbeard, who considered himself the rightful heir of Harthacnut.

Elliseva (Elizabeth), daughter of the King of Kievan Rus, wife of Harald the Landwaster. Through his marriage, Harald became brother-in-law to Henry I of France, Andrew I of Hungaria and the daughter of Constantine IX. Elliseva's sister **Agatha of Kievan Rus** married the exiled heir to the English throne and was the mother of Edgar the Ætheling (king for 33 days in 1066) and the Lady Margaret, later Saint Margaret of Scotland.

Emma, sister of the Duke of Normandy, married (1) to **Æthelred the Unraede,** and (2) to **Cnut the Great,** and twice crowned Queen. Five children. Edward, Alfred and Godgifu (to Æthelred); Harthacnut and Gunhilda (to Cnut). She had been Queen of England, Denmark and Norway and even Regent for a while when Cnut was in Scandinavia. Two of her sons, Harthacnut and Edward became kings of England and she continued to dominate state-craft until her death in March 1052. See *Enconium Emmae Reginae* and Elizabethan drama *Edmund Ironside.*

William of Normandy, the Bastard, nephew of the Duke of Normandy and his heir. Emma's nephew and cousin to King Edward. Married to Mathilda of Flanders.

Judith of Flanders, cousin of William of Normandy, niece of his wife Mathilda. Married to Tostig Godwinson.

The House of Mercia

Leofric, Earl of Mercia, deceased. A very powerful Earl, rival to the Godwins.

Lady Godgifu [Godiva], wife of Leofric. Famous for the legend of her naked ride through Coventry.

Ælfgar, their son, deceased, after being outlawed as a traitor. He rebelled against King Edward and the Godwinsons after the king gave the earldom of Northumbria to Tostig rather than himself.

Edwin, Earl of Mercia, grandson of Earl Leofric, brother of Morcar.

Morcar, grandson of Earl Leofric, made Earl of Northumbria after the removal of Tostig Godwinson. Together the brothers controlled the north of England and the midlands.

Ældyth, Queen of England 1066, sister of Edwin and Morcar, married first to King Gruffydd ap Llewellyn of Wales, who was killed in battle by Harold Godwinson. Mother of a daughter, Nest, by Gruffydd ap Llewellyn, and a son Harold Haroldson.

The House of Godwin

Earl Godwin of Wessex – a rich earl raised up by Cnut and Harthacnut.

Gytha – Godwin's Danish wife, sister-in-law to Cnut the Great.

Queen Edith their daughter. Born Gytha Godwinsdottir, her name was changed to Edith (considered more Saxon) when she married Edward the Confessor.

Harold Godwinson, King Harold II of England 1066, Earl of East Anglia, then Earl of Wessex after the death of his father.

Swein Godwinson, Earl of Herefordshire, Harold's older brother, abducted and raped the Abbess of Leominster, murdered his cousin Beorn and was banished. Died on a barefoot walk to Jerusalem to absolve his sins. One son Hakon by the Abbess of Leominster, held as hostage in Normandy, but back in England in time to die at the Battle of Hastings.

Tostig Godwinson, Harold's younger brother. Earl of Northumbria 1055-1065. Confidante and companion of King

Edward. Married Judith of Flanders (a relative of William of Normandy).

Gyrth Godwinson, Earl of East Anglia, Harold's younger brother. Married to Theo.

Leofwine Godwinson, Earl of Kent, Harold's younger brother and his closest ally. During their exile in 1051 he and Harold took refuge in Ireland with the King of Leinster. Married to Hilde.

Wulfnoth Godwinson, the youngest brother. Held as a hostage by William of Normandy after his father and brothers had been exiled by the king.

Eadgifu Swan-neck, Anglo-Danish wife to Harold Godwinson, wealthy owner of considerable land and property in East Anglia. Six children to Harold:-

Godwin, Edmund, Gunhild, Magnus, Gytha, and Ulf.

Gytha Haroldsdottir went into exile with her mother in 1066 and was married to Prince Vladimir II Monomakh of Kievan Rus, beginning a new Anglo-Russian dynasty. Through her son Mistislav she was the ancestor of Philippa of Hainault and Edward III of England and all subsequent monarchs of England and Great Britain.

Harold Haroldson, Harold's only son by Ældyth of Mercia, fate unknown.

Earl Ulf - brother of Harold's mother, who married King Cnut's sister and was the father of Beorn, murdered by Swein Godwinson. Earl Ulf was murdered by a hearth-carle on the orders of King Cnut after an argument over a game of chess, though it was really about rivalry for the throne.

Other Characters

Hannë/Hari: Daughter of Earl Magnus of Denmark, granddaughter of King Magnus of Denmark.

Thorkild Magnusson: her brother.

Arthur, youngest half-brother to Edwin and Morcar, by a concubine.

Acknowledgements

Although this is a work of fiction, I've tried (a biographer by trade) to stick as close to the facts as I could. But facts are slippery things and sometimes difficult to establish. History, over a thousand years of telling, becomes murky and distorted. The truth of a story often depends on who is telling it – usually the winner of a conflict. Much of the story of Harold and his family has been manipulated by Norman propaganda. Some sources are more reliable than others. The Anglo-Saxon Chronicle has been compiled from three or four different monastic originals, but it is contemporary, there is usually consensus, and it is generally a fair indication of the truth of an event. Disentangling truth from a thousand years of myth and legend, reportage and propaganda, has been a difficult task. There are huge gaps in the narrative, but these give a novelist leave to fill them with a story that seems logical and possible.

The Battle of Hastings is a good example of an event that has been distorted and confused in the telling. William of Normandy needed a story that excused his unjustified invasion of England (even his allies in Europe warned him against it) and the assassination – because that's what it was – of an anointed king. Some of the accounts of the battle and the death of Harold were written from that point of view. They are in conflict with other accounts, from more impartial narrators, as well as the wider historical context. The closest account is a poem, the *Carmen de Hastingae Proelio*, very recently discovered, believed to have been written in 1068 (within two years of the event) by the Bishop of Amiens, Guy de Ponthieu, who was a brother of Hugh de Ponthieu, one of the knights who, according to the *Carmen*, slaughtered Harold. His account completely contradicts the story of the 'arrow in the eye' that is one of the best known historical 'facts' in the public domain. It was Harald Hadrada, King of Norway, slain three weeks earlier at Stamford Bridge, who died from an arrow in the face or neck. Somehow these two Harolds may have been confused. The first mention of it is in the 12th century account by the Norman William of Malmesbury.

The Bayeux Tapestry has also been used to justify the story but seems to have been another victim of this ubiquitous but unreliable tale. In 1729 a Georgian antiquarian made a drawing of the section of the tapestry relating to the Battle of Hastings and what is now an embroidered arrow was then the shaft of a spear or javelin held by an Anglo-Saxon soldier. When the tapestry was restored in the 19th century, this shaft was restored as an arrow to align with the popular story. There are two Saxon men under the words 'Harold was killed', and both have been believed to be different versions of Harold. But the warrior holding the shaft is dressed differently to the figure on the ground under the word 'killed', a figure who is being sliced across the leg with a sword – just as recorded in the *Carmen*.

The burial of Harold is another mystery that seems beyond solution. There are so many different versions of it they can't all be true. Some involve his mother Gytha, many more his Saxon wife Eadgifu Swan-neck. Some have him buried on a headland near Hastings by William, some at Bosham, some at Waltham Abbey, some at Bishop Stortford.

In others his heart is removed and kept as a relic. One even has him surviving and becoming an anchorite. In the novel I've employed what little evidence there is to create what I hope is a plausible story.

I've been helped in this by Paula Lofting's carefully researched *The Search for Harold Godwinson*, which is level-headed and as accurate as it's possible to be on the historical evidence. Other books that I've relied on can be found in the bibliogaphy below. I read Anglo-Saxon and Old Norse language and literature as part of my first university degree, falling in love with both. This novel has been a long time in the making. Any errors of translation, or of fact, are mine.

As for Hannë/Hari, there is considerable evidence of female *scops* during this period, particularly in Norway and Denmark, among them Hildr Hrólfsdóttir, 9th century, Jórunn Skáldmær, early 10th century, and Steinunn Refsdóttir, late 10th century. And then there is the Geat woman in Beowulf, raising her voice beside the king's funeral pyre in a 'wild litany of nightmare and lament'. The poets were often the recorders of history, as in the Norse Sagas, and so Hannë/Hari in this novel is the one committing what s/he witnesses to memory and composing poems and sagas to pass down through time.

Thank you for reading my book. I hope that you've enjoyed it. If you have, I'd be really grateful if you could leave a review on Amazon, Goodreads, Facebook, Bluesky or any other public platform. It makes authors very happy to know that readers have enjoyed their work. You can find me on Facebook at kathleen.jones.10485, or on my website at www.kathleenjones.co.uk

Some Sources

The Anglo-Saxon Chronicle - Translation ed. Bob Carruthers

Carmen de Hastingae Proelio, (The Song of the Battle of Hastings), ascribed to Guy de Ponthieu, Bishop of Amiens, 1068.

Vita Edwardi Regis (the Life of King Edward) Trans by Frank Barlow

Enconium Emmae Reginae, (the Praise-song of Queen Emma) Ed. Alastair Campbell

Helmskringla, Olaf's Saga and Harald's Saga, Snorri Sturluson(1179-1241)

Christine Fell - *Women in Anglo-Saxon England*

Seamus Heaney - *Beowulf*

N.J. Higham - *The Death of Anglo-Saxon England*

Paula Lofting - *The Search for Harold Godwinson*

Marc Morris - *The Norman Conquest*

Eleanor Parker - *Winters in the World*; A journey through the Anglo-Saxon year.

Annie Whitehead - *Women of Power in Anglo-Saxon England*

Podcast: *The Rest is History – 1066*

About the Author

Kathleen Jones is a *Sunday Times* best-selling biographer, whose subjects include Christina Rossetti, Katherine Mansfield and Catherine Cookson. Her award-winning account of the lives of the women associated with the Lake Poets, '*A Passionate Sisterhood*' was a Virago Classic. She has also written 3 Historical Novels and 4 collections of poetry. Kathleen was born and brought up in the English Lake District, worked in broadcast journalism and has taught creative writing and women's studies in a number of universities. She became a Royal Literary Fund Fellow in 2007.

www.kathleenjones.co.uk

http://www.kathleenjonesauthor.blogspot.com

https://www.facebook.com/kathleen.jones.10485

https://tinyurl.com/22y3b3yy

Other Books by Kathleen Jones

Poetry:

Hunger

The Rainmaker's Wife

Mapping Emily

Not Saying Goodbye at Gate 21

Unwritten Lives

Biography & Memoir:

A Passionate Sisterhood: The Sisters, Wives and Daughters of the Lake Poets

Katherine Mansfield: The Storyteller

Christina Rossetti: Learning Not to be First

Catherine Cookson: The Biography

Finding Alexander: The Search for Catherine Cookson's father

A Glorious Fame: Margaret Cavendish

Norman Nicholson: The Whispering Poet

Margaret Forster: A Life in Books

Reading My Mother: A Memoir

Travel:

Travelling to the Edge of the World

Fiction:

The Sun's Companion

The Centauress

Mussolini's Hat

Three and Other Stories

As Kate Gordon:

A Practical Guide to Alternative Weddings

A Practical Guide to Alternative Baptism and Baby-Naming

A Practical Guide to Alternative Funerals

What Readers and Reviewers have said about Kathleen Jones' books

'I found the Sun's Companion an engrossing read, hard to put down. If you like to "disappear" into the world of a book you'll find this a satisfying read.'
  Linda Gillard, author of 'Cauldstane' and 'House of Silence'

'Poet and biographer Kathleen Jones' move into fiction should be celebrated by readers and writers alike.'
  Best-selling novelist Wendy Robertson

'I . . quickly became captivated. I think Kathleen Jones has done a great job. . . And she has a good deal of passion herself, tho' strictly controlled. . . her use of quotes from the womens' letters etc was what I admired most. I know to my cost how hard it is to do. . . what a wonderful story it is.'
  Margaret Forster [A Passionate Sisterhood]

'Kathleen Jones is such a good writer and never more so than when she is writing about people engaged in the creative process - sculptors and painters as well as writers.'
  Biographer and novelist Julia Jones [Three and Other Stories]

'Utterly gripping and I didn't want it to end.'
Debbie Bennett [The Sun's Companion]

'A compelling narrative of a writer's passion for her work'
Helen Dunmore, [Katherine Mansfield: The Story-teller]

'I read it with huge enjoyment - I think it's by far the best biography yet.'
Jacqueline Wilson, [Katherine Mansfield: The Story-teller]

'It kept me reading long after I should have turned off the bedside light!'
Amazon Review [The Sun's Companion]

'This is an extremely well-written novel, and exceptionally enjoyable. It's difficult to put it down once started.'
The Kindle Book Review [The Sun's Companion]

'I have been unable to put down this compelling autobiography and have found it a total delight... Kathleen was born to write.'

'This book is a story of reading and writing and the impact it has on our lives... I loved this book; it will stay in my mind for a long time.'
Amazon Reviews [Reading My Mother]